Three Craws

Three Craws

James Yorkston

Published by Freight Books, 2016

Freight Books
49-53 Virginia Street
Glasgow, G1 1TS
www.freightbooks.co.uk

James Yorkston acknowledges support from Creative Scotland towards the writing of this book

A CIP catalogue reference for this book is available from the British Library

ISBN: 978-1-910449-76-9
eISBN: 978-1-910449-77-6

Typeset by Freight in Plantin
Printed and bound by Bell and Bain, Glasgow

For Linda, Bob and Magee

'You hated the land and the coarse speak of the folk and learning was brave and fine one day; and the next you'd waken with the peewits crying across the hills, deep and deep, crying in the heart of you and the smell of the earth in your face, almost you'd cry for that, the beauty of it and the sweetness of the Scottish land and skies.'
Sunset Song, Lewis Grassic Gibbon

Sweethope Cottage
Burnoch Farm
Strathhillock
3 May 1994

Johnny,
I got your address from your mother who asked I'd say hello. I hope everything is going well for you. I'm back in Fife now, my uncle and aunt both dead, maybe you heard, maybe you didn't so. I have their cottage. I was going to sell but thought I may live there a while. I have room for a visit if you ever should fancy a muster. It'd be good to see you.
Stevie

And that was all it took to shoogle my shallow London roots and lead me ambling back home. London was just a bridge from a then to a now. Sure, I've had my adventures and made a few memories, but mostly those memories involve struggling to get to Art College on time, struggling to stay awake when I arrived and then struggling to work enough hours through the evening and into the night to keep out of debt. Just for it all to begin again the following day.

When Stevie left Fife originally, it was the final push for me too. He'd warned me of his plans and I could see myself being stuck with my mother in our tiny, rented but 'n' ben cottage. I began looking for an escape, somewhere I could go, something I could do. Since my father had swanned off years before and my elder brother Rab a few years after – what, when I was ten or so? Well, my mother's once exuberant, socialite life had slowly constricted and boiled down to a thick broth of sadness and gossip, short temper and regret. But who can I blame for that?

She would always paint though, and through her skills, I learnt the same. But I was – I am – a lazy painter. I wouldn't even use the word *artist*. I'm just a guy who can do pictures, that's all. It didn't interest me, not much anyhow, but see at school? I was good enough that I could just sit in the corner of an art lesson and scratch away, enjoy a few hours of peace in the week, serenity amongst the rumbustious nature of the remainder of my otherwise oppressive school day.

With my mother's help – she saw Art College as a result, perhaps as a *fuck you* to my more money-fixated distant memory of a father – we managed to get me accepted down here. I was just delighted to be leaving Fife, and *Art College in London,* well it sounds good, doesn't it? It sounds good leaving her lips and snaking round the coffee mornings of the East Neuk. It sounds better than *stacking shelves* or even, dare I say it, *staying on at the farm.*

I've fitted in okay here, wasn't the worst, there was no great collapse of confidence. I drew things reasonably well, followed the coursework, played my part – but it didn't excite me. The college itself was a 1950s new build with huge glass windows that magnified the sun's rays and slowly boiled me alive. There was no historical glamour here, no romance, no architectural wonder. The other students I was more comfortable amongst. Sure, there were eejits there whose work I couldn't understand, feather-haired and rebellious, creating cows clothed with pictures of dead servicemen, swathes of black canvas *accurately displaying their inner souls* or more commonly, naked pictures of themselves, blown up and magnified, titillating and on display to their delighted colleagues, visiting parents and grinning tutors. But there were others, also. Like me, just drifting through their years.

For the exhibition of my final exam, I pencil-drew a cow. Very detailed, but just a cow, in a field. Not too big, not too small. It warranted a passing glance and a pass mark. I got my BA (Hons) in Fine Art. A waste of time if there ever was one, a scrap of paper informing the world I am average at the scribble business.

I did actually miss the college when we left. There was an inbuilt comradery with the other students, even with the tutors themselves. I had friends, nodding acquaintances. When we discussed art I switched off a little, but there was plenty more – music, some literature even. Humour. The humour of the collected outsiders, the artists, the people who don't *really* know what to do, sent here in desperation by concerned parents, as if *Art* was a thing to be valued, a thing with any actual use. And as a youth my mother had forced a few library books onto me – she thought my secondary school was terrible, made it very clear I'd be somewhere better if my father hadn't flitted... So I could talk *Chekov* or *Pinter.* Not to a huge depth, mind, but I knew how to pronounce their names and sometimes that is enough. Mostly, though, it was a relief just to be in a room with people who'd listen to something beyond whatever crap was playing on Radio 1. Or worse, Radio Tay.

Come the final term and I could feel those bonds slowly loosening, people pairing together or cutting themselves off, making plans for their next big steps. And that spring, nobody paired off with me. I fell the other way, I asked for more hours in the bars and in the hotels I was working. And then when the ludicrous bubble of Art College burst I quickly became stuck in either a tiny bedroom or behind a tiny bar, a captive mouse scurrying on a wheel, somehow helping to keep the bright lights of London burning.

I kept my final exhibition cow picture, as no-one deigned to buy it. For a few years I had it on display in my various bedrooms – not on the walls, just down at floor level, but certainly facing outwards. Eventually, with successive flat moves, the glass became cracked, the mounting loose and the cow upped and left its frame, its preferred position being stuffed behind radiators where it crinkled, dried up and finally became nuisance debris. Looking the other way one morn, I scrunched it into a ball and threw it into an egg-soiled, jam-sticky, tea-stained bin.

Chapter Ane

I am way too early for the bus, even though the walk to Victoria Station can easily take an hour. I could afford a tube, but I want to take in the streets one last time. And I want to be tired for the lang bus journey back to Scotland. I'll need to sleep. And I'll need a small quarter bottle of vodka to take the edge off things. And maybe a sandwich. I can justify my walking, oh yes.

The nearest grocer's shop, a place I've visited frequently, is just along the road. They have a sign saying *Please do not ask for credit, as you will be refused.* But I know they'd smile and give my familiar face credit. I've never asked – of course not. They are grown-ups, running a business. They ask how I am, they offer me the best deals, the cheapest drinks, the food they are about to throw... I am loyal to them and they to me. The lady of the house is serving. She's wearing her usual sari and smiling, generously. *A quarter bottle of Flying Horse, please.* She reaches down below the counter and up it flies, this pale red be-winged stallion, straight into a brown paper envelope. *Will there be anything else, Johnny?*

Aye, erm – have you any of yesterday's sandwiches?

Again, the smile. The bread is out of date, the filling suspect. *Only this today, Johnny.* There's one left and it's egg.

An off-egg sandwich on the bus will not make me a popular man.

Aye, okay.

Christ.

We share a grimace, a comical look of *Who'd eat that?* and make to go. As I'm leaving, her husband is entering, carrying two boxes of confectionery. He sees my stash and grins. *Have a good evening, John.* I stand back a bit, allowing him passage. *I will, I will.* Then, to both, *See you next time.*

Deep exhale, then out I go, straight up to the speed of my fellow pavement walkers, not wanting to be the slow guy causing folk to overtake.

It occurs to me that there was no way my friends in the shop would have known I was leaving *for good*. I'm only carrying a small rucksack, after all. I have my heavy coat on, but I wear that most of the time, most of the year. Except in summer. I wash it then, before drying it, ready for winter once more. I wonder if they'll miss me?

What happened to Johnny?

I don't know, but it's egg sandwich for tea again.

I sure do miss Johnny.

As I walk away from all this, there's no voice in the back of my head telling me *If only I'd made an effort with the art I could have been someone, done something…* I am not leaving a lover under duress, I am not being forced to flee a house consumed with fire…

I don't see anything I want to draw, sketch, comment upon. I see the sheen of wet on the paving stone, I smell the wet of the paving stone, I continue on my way.

On occasion in college reality would intervene and we'd be offered the chance to try for some outside work. I guess companies with scant resources would conclude – *We can't afford to get this illustrated, so let's hand it over to the students – get it for free*. We were once asked to attempt the illustrations for a sexual-health manual aimed at young teens. It was, my tutor told me, *A shot at having a shot. See if you can grasp the opportunity*. The opportunity to draw condoms and VD clinics, cocks erect yet somehow flaccid and most definitely friendly, all aimed for a young, young audience. I thought of HH Geiger – perhaps his famous cock-fests had once been seeded by such a request. I doubt it. All I know for sure is that I had been asked to draw some cocks.

I tried – I did. It would have been an *in*, perhaps. But I had little practice of the cock-drawing, it's more complicated that one would think, if one had never attempted it previously. I mean, of course, anyone can draw a bus-stop cock, but it had to be slightly beyond that, didn't it? So, I drew cock after cock. Very quick, disappointing work that soon filled my sketchbooks. The best cocks, the most successful, the most accurate yet friendly, the most unlaughable yet of *youth interest* I copied, using tracing paper, into a smaller, more presentable notebook, to be handed to my tutor and if considered suitable, onto the *client*.

A flatmate walked in at one stage, to see me tracing cocks. He looked on incredulous. *What are you doing, Johnny?*

Ah, you know, just tracing cocks.

My work wasn't accepted. I wasn't the chosen prick, thank God. My career, although still unstarted, had at least not got off to a start with such a shaming dignity. The girl whose drawings were chosen – a young Newcastle thing called Jody – she seemed rightly embarrassed that her drawings of male genitalia and their surrounds had outshone the rest of us. And when the booklet had been printed, there was her name, coolly displayed on the back cover, amongst that season's sexual terms of endearment, all floating in thought bubbles, coming from the heads of a young black teenage boy and a young white teenage girl. She was proud as punch was young Jody. A foot on the ladder to the heaven of cheaply paid advertising skits.

All I got out of it was my reasonably expensive sketchpad had been filled with badly drawn wangers. Ya beauty.

* * *

I turn a corner, spy my once local-away-from-home, consider my finances and duck inside for a one-er. A pint, no more. During my London stay, I have worked in many bars, providing me with a meagre income. Never this one, but its opening hours and proximity to my flat meant I often popped in for a night cap after finishing my shift who knows where, whichever bar or hotel I was juggling in, and thus I have never been anything other than a well-behaved, quiet when drunk, passive regular. I have been involved in many a lock-in, simply as I was a good audience to the boasting and cajoling that went on around me, the local Big Fish, small-time businessmen. Their leader by volume, George, an overweight, tracksuit-wearing, small-time property developer always looking my way, making sure I'm listening to his tales of subterfuge. *Just let Johnny hang around. He won't cause any bother, will you Johnny? Eh? Ee's a good old Sweaty Sock!*

What a fud.

Jan, the barmaid, would catch my eye briefly. She's Scottish herself, late twenties, early thirties maybe. Bonny enough, quiet, serves the drinks, puts up with the shecht to keep the establishment busy, her regulars happy. And of course George also gets the drinks in, so welcome here he remained, gurning away.

I, on occasion, would pitch in with something almost-witty, making sure I was a friend who chatted, happy to be a member of the common people, sharing their tales of ripping off the Yellow Pages advertising systems and getting cut-price paint from a man George knew down Marylebone. This man he knew, I was fairly sure, was actually Dodge City Warehouse, where at best George had a trade account or whatever, but anyhow I let him tell his tales. The drink would warm and comfort me, worth sitting through the crud to catch a few whiskies at the end of an evening. Happy to attempt my round, to start things off, I'd count my pennies visibly – *Can I get a round of the house, please Jan?* – but George would butt in, of course – *Eh? Nah mate, we can't be having that muck. I thought you Scots knew your whisky Johnny boy! Let's get the good stuff – Jan, Bells for all please love ha ha. Like that sound, I do, the Bells* – and we'd be straight onto the whisky I've known since it was first placed in my mouth as a child, soaked in cotton wool, to ease an aching tooth.

Today though, opening the doors to enter, no-one turns, there's no commotion. It's a different clientele, this early evening. None of the hardened drinkers are in – they'll be at home, lolloping up a few tinnies before making their grand entrance. That way, they're only ever seen as having *One or two pints – perhaps a whisky* a night by Jan or their buddies or whoever – and similarly, although alcohol is a regular guest in their supermarket trolley or corner shop, it's never seen as *a problem*. We're all above board here. We're not the people with the problems the politicians and newspapers warn us about, oh no.

As I walk over, Jan's there, behind the bar, drying a glass. She looks up, but no double take.

Oh hello Johnny. You're early.

I smile – *Hey* – ignoring the almost-question.

Just a lager, please Jan. Pint of Four X.

A chap at the bar – I guess this one an early-eve regular – turns from his stool and looks at me, curious how I know *Jan*. Blank. No recognition and then he's up and off for a piss. I await his departure then say –

That's me going home Jan.

She looks up.

Ah, that's a shame. For good? Well, you never know, I've seen it many a time Johnny, folk down and back, down and back. Fair enough though. You never really sat in with this crowd.

She's slicing some lemons now. A basic skill.

So. Have you something to go back to? Any work maybe, Johnny?

No. Nothing. Well – maybe a place to bide. We'll see.

That doesn't sound too concrete, Johnny.

I sip at the lager. I can taste the detergent used for cleaning the glasses.

Aye, there's more jobs up there. A Jobcentre I can visit. Maybe get some farm work. My mate Stevie…

Farm work?

Aye, I did enough of it as a kid. Who knows? Would be good to be working outside again though… maybe I'm, I don't know… guessing…

I trail off.

Slice, slice, slice, then a look, briefly, then back to the slice.

Aye, fair enough Johnny.

The guy who was at the bar returns and scrapes his chair. Even within the bar's ever-present fug of cigarette smoke, his great grey flannel jacket is still noticeably giving off an ash-tray reek. Here sits a veteran of smoked tobacco stench.

Jan speaks – *Johnny here's away back home Tam* – wiping hands – *Aye, it's not worked out for him down here.*

Tam turns and looks at me, and me at him. He looks like a fish. An aged fish, big mouth, trout mouth. He speaks, a short sentence, but full of phlegm and grizzle, the years of alcohol and nicotine toil on his throat quite evident.

Is that right?

There's no sign of a younger man lurking in there. It is just him – Tam – early sixties, I guess.

Aye, I went back a few times, but always escaped heh heh. Fuck that up there.

He turns and sups his beer.

Every time, see…

He's pleased of the audience, however small, and is making the most of me. I guess if he's been as regular to this bar as I suspect, him and Jan will have said all they needed to long before now.

...every time I went up there – home heh heh – I'd see the same bunch of bollocks – excuse me Jan – that I tried to escape. And aye, they'd judge me just the same...

And no doubt he'd be found wanting, I'm guessing.

So I stopped going. Even to the funerals, family excepted. Ach, I can always wash and scrub up for a dead aunt can't I Jan heh heh!?

Aye, you can that Tam.

She's barely listening, just letting him ramble.

But the thing is though Jimmy.

Johnny...

Aye, Johnny, the thing is... when I'm down here, I could be anyone – he gestures around the near-empty bar – *naebody's looking, naebody's judging. But when I'm up there* – sup of drink – *When I'm up there, well – I'm sneered at. A fuck-all. And I tell you Johnny, there's a big difference between being a no-one – anonymous – and a well-kent fuck-all failure, I tell you that.*

Great.

So you're off back up eh? Well, folk will be happy to see ye crawling hame. Thing is Johnny – just the getting away, that's success. Staying up there and rotting – that's the failure. And that's why – throat gurgle – *that's why they'll've wanted you to've failed. So they feel better.*

I'm not sure if I can live with that, accept that, just yet.

I'm only twenty-three, that's a bit premature to imply failure. What are you? Sixty? Seventy?

He recoils and looks at me as though I've thrown a dart at him. Then silence. He's leaving it for the drama, I'm sure of that. His breathing sounds like a motorbike – a small motorbike though – perhaps a hamster's motorbike. The image plays in my mind.

I'm fifty-fucking-five ye fucking cheeky cunt.

Ah right, enough, I'm aff. I finish off the soapy pint, pick up my bag and wait for Jan to catch my eye. She's well aware of my leaving, regardless of her being faced away, no doubt avoiding another bout of Tam's wisdom. She half turns –

Well, good luck to you. You're always welcome back here Johnny.

And a genuine smile. Good lass.

I stop for a second, consider staying for a whisky, but then I'm gone.

I Mean, I'm Mair A Train Man

These buses man – they're no' for me. I'll be honest wi' ye. I mean, I'm mair a train man, ken? Fucking easy ride, the train – but picking up that speed wisnae the smoothest, it turned out. Christ, the boy wee Keith – the drugs boy, ken? He's only para about being watched by the polis! I didnae ken nought about it, but, aye, he telt me sure enough, once I'd paid, once the stuff was in MA bag. Telling me "Aye, I reckon they're efter me – keep yer eyes peeled open" – I reckon it could jist be the smoke, ken, making him delusional – beasties in the cushions and a' that – but here I am, slinky likes, aff tae the bus, mebbe safer, mair… anonymous. And it got me thinking – just imagining, ken – in the back o' ma mind – well, mebbe I could take wee Keith's place, if he's keiching it – heh heh – Keith the Keich… Got tae be better than the fish market, eh. Fucking stinks, that malarkey, let me tell you. Ken, if I made a wee bit of cash I could mebbe even just get a wee bit flat tae masel somewhere – keep it clean, nae parties an' that. Nah, fuck 'em, nae cunts getting tae Mikey's pad. Fucking party round at theirs, sure enough, sure I will. Won't even tell these cunters where ah live. Keep it cool, keep it backstage, mysterious like, in and oot of their lives, keep the scent o' the polis that Keith's so feart o' far away. "Who, Michael? No, I don't know where he lives Boss, or even if that's his real name. Scottish, or Welsh, maybe." Aye, that'll do me, keep me shipshape, tip-top, fully fit, fully formed, happy and healthy… I reckon I'll see about selling this wee lot up in Dundee, or maybe further along the coast – keepin' ma name clean in ma hame town isnae a bad idea… Mebbe I'll make a new contact or two, mebbe go down that route? It'd be on MY terms, sure enough, if I do onything – no' letting nae cunt push me around… Ach – but I'm jist thinking aloud, I'm aware o' that. Thrawin around ideas, ken?

Gub

Victoria Station arrives. At this early evening, the crowds are thinning out, most folk home after their tea or in the pub already, but Victoria is still well stocked with travellers from all over the world – a flurry of Spaniards, young girls with rucksacks, young boys with rat-tail haircuts, bus-loads of French students, the occasional responsible adult looking stressed and out of depth. In amongst all this youth and excitement there are the commoners who use this station daily, more aged explorers, some of whom look life-battered and weary, the long-distance travellers such as myself and tramps, beggars and hawkers.

I spy my stand, observe I have forty-five minutes, make my way over, sit and wait.

At the end of the platform I spy a wee guy weaving his way in my direction. Although he's a good bit in the distance, I can see the grease in his scraggled hair shining clearly. He looks gnarly. Folk are clearing a path for him, his once blue jeans, haggard leather jacket and bulging, worn Rucanor sports bag. I know, I just know he's going to park himself beside me and of course, of course, he does.

And at this very moment he arrives, he opens his mouth. It's obvious he's keen to divulge his all, telling me about his *lang deid folks*, his drug taking, his squat. He's on his way to up Edinburgh and I fear I'll be stuck with him now. He's smoking – a weed/tobacco cross, I reckon – and has the urine smell going on alongside. Or is it fish? Not overpowering, but there, for sure. Fuck London for its spitting out of worn-out Scotsmen. *Draw?* He offers me the stub of his rolled joint/cigarette, but his fingers are grimy black and yellow and I tell you this – I wouldn't kiss him, so I won't be sharing his dowp. And for the first time, I speak –

No thanks, I gave up a while back.

He twigs my accent, not as thick as his, but there's no escape – *Are you a Fifer, then?*

I don't need this. I need to be left alone to stew, work things out, what I'm going to be getting up to once I reach home, what I'll tell folk, how I'll greet Stevie – I just need time, you know? I don't need to baby-sit anyone.

I consider moving; any excuse – for a drink perhaps, or to *grab a newspaper,* but the heroes arrive; the polis, and in-between his face rubbing, jittery shoulders and involuntary twitching, he spots them a good fifty yards away. For whatever reason he's up and off, considering leaving me to *guard his bag* but no, taking it with him and bounding away. And straight over to us they come, or to me, now he's gone, asking me to stand up, sniffing the air, checking the dowp on the ground. *Is this yours, sir?* But I show them my lang, thin, clean hands, blue-white fingers and no, quite clearly it's not. *I don't smoke, I gave up lang ago.* They're looking this side and that around me, talking but paying no attention to my answers. *Would you mind if I checked your bag?* And I wouldn't, so long as they don't disturb the off-egg sandwich or confiscate my genuine Russian vodka. Folk are giving us looks, but that's no concern of mine. I glance back towards one older interested lady and smile, just then seeing she has a small lapdog, consoling and comforting her in these trying times. I hope it doesn't piss on her, or if it does, it gets it done now and not on the bus. Bus journeys with wee streams of pish aren't the best, knees locked firmly to the seat in front, blood cutting off, bum freezing and numbing, lower back screaming with pain, just for the avoidance of the dog pish, or worse, crawling onto my well-worn and certainly not watertight Converse.

The polis lady is routing through my bag, but there's nothing there to worry her, just a few shirts, some grey underwear and an oft-opened envelope containing Stevie's letter and its short follow-up. I've read and re-read them – *he does want me up. He does. But I don't HAVE to come up.* A lukewarm welcome from a half-friendly welcoming committee would be enough for me.

The polis radios start chattering away – I can't decipher what they're saying – and that's them done for now, called to more important things. The lady looks at me – *Stay right here* – but there's no chance of that. My bus is soon boarding and the moment the polis are out of sight I nudge to the front of the queue and climb on board, make my way upstairs and find a seat, pull my black woolly hat down hard to my eyes and scrunch down into a corner near the back. I rub my face, pleased to be on board and pleased to be leaving London, finally, glad that dowp duffer was chased away so I can get some peace. I keep an eye on the outside, but can't see the polis folk anywhere and slowly, slowly, the bus fills up. I guess there's more attractive seats to occupy than the one beside me as it remains empty, suiting me fine. Eventually the doors close and I sink further into my seat, the diesel engine revs up and the bus pulls away.

But a second later there's a clatter on the door and the bus stops. I look down outside, knowing who it'll be and yep – it's that erse from earlier. There's no escape now. I pull my bag out from under the seat and place it on the seat beside me, curl up with my head against the window and feign sleep.

My eyes are closed. My hand is resting on my ears and I am listening to the sound of my breathing. There is no disturbance and I am relishing these few moments of peace. I am relishing my return to Scotland. But I know, oh yes, that this will soon be broken. In mere seconds, if my luck is out, this twinging oaf will appear and assume his place beside me.

Hey boss, and now I only have half a second, if that, in which to luxuriate, pretend to be asleep/waking. *Hey pal, gaen move yer bag eh?* And that's it. Exhale. Open my eyes and there he is, grinning, the bus's ceiling lights reflecting on his oily flapjack hair. His skin thick and creased, his eyes wide open, flickering left and right. Then he starts, moving my bag, handing it to me – *Ah man, did you see the polis?* Of course I did. *Man, man – I had to leave.* I know that. I turn away, one last chance to attempt to pretend to sleep... *If you'd excuse me* but no – *Fucking...* and some rustling away in his poly bag – *fucking...* I open my eyes and glare at him. He stops routing through the bag and glares at me, whispering *Man, I had tae gub a' ma speed. I'd a bunch tae sell up in Dundee, but fuck it with the polis jist there efter me fer sure and me, well, fuck, I wisnae gaen tae flush it away, so, aye, I had tae take it eh?*

My eyes widen. Ah great, he's taken a significant amount of amphetamine. That'll help the journey go peacefully, for sure.

His name is Mikey. He knew me, it seems, once he'd ran off. He remembered me. Knew my elder brother Rab from school. He'd recognised me.

How is he eh? How's the Rabster?

I look away. I've not seen Rab for years now, in fact I barely knew him as *Rab*. He caught the emotional flack when dad pissed off and as soon as he could, he pissed off too, leaving little ol' me and dear ol' ma. Mother calls him Robert, of course. He's ne'er been in touch with me, all this time. I mean, I know I've been away and such but... My mother occasionally gets letters, I think, although I've never seen one. Little snippets of news reach my ears, almost always through her. I suspect she may make a few of them up.

The vodka bottle I bought earlier is caressing my heart with my every breath. Its beauty and cool touch is intact and I can sink into it, retire to the on-board loo and drink it down, as soon as *Mikey* becomes too much. But every sentence, every word – with every utterance he's breaking new boundaries of *too much. I'm fucking aff ma tits man, I'M AFF MA TITS*. He's almost shouting now, hands on the neck rest of the seat of the poor fellow in front, who's no doubt thinking *Christ, of all the luck, these fucking night buses...* I've barely opened my mouth and I don't feel the need, Mikey is doing all the talking.

I'm looking outside, watching the lights of London wave their goodbyes to me, the same lights that seemed so welcoming those few years ago. I've dragged my Walkman from my bag and have slipped the headphones over my ears, Mikey oblivious to the affront, still chatting away, looking at me when I open my eyes, at one stage pulling an ear-piece off my lug and asking *So what did you think I did? Eh?* And me answering *I...* but he's off chatting again, pulling the seat in front back and forth. The guy in said seat turning round and occasionally letting off a *Give over* or *Let it be* but Mikey's paying no attention whatsoever.

Then there's calm. A silence, for three, maybe four seconds, before Mikey's off up his seat and running down the bus stair, only to re-appear a few seconds later, run to the back of the bus, turn around and down the stair again, over and over. The third time, before he disappears again, Mikey grabs the hand rails that run along the ceiling and begins to lift himself up and down, up and down, like pull-up bars in a school gymnasium. The guy in front lets out a *What the fuck?* And folk all around are staring at this obviously highly trained Olympian at the height of his powers, showing us all his prowess, showing us slovenly folk up for our lack of strength and desire for fitness.

He's no Olympian though. He's just speeding off his noggin.

As Mikey disappears down the stair once more, I count the time he's out of sight, slowly and considered… and eight seconds later he's back, grinning at me *Fucking hell man!* To the back of the bus and away, lifting himself up and down, up and down, wired and occupied. As he runs out of sight, I grab inside my jacket and open the vodka bottle, ready for a quick swig on his next departure. He's grinning at me and me back at him this time, my hand under my arm, awaiting the chance to grab my fix, then he's gone and the bottle's out, I get three, four good swigs before he's back up and passing me, the vodka hidden on my lap, under my hat.

And it continues long past me finishing the vodka. Everyone – the whole bus – must have settled into his rhythm. It is collectively decided that he means no harm, that he is a mere loon doing what loons do. Every brush of an arm as he horsed past was followed by a *Sorry,* he'd wait in the isles, jogging on the spot to make way for whoever was making their way to the loo. I close my eyes and doze.

I Dream Of Stevie

That evening, we caught the early bus – the 7:15pm – into town. Just the usual accompaniments: Stevie had a bottle of various alcohols, carefully distilled from his uncle's larder then mixed with Ribena; I had my usual quarter bottle of vodka. £2.50. A quarter bottle was enough, I found. A half bottle better, but a wee bitty dangerous as it tipped you into seriously drunk land, unless you shared it, and I had no desire to share my bottle with anyone else. Compact, also. Slips into your pocket like a true gentleman's drink. Stevie's raspberry surprise however was a rank-bad concoction – too much Ribena in the mix and it was a sickly sweet medicine drink and too little? Well, all you could taste was the headache of the gin and the gurning of the cheap black rum. The Ribena stained Stevie's lips and before too long he had a wee red circle just above and below, as if he'd been caught out by some bairn's kissing game or something. I kept telling him to wipe it off, but after a while, after we'd both had a drink or a sip or two, I'd not bother and he'd just sit there like an Aunt Sally, all rough hair and big red lips, burning red lugs and watery eyes from the cigarettes he couldn't yet smoke. He'd steal two or three from his uncle through the week and that was enough for him, easy, he'd only light up if there was a group of lassies on board the bus or if we were going to the off-licence. I always sent Stevie in – he was a stout lad, wearing that peculiar black leather jacket of his – expensive, sure, but intended for lassies, equally sure of that – elasticated waist pulling in and creeping up his frame, bottle red lips, big lugs – they always served him. He looked odd as fuck, let's face it, like a big old drag queenie, walking around this most undrag-queenie of towns.

First, the bus. Running the gauntlet to town and back, unaware and ill at ease with whoever we may find ourselves beside or broddling against. It's always against. Most of the folk to be avoided have gotten on by the time the bus reaches our village – the teuchters from the fishing villages further along, who look down upon us mere farm boys... They wear the mullets, the obligatory badly grown fifteen-year-old's tash, the nasty yellow golfing tops, all diagonal striped like drunken blurry bees, gauche pinks and Space Invader prints on their coats. I'm a' fu' o' New York clothing nonsense ideas, read second-hand in some music magazine or other; dressing like someone who may have had an idea of what fashion may have been seven or eight years ago – but in comparison to the fisherman boys – jings, I'm cutting edge, for sure.

We climb on, paying full fare, and walking down to the end of the bus, keep an eye on who's left and right, but it's just auld folk, church folk, no-one to concern us. Right down the end though, there's three folk we ken a' too well, three lads we run into most weeks – sons of fishermen they are – and most weeks get abuse from them. *Aye here come the benders richt enough,* they say, loudly. My cheeks flush. I want to tell the normal folk on the bus that we're no' *benders,* that we're as straight as all of themselves, but we just keep on walking down, stiff-necked. Stevie's turning bright red and his eyes blaze at our accusers, but he's so shy he can't get a word out in their direction and they know it fine. When he sits down I sneak in beside him and await the onslaught and sure enough – *Well hello Steven, yer looking beeeuuutiful this evening, what a laaarvly jacket.* Stevie's fuming already, his lips are pursed and he's slapping his tight black stonewashed knee with the inside of his palm. I know not to bother him when he's like this, he'd just be full of stutter and accusation. I wasn't scared of Stevie, although he could have battered fuck out of me had he been that kind of guy, but I was a little wary of him, in the same way we were wary of bulls. Just don't take the piss and you'll be okay. *Hey Steven, are ye gaen dancin' the nicht? Ye an' yer wee boyfriend?* But, after a few more minutes, the fisher boys, all high on cheap cola and vodka, run out of onslaught and the remarks come less frequently and less full of threat. They begin talking of conquests and fights and all sorts. I can tell Stevie is riled up and tuned in, awaiting a word about himself, and I try to distract him –

That mudguard o' mine's puir fucked by the way.

Eh? How?

Aye, from the crash, ken?

We'd been out on our mopeds earlier that week – I had a C50, Stevie a more powerful C90 – and I'd fairly come off my own. We were horsing around in the wee woody bit just beyond burned down Blair Malcolm House, Stevie way in the lead, a better driver, more powerful bike, and me trying to catch up, so taking a *short-cut* through some long grass. Unfortunately, as ever, there was a reason why no-one used this short-cut, the reason being a great muckle tree stump, hidden in the greenery but solid and obstinate enough to send me heels-over-head, at one stage flying fully upside down, looking behind me at the unimpressed foliage, me wondering where I'd land if I let go, preferring not to let go but the twisting of my arms making it a necessity, turning full back around and landing on my knees just beyond the stump, falling forwards into head-bowed and praying position. I'd stayed like that for a while, wondering when the pain was going to kick in; wiggling my toes (back not broken), turning my neck, slowly (neck not broken), raising my shoulders (arms not broken) and then slowly, slowly, standing. Sore left knee, but. Twisted, maybe. It was dramatic, but Stevie wasn't impressed, either then or now.

Ach, it wisnae a crash, just a wee dint. Ya dowp.

We're quiet then, the kids at the back muttering away. I change track –

See James Bray's got one of those new Fizzys?

Despite my moped heroics, I wasn't really a motorbike lad like Stevie, I was more just *joining in* and he knew it, but he could see with my chat I was trying to pull him away from the dafties at the back, and this time he responds – *Aye, just 49cc but, sounds like a bag o' stanes being dragged through a church* – but the fisher boys have tuned in again now and straight away they're off – *Listen tae the teuchters, talkin' aboot the mow-peds* – elongating "moped" to make it sound posh – What the fuck did they know. One of the lads says *Aye Steven, I can just imagine you twa lovebirds, riding aff intae the distance.* Involuntarily, I close my eyes tight and smile, covering my mouth with my hands. *Fuck.* Stevie's right up, standing, but held in by my legs, turning right around and stuttering at them, red-faced *Aye you* – pointing now, pointing like a darts player – *Aye you, you just shut the fuck up or I'll came richt o'er there an' belt the fucking shite out ye.*

The bus goes quiet, the kids on the back seat go quiet and I stay quiet. My eyebrows raise up to the roof, my eyes widen and I examine the hard blue and orange fur on the seat in front of me. Still silence. Stevie sits down, jumpy, agitated, but sitting down at least. The fisherman lads are mumbling now, but every now and then, to show defiance, we'll hear *fucking prick* or *I'm no' scared of that fat poof.* But Stevie's shut them up. He scared them. He scared me. He's a big lad.

We take the easy way out, come St Andrews. We climb off before the centre of town, so we're not waiting them walking by us, no chance for them to scuff my hair or spit or whatever. Chuggy in my hair. Can you imagine that? No chance. So we're out, just past the outskirts. There's a few wee comments and such but Stevie knows he won the exchange and we're pretty happy with ourselves. We're off into the early evening light and make to walk away, but once the bus is gone, we're all squealing and smiling and almost hugging. We're kids again. Primary school heroes, playing soldiers. I squeeze his arm and he shakes my hand aff, embarrassed. Full of the talk of the big event. Full of the talk of Stevie fighting back. I was nothing, just a wee quiet mouth, nothing more, but Stevie did it all and his face is a wonder – wide smile, freckles bouncing about his cheeks as his jaw extends, almost tears in his eyes, but happy, full of adrenalin us both and tales of bravery. *I could have those cunts* he's saying. I know he could, but now Stevie knows it. *I could take those cunters richt doon. Did ye see them quieten doon? Bunch o' wee shitebags, nothing mair.* And he's rubbing his giant hands together like he's just done the deal of the decade. Good man. We begin the walk into town.

We stop off at the Star Bar – an easy place to get a drink as an under-ager – and order two lagers. Stevie preferred cider, but it was seen as a wee boy's drink, so lager it was. The other week the barman had asked me how auld I was and I'd said twenty-one – I was unsure of the licensing laws – and he looked so dumfounded he hadn't asked for ID. There was no way I was twenty-one. I looked nineteen at a push. Maybe sixteen-and-a-half, which is what I was. Big though – not fat – but tall. No beard, but low voice. No baby-face and no bum-fluff moustache. The fisher boys had their bum-fluff moustaches and they looked total pricks.

We have a game of pool and Stevie's whacking the balls with all his might and just laughing as the white scoots off the table or if he pots three of my balls or two of his own or anything. He's in a light delirium. I'm going along with him, but not as loudly, aware that his exclamations are drawing attention to us and occasionally catching the eye of the barman as he peers over at us – making us look all the more guilty. He steps over. *Hey lads.* Then he looks in the ash tray, pokes it a bit with a pen, to see if we've been smoking roll-ups – evidence of druggery to go along with Stevie's heightened state of reality. *You been taking something?* His nose is up a wee bit, his mouth open, short black hair greased back, plook-marked cheeks stretched, jaw down. I wonder who he was at school? A wee lad, no doubt, a wee bullied lad, but quite tall now, quite lang and thin. *No,* I say, *don't worry, Stevie just had some good news, that's all.* Stevie fires in a long red. *Aye, I did that,* he says. But the barman doesn't believe us. I'm smirking, just a little too much, whilst Stevie's ignoring him and hitting shite out of the balls. Plus we're both mostly dressed in black – which is code for drugs, surely. *Guys, I cannae have ye in here if yer on magical mushrooms, ken?* Stevie bursts out laughing *Magical mushrooms? Ya dowp. We're on nothing of the sort,* but it's too late and the barman's picked up our drinks, one-handed – I spy a lang white index finger dabbing in my lager – and motioning us towards the door. He doesn't want any trouble. *Now you guys ken yer welcome any day, but no' when you've been elsewhere first, eh.* He winks at me. He's trying to be cool, considering his language, talking *street.* We leave, laughing away, saying *Goooodbaaye* to the locals, with exaggerated Thatcher vowels.

We're walking again now, brisker, keen to get into town, the energy and adrenalin slowly wearing off. *Christ, what a fud that boy is,* says Stevie. We cut along by the burn, turning right so we're walking on its verge, reeds and fencing on one side, burn on the other, hidden from view, on the way up to the hill into town.

And then they're all over us. Came out of nowhere, well, from behind a bush and some big bottle bins at the back of the pub that edges up to the burn. My instinct is to go down and I do just that, down amongst the gravel and the dog shit, face hidden behind hands, body screwed up as the kicks come raining in, aimed at head, body, baws, legs, a few stamps on my feet, but then it stops and I'm left cowering, just hearing the continued sounds of fighting. I'm guessing Stevie is on the floor too and getting his share of the kicking, I'm guessing that soon enough they'll stop on him as they stopped on me, but the noise of the ficht continues, the feet against back, the scuffed shoes on the ground, the grunts and shouts, swearing – it's the guys from the bus – of course it fucking is. *Cunts.* Stevie's coming in for worse than me it seems – I'm long since ignored, curled up like a baby, breathing fast and shallow, sweating through my clothes. I hear Stevie call out *Johnny!* I ignore it. *Johnny, for fuck's sake Johnny, get up!* I take a huge deep breath but my muscles won't move. *John!* Stevie's getting the blows, I'm taking a rest. I'm thinking about what I'll be telling my folks about any mottled bruises and the scuff marks all over my clothing. Stevie's still getting it hard, three guys, I guess, all on him. *JOHNNY YA CUNT GET UP* and I'm up in a shot, losing my bearings for a split second, and there's Stevie, standing, just, two guys holding him back, one guy pummelling him with his fists, aiming all over like a scattergun, sometimes his face sometimes his body. I'm not a fighter, but this is Stevie. *Ah, for fuck's sake.* I charge at the fists guy and do what I know how: grab him around his lower legs and rugby tackle the fucker straight down, my head resting on his stonewash jeans as he falls, his head scraping hard against the gravel. I caught him sideways and knocked him hard. I get up quickly, expecting kicks in the head from behind, but the other two cunters have been stunned momentarily by their high heid yin being banjoed onto the floor. I stamp on his ankles, hard. More for effect that anything, but it must have hurt like fuck as he screams out, way beyond the force I'd used. One of the other guys is screaming now and I turn around – Stevie, face all bleeding and spittled, has got him in a bear hug and is carrying him towards the burn. It's not a straight drop though, not an easy throw and pretty soon he's rolling down the burn bank, through the weeds, stopping just short of the main body of the burn in a murky brown puddle, the soft mud enveloping his hands. He starts to scream *I'm falling in man! Help me! Fucking Davo! Help me!* But Davo is either rolling on the floor grasping at his ankle and crying his eyes out or is running away up along the path, towards the chip shop. Stevie's glaring at burn guy, pushing him further in with his mad, wide, reddened eyes. *We should help him* I say, but Stevie turns around and SHOUTS at me *FUCK THAT GUY, LOOK AT MA FUCKING PUSS* and he points two fingers, one from each hand at his pizza-faced, blotched-up, fucked-up face, bleeding and sore, lip split, eyes bloodied. *AND WHERE THE FUCK WERE YOU JOHNNY, EH? WHERE THE FUCK WERE YOU?* I'm walking backwards, away from Stevie, my arms hanging down on both sides, raising one hand slightly to point at the broken ankle guy, my eyes questioning and feart, my mouth open but silent. Stevie's turned away though and has picked up a half brick from the path. He raises it above his head and makes to throw it hard down onto the burn guy, who screams and rolls into the water – only a metre deep, I guess, and it's as well he does as Stevie's brick lands just where his legs had been. He stands up then, soaked but silent, still scared about what Stevie will do next. Ankle man is whimpering away and Stevie turns to me, calm now, *Come on Johnny. C'mon the fuck away.*

Stevie's a mess, a real scuffed-up, bloodied mess. I must look a bit worse for wear, but I'm not the guy people will be staring at in the street. We hurry up the wee path that snakes between the gardens away from the burn, through the ancient snickets which border the big auld houses here, dart over the main street, through another snicket, down past the university, over the golf course and into one of the caddie huts. Not saying a word. Not even looking at each other, just letting the events flood through. Stevie's greeting now, not a lot, but sobbing, wiping his eyes, covering his sleeve with blood and snot. *Look at me Johnny. I'm fucked. My clothes are fucked.* His elasticated black leather jacket has ridden up his body and is sitting, high waisted, like a black bin liner brassiere. He looks daft. I'm not laughing though. I'm white-shocked, exhausted and getting cold. I reach into my pocket and search for something to clean the blood off, finding only a bus timetable. Stevie takes it and starts to clean up his face, but the timetable isn't absorbent and he's just mushing his blood, snot and tears around and around. He looks like a toddler, covered in jam. *Ah, for fuck's sake.* And relax. He's head down now, head between his knees. Silent, except for our breathing.

A minute or so later, he's facing me, right close, and I'm using the same bus timetable to scrape the clart from his face. Underneath the muck he looks okay, the usual blue-white freckly skin, a few bruises coming up, but really okay. One of his eyes is cut, sure, and his nose is well kicked, but it doesn't look broken.

How does it look Johnny?

You look okay Stevie. You look okay. A bit fucked here and there, but the blood's coming off fine.

He looks at me. *Will we be able to get on the bus?* I have no idea. It's still early, anyhow.

I'm sorry I shouted, Johnny. It was fair pish though. I thought I was going to die – they had ma hands pulled richt back and that guy was just chucking punches. They weren't even particularly hard, but they were stinging and I could feel my eyes warming over and you were just…

I know. But I got the guy, which must count for something. *I'm no' a fighter, Stevie. I'm not that type of person. I wiz feart.*

Silence.

But I got that guy, did I not?

Stevie laughs. A laugh. Thank fuck. *Aye Johnny, you got that guy. I think he's well fucked, judging by the bleating that was going on* and we're laughing and pretty soon reliving the whole episode. *Man, his jacket will be ripped to shreds – did you see him fall on that gravel?* I'm smiling. I reach into my bag, pulling out my wee quarter bottle of vodka. I offer some to Stevie. His jacket is sodden with the stench of the broken bottle that split at some point in the fight. The pink Ribena stain barely visible on his black jeans, but not helping the general appearance, that's for sure. He takes a lang swig of the vodka then hands it back. I do the same and the bottle is finished. Grown-up as fuck. Twa men, twa drinks, bottle empty. *So what are we going to do now then, eh Johnny? If the polis see us now and they ken about those boys at the burn, we'll be lifted for sure.* The pub. We'll go to the pub, get cleaned up, relax a bit and then decide.

We're walking pretty quickly now, but not enough to make us stand out, I hope. Maybe we look as though we're after a bus or are late for something. There's a wee bit of nervous small talk going on and Stevie's carefully feeling his jacket pocket as we walk, as if he's got a wallet in it which needs protecting or fondling, as if we're off doing something important. Every now and then his hand will emerge with a wee shard of glass which he'll drop on the floor. A polis van drives past us, going the other way.

A few minutes later and we're at the bar in an Auld World tourist pub. The lighting is always so low here that most of Stevie's indiscretions are ignored – though the barman does look at him a tad queerly. *Is he okay?* He asks as Stevie takes our drinks away, over to one of the darkened booths that overlook the small car park. *Aye, he's fine,* I reply. *He just fell over and cut his cheek a bit.* I smile. The barman hands my change over. *Aye well, so long as he doesn't fall over in here, eh.* A wry, knowing look. I smile and head over to the jukebox, put in my 50p and choose my songs. A good selection for a wee town like this. Some Sex Pistols compilation album, The Smiths' *London*, Bob Marley *Redemption Song*, The Beatles *Helter Skelter,* Adam & The Ants, Pixies, The Primitives… I sit down and Stevie's halfway through his pint and looking outside in a dwam, fingers drumming on the table. *You okay?* I ask. *Aye Johnny. I am.* He rubs his face with his hand and says, *I'm aff in tae the cludgie tae clean masel up.* And he stands up, a big, wide man, squeezes out of the booth and into the lavatory. I hope he doesn't get too freaked out by what he sees in there – other than the permanently flooded urinal and the numerous families of flies that make themselves known upon entrance. I'm supping away at my drink and watching outside as the nightlife passes by. Same old faces, folk from school, students, the occasional suited worker, taxi drivers. I see folk who've left school but still live here – imagine that. Imagine staying here in this backwater shitehole when you've got the opportunity to leave. Imagine getting a job in the burger bar and getting a wee flat somewhere 200 yards from where you went to school. *Jesus Fucking Christ Almighty.*

A guy zips by, a year or so above me at school, now with a terrible moustache and heavy shoulders. *What now? Is this it?* What plans has he got then? Other than to make it through this weekend and into the next? I wonder about my own plans, which don't exactly add up to much, other than I'll be doing my best to get the fuck away as soon as I can, as soon as school's over. Maybe I'll move to Edinburgh. Maybe try and get that art going somewhere. Or more likely get a job in a bar. Wha' kens? I guess Stevie will be going straight into the farming.

Barely any need to study at school at all for that, he's been learning all his life. What use is French to him? What's French for neep? Ach well. I look down and see I've finished my drink.

Stevie returns, looking pretty good, though his face is redder than ever. *Worst pub we couldae chosen. Nae hot water, thick paper towels. I feel like I've had a ficht wi' a scouring pad.* He's grinning and, seeing my empty pint, is off to the bar, returning soon with two drinks, one for him and one for me.

I Wake With Mikey

Fucking… I cannae believe it. I necked half ma stash man, half ma fucking stash. I left a wee bit – personal, ken, the polis would think it was personal, no' fer selling – jist fae ma sister, likes – I cannae jist turn up wi' a bairn's saft toy – but fucking… Aye. I gubbed half ma fucking stash. And now I'm bouncing up and down these steps like a kangaroo, looking like a richt fitness freak, toning ma muscles, or mebbe a guy puir desperate fer the cludgie… Still, maist folk got their eyes shut as fuck, no' wanting tae see the freaky running boy, up and doon the stair, but I'm fucking a' fu' o' the speeds o' life, let me tell you that, the joys o' life are richt here inside me and ma legs will be aching by the morn, fucking polis cunters fearin' me up like that. But the bright side, the bright side – a' fucking cunts look fer a bright side, no' jist me, I'm no' a saftie or ought – aye well, the bright side is I got a seat next tae fucking Fenian Rab's wee brother, and he seems like he may be sound likes, he's no' tae bothered wi' ma antics. Ken if ma wee sis is busy or what I could mebbe even take a pint wi' him, pass the time o' day…

Fleeting

Come the lights of Forton services, a good five or six hours later, the effects of Mikey's speed must be wearing off. Everyone else is fast asleep – it's, what, 4am now? And the bus's lights are dimmed, sending a fuzzy orange glow over the seating and the passengers. Mikey is still up and out, but – I'll give him this – he's pretty sleek. Quiet, more walking than running now, no longer grabbing at seats, on occasion taking a swig of his water and wiping his mouth with his jacket, studying the seat in front of him for a moment, maybe thirty seconds, then off again. He must be exhausted. He's practically run a marathon, up and down the steps these past six hours.

And then, without warning, he slumps back into the seat beside me. *Ah, man.* His neck creases, shoulders collapse, head back and then he's asleep. A light snore, mouth open. Three or four deep breaths to be sure he's asleep then I squint at his face in the gloom. Unshaven, spidery black hairs creeping out of his cheeks, unkempt teeth, one solitary sailor's earring, his hair as thick as horse hair. I'm guessing he must be approaching thirty? Older than me, anyhow.

But he still smells. More so now, in this enclosed space, after his hours of enhanced exuberance.

I rest my head as far from him as I can, in the crack between the seat and the window, close my eyes and attempt to drift back off, the cold from the outside peeling in through the window frame's frayed rubber edges, tickling down my neck, bringing memories of childhood.

I have fallen between doze and dream, asleep and awake, the Mikey creature's smell somehow quite lulling, despite the sweet acidy tickle it produces high inside my nose. I occasionally tweak my eyes open to watch the early morn traffic pulling through the motorway lights, to watch Edinburgh as it gently begins to surround our bus.

When we finally park, all around me folk leap up, eager to get off, get away from Mikey, begin their civilised lives away from the cramped positioning of the bus seats, away from the fellow cheapskate bus folk, eager to make their mark as individuals. I, however, am stuck beside the snoring lummox.

I nudge him, softly first – *Mikey.*

I am aware that me saying his name implies knowledge of who he is, perhaps friendship. It somehow apportions a part of the blame to me.

The bus is thinning out, last few people now, and me, wedged in my place. I consider climbing over the seats – I reckon I could do that? Yep. Fuck it, let's do that.

Belongings gathered, I push my bag over onto the seat in front, then attempt to get through myself. But these low slung luggage racks don't leave much room and it's a bit of a struggle just to begin. By the time my head and shoulders are through, my feet are having to shimmy up the back of my seat, slowly edging my body forwards. When I get to my lower stomach, gravity takes over and I slip – or fall, I suppose, it could be called a fall – onto the seat in front. My legs follow me and I'm soon curled upside down, foetus-like.

What the fuck are YOU doing, Johnny boy?

Mikey's awake and smiling.

My face is bright red from the blood rush and embarrassment of discovery. I struggle to escape, but find myself with my hands crawling along the floor, my feet sticking up against the air vents and my jacket falling all around my head, my shirt up around my nipples and my belly sticking out, rubbing against the cold bristles of the seat. Mikey steps up –

Here –

He offers his hand. It is filthy. But what else can I do? For a second I marvel at it, the dirt between the creases, the broken nails, the yellow-brown, nicotine-dyed thumb…

I take it. Of course. And he's a strong one, I'll give him that. Picks me up, almost, lifts me round, holds almost my entire weight for the second my body and legs readjust themselves.

And then I'm upright, but shaken. I pat my hair down, adjust my shirt, straighten my jacket, get my rucksack, turn and make my way off the bus.

Hey!

Fuck this, keep on walking…

Hey – Johnny!

Down the steps to below…

Johnny!

As I approach the exit, I turn just for a second, and see him. He sees my eyes and slows. He has a hurt, put-upon look and drags to a stop. Years of practice no doubt, but he's got me.

Shall we – eh – shall we take a pint?

Um, aye, sure, why not?

Grand.

And he overtakes me, bounds down the stairs and off the bus, straight to the toilets. Who knows? I smile at the bus driver, who's waiting for me to depart, last man off. I'd guess he's in his early sixties, small, wiry, the grey-blue uniform bagging around him, filling him out, just, like a partially inflated balloon.

Christ pal what was your mate on? Fucking wang-danged that boy.

Aye, I think it was his sugar levels. He's diabetic, ken?

Diabetic is he? I doot that. I've ne'er seen that behaviour in a diabetic.

He smoking a roll-up through toothless gums.

Aye well. That's me aff back to ma bed noo. I stay up here, ken, jist drive up an' doon, up an' doon.

He takes a draw on his cigarette.

Guid work, ken, guid money, but ahm fucking sick o' it. A joab though, eh.

He spits a green-brown phlegm on the floor.

Aye well. There was nae fucking tips today though eh. Sometimes there is, sometimes there isnae.

I nod in sympathy. I am not giving him a tip though, oh no. He watches me, for a second longer, then –

I guess I'll make sure that's a'body aff, grab a coffee an' make ma wa' hame.

Okay. Oh – hang on – Where's the St Andrews bus leave from?

He points –

Doon there. Aff tae the Neuk are ye? Well, it's X60, I think. Leaves aroond 9am.

And he's off, waggling his rickety legs towards the staff canteen.

Wee Felt Beastie

Jings, my wee mind's taken a bit o' buttering. I need tae wash up the now, clear ma thoughts, clean ma face, wash the speed oot, the spiders oot. Open this bag, jist mak sure nothing was taken when I kipt, ken – claes, aye – underneath – saft toy – whit is it anyhoo? An elephant, mebbe? Big trunk anyhoo – unless it's a nose... Speed... speed, whaur's that speed...? Aye there it is, in ma wee tea tin. I was telt that the smell o' green tea puts the sniffer dugs off, eh. No idea if it's an urban myth though. Thar she blows richt enough – a wee bit fae sis, a bit fae me – is there ony left tae sell? Ach maybe – maybe a sampler. A fucking sampler? I'm no' a carpet salesman, Christ. Aye well, better get done, wash up, go and meet Rab's wee bro'. Whit was his name? Johnny, aye, Johnny. Go and meet that fella. Maybe take a drink or twa eh? Calm things doon... Aye, I could dae wi' that.

A Lang Spoon

I'm not meeting Stevie here in Edinburgh. I have a two-hour wait, then a short bus hop to St Andrews bus station. Two hours that bus, maybe. Common sense would have me eating breakfast somewhere more suitable than a bar, but here I am, juggling responsibilities between myself and Mikey, who really should in no way be *my* responsibility.

Aye, erm – a vegetarian breakfast please. Eh? No – erm – just no bacon or sausage.

I'll hae that! Just take it Johnny, I'll eat it.

Oh – okay, then – put them on a different plate please. For this guy. I'll have the beans, egg and toast.

And the mushrooms? What plate do you want those on?

Mine, eh?

No, fuck him – put them on mine, I'm the one paying.

The barman laughs.

Any drinks?

Aye, just a pint of Tennents please.

Just the one?

Mikey's looking at me, expectant, barman the same. But I'm not biting. No chance.

Aye, just the one.

Then Mikey kicks in –

Oh, and one for me eh.

He can pay for that.

He's visibly reaching in his filthy pocket for some change, pouring it onto the counter. Cheeky sod was going for a free breakfast/drink combo.

⋆ ⋆ ⋆

It turns out Mikey's on his way up to St Andrews too. When he decided this, I cannot tell. He asks me if I have anywhere to stay.

Aye, kind of, but no space for others – it's at a mate's.

Who's that? I'll ken him?

No chance. He's a farmer buddy of mine. Doesn't drink. (Lie.) *Very Straight. Wouldn't be happy if I turned up with a buddy.*

I regret the use of the word "buddy" instantly.

Fair enough.

His hangdog eyes stare into his lager.

Aye, I've missed this.

But how? It's a pish drink. Chosen by me only for its relative lack of alcohol. I do not need a foggy head on top of a night of bus-broken sleep.

Within time, our food arrives and is finished. My helping was significantly larger than Mikey's. I suspect the barman disapproved of his scrounging. I think I even got extra toast.

Can I…

No. I'm hungry. Buy your own.

During the meal, I learn that Mikey has a sister still in St Andrews, who he'll do his best to stay with. *She'll be delighted*, I think. And, *I hope she has a shower.* I also learn that he had necked almost *twa-hunner squid* worth of amphetamine.

I've got it planned. When our bus arrives, I'll tie my lace, get Mikey on board first, then sit elsewhere. Well, not too far elsewhere, but just not in the *buddy* position. More relaxed. Room to breathe.

But he won't get on first.

Eh – Mikey – just get on, I'm tying my lace.

And he's just standing there, staring at me, smiling. I'm done. Should I make to do the other? Why not –

Mikey, get on and get a seat, eh. It's still two hours on this bus. Can't be standing.

There's a slight change in his face, a realisation, perhaps, maybe offence, that I'm ushering him on-board solo. He's stock-still for a moment, then joins the small queue. By the time I'm done undoing and redoing my second lace, he's up inside. I wipe my face, look over to the bar we've just left. Maybe I should pop back inside? I stand, my legs aching from the short time I've been crouched, stretch my back and look over. It's tempting. Lose some excess baggage. Relax for an hour. Arrive at Stevie's at a reasonable time. It's decided. I make to leave – and then – *and then*, Mikey knocks on the window of the bus, the half-full bus, lifts his bag from the seat beside him and points down towards me. He mouths, I think, *I've bagged you a seat*. I smile and make my way on board, the doors slipping closed behind me.

* * *

You know, I'm no' too happy to be back.

Aye, me neither.

Seriously? You look sorted! A clever guy.

Ha. How, exactly?

* * *

I like London, good place tae be wi' a bit o' money, eh? Ne'er a problem fer me, always got a wee scheme gaen, ane thing or anither…

* * *

I'm seein' ma sister. She bides in San Andres.

Aye, you said. What does she do?

Cannae mind. Last I heard she was working in that chippy at the end o' Merket St.

Greasy Joe's?

Eh? No. The other ain.

* * *

See this wee town we're passing now aye?

Aha.

This wee place was built on top of a rabbit warren of old mineshafts. I wouldn't live here if you paid me, no chance.

How about being on a bus, driving over the shafts? How does that feel?

Fuck it, we'll be aff it soon enough.

* * *

Aye, she's just had a bairn, ken?

Who?

Ma sister, mind?

Oh aye.

Aye. I've no' seen it yet.

How come?

Eh? It's just wee, likes. No' even twa year auld yet.

Oh. What's her name?

Ha, aye – here's the thing – I cannae mind. Tracey, I think, or Dierdre. Ane o' those types o' names. Here – look –

He reaches into his bag – *I got her this wee doll eh.*

Ah right – is it an… is it an elephant?

Aye, I reckon so. You reckon so?

Could be, could be.

⋆ ⋆ ⋆

I mind that bar. I've been drinking in that bar. Here – look…

⋆ ⋆ ⋆

Are you into the football game, eh?

No. Not one bit.

Ah. Aye well, me neither. Fuck all that Rangers Celtic pish.

So…

Aha?

What team are you then?

⋆ ⋆ ⋆

Christ, I could go a slash for sure. That Tennents eh? Fizzy – rushes through you faster because it's fizzy, ken?

That's not true.

That's what they say…

Who?

It's a well-kent fact. Like food with roughage does the same, eh?

⋆ ⋆ ⋆

Are you no needin' a pish?

I am. All this talking about it isn't helping.

No, not really.

He's jittery, looking at me, then up to the driver, then back to me.

Do you reckon he'll stop and let me aff to pee in a bush?

No chance. Unless you tell him you're going to wet yourself. Like a wee bairn.

There's terror in his eyes.

No. And I wouldnae. Not yet, onyhow.

⋆ ⋆ ⋆

Kirkcaldy arrives. Lang, grey Kirkcaldy, luckily perched on a beautiful lang beach, a beach entertaining several morning dog-walkers.

Fuck it, I'm getting aff here. I'll dash in, quick as fuck, then pish in the bogs and get back. Haud him here eh – haud the bus here.

The bogs here are closed. They've been closed for months.

I'm winding him up.

Eh?

Smile.

We pull in to the station, anonymous, small fleet of assorted buses slotting into bus-sized slots, grannies climbing on and off. The driver announces, *We'll be here for ten minutes but, so if you want to avail yourself of any of the facilities, be quick – and mind to keep your ticket stub.*

Thank fuck for that.

Mikey's off and down to the front of the bus quick as he can. I wait a minute, let everyone else who wants to stand and depart, then do so myself. I have no desire to be buddying Mikey to the cludgie.

I cross the forecourt and arrive at the toilet block just as he's leaving, a beaming grin on his face. For some reason – for no reason – he blurts out particularly loudly, *I thought you didn't need a pish Johnny?* A trio of grannies, just themselves leaving the ladies, stop walking and look over, first to Mikey, then to me. We're all still, the five of us caught in a dwam, before one of the grannies speaks up – *Well on you go son, don't let us stop you.*

San Andres

We climb back on, me first, Mikey disappearing for a minute but returning soon enough with four tins of lager. Horrible lager, supermarket lager. But I am grateful, although aware my accepting is knitting us closer, closer together. He opens *one for me* and then *one for you*, so I have no choice really. *Dive in, Johnny boy.*

By the time we reach St Andrews, despite myself I'm laughing away at some far-fetched story he's telling: a squatter friend of his who'd worn his boots for over a year without taking them off, only to discover upon attempt that his skin and hair had grown through his socks and into the boots themselves and they needed to be surgically removed. *Aye, mad George – crazy guy, big speed freak – and acid too. Man, he loved the acid.* I didn't really believe the story and was just as incredulous about the telling of the tale as I was the tale itself, but we're still talking about it when we get off the bus last, letting all the grannies off first, then us two, both with luggage and tin of lager in hand.

Now, I'm not sure if Mikey pushed me, or fell down on purpose, but just at the awkward moment, legs half-bent navigating the stairs, he came tumbling down on top of me, him giggling away, me trying to get out of his way, what with the stench and the unfamiliarity and all, but ending up falling out of the bus, down onto the tarmac between the pavement and the bus, Mikey straight on top of me, his lager open and splashing liberally, me in the most undignified place I could be, a rare old welcoming to this haughty old town. Mikey laughs himself off and rolls down from me, but I'm stuck here, my bag perched on my back like a turtle shell, raised up over my neck and head, the lip slightly open and cassettes, pens, a' sorts falling out around me, onto the ground, joining the dowps and the ground-in old chuggy.

My face is red as I sit up, Mikey sat on the pavement, laughing away. I scrabble around, picking up this and that, gathering it all then finally standing up, turning and offering my hand to Mikey, pulling him upright, trying to straighten the situation, minimise my embarrassment, move on, move on.

Is this what you've become then, Johnny? Eh?

I turn around and it's Stevie. Just. I mean, it's him, of course, but he's older – it's what, four or five years since I saw him last? He's grown – filled out, muscular, a bigger lad now, but clean, as I would normally be, sober, as I would normally be, angry at what he's seeing – as I would be. As I am. There's no smile, he's pissed off. He must have been there the whole time, watching me horsing around with the jakey.

Hey Stevie…

I make towards him, but he backs off, then –

Who the fuck is that?

Looking, nose scrunched, slight nod of the head, disgusted. Looking at Mikey. I see Mikey once more as the first time I'd seen him. A greasy, slovenly, dirty mess. Except now we can add alcohol-fuelled. Oh, and don't forget the smell. Can't forget that.

Oh um, that's Mikey. He's um…

Mikey's looking at me, seeing what he is to me.

He's a guy I met on the bus.

Which is true. Stevie speaks.

He's no fucking coming back to mine.

Ah no.

I guess he's not.

Calm down mate.

Mikey now –

Calm down mate, I wouldnae want tae come back tae yours. Pause. *Ya dobber.*

Mikey comes towards me, close, shakes my hand and looks in my eyes, his own scrunched up, studiously, looking for a reaction. *Aye, good to meet you Johnny boy. See you around. We can catch up eh.*

He holds my hand for a second longer than he should, perhaps waiting for me to go *with him.*

Then he pushes me away, gently, and he's off, patting a recoiling Stevie on the shoulder as he passes.

As We'ans

What were you doing at the bus station?

Eh? Nothing. I asked which bus connects from London. I was in town anyhow.

You missed me?

Shut it.

⋆ ⋆ ⋆

Are you pissed off? How come?

How the fuck do you get aff rolling around the floor with that guy and how does that fucking guy get off calling me a dobber? The wee shecht. Kind o' welcome is that for me? I kent folk in that station and there I was – meeting the twa tramps.

⋆ ⋆ ⋆

I didnae ken that guy from Adam, by the way. Couldn't believe you had such a hissy fit.

Ach. I cannae stand filthy folk like that. Scroungers. Get a job man – and a bath!

Hold, I've only just arrived…

No, not you – well, aye, you – but him. Christ. What a mess to get yourself into.

⋆ ⋆ ⋆

Mind when Fat Karen ate those three Creme eggs?

Aye. What aboot it?

Nothing. Just… mind?

⋆ ⋆ ⋆

Is this the bit lang Suzy Rob went skidding down on her erse that winter? Landed in the burn?

Ye ken it is.

Mebbe a hint of a smile.

* * *

Christ man, cheer up. You're like the most miserable taxi driver alive. It was YOU who asked me up, mind. I was happy as fuck down in London.

* * *

We knew each other a wee bit as kids, Stevie and I. We'd been brought up right beside each other, him on the farm his uncle worked, me in a wee cottage on the big estate nearby. Stevie had gone to the local village school, of course, whereas I'd been sent into town with the Catholics, for a medieval Catholic primary education, which I'm not sure did me much good. Come secondary, we ended up together, in a faceless 60s monstrosity perched on a hill on the outskirts of St Andrews. I didn't delight in the place, but I kept my head down, getting along okay. Stevie though, well, Stevie had other troubles. Mainly due to his slight stammer and village shyness, he found himself the subject to first just a wee bit of bullying and then just a wee bit more. Stevie was always a saft lad, despite his size, but that size seemed to attract trouble more than keep it away. I slowly fell closer in with him on the bus home, mostly. Through the many long journeys to and from school, we found we were both pretty similar, just happy with a quiet laugh and away from all the muck of the school, the Protestant/Catholic shite, the football talk, the pressure of girls, the lazy violence of the slower, less selfless pupils.

So... Sorry to hear about your aunt.

And ma uncle.

Aye, and yir uncle. Sorry.

Aye, well. Fuck it, there it is.

Silence. Out of town now, on the way back to his auld familiar bidings, his uncle's auld bothy farm cottage, Stevie now lord of the manor, or owner of the enclosed cottage, surrounded by farm buildings.

The car smells of stale cigarettes and dog, but it's clean – narry a dog hair to be seen, no dowps in the ashtray. What a reek, but.

Jings Stevie, good car and thanks and all, but, well, it's surely fragrant.

He looks over. A tiny smile, maybe.

Aye, my uncle's dug. Pined for him a wee bit, but auld as fuck itself. Started pishing in the car, but that smell – smell it?

I can. I think. In between all the other smells there is a champion smell, cutting through, making itself known.

Aye, that smell was when the daft thing started being sick in the car. Took it to the vets – being sick, pishing, auld, blind. Vet boy put him doon right there.

Called him a dirty mongrel?

Aye, Johnny – unamused exhale – *he called him a dirty mongrel. And mair.*

Past the garage, out along the low straight –

Lovely dog, mebbe, when he was a pup. Mebbe.

Up the hill, past another few farms, holiday cottages and the like –

So, is it just you in that hoose now?

He looks at me full on, then –

Aye. Mebbe.

Cool.

So, am I in yer auld room, or yer uncle 'n' aunt's?

My auld ain. I couldnae be in there. Well, I was, for one night. Then, fuck it, put a' their crap in the wee loft, cleaned the hoose tae billyo, threw oot all the auld food, milk lang since aff, most of the cookery books, all oot. Well, kept a bit, mind, but mostly all. Looks good now, I think.

Down the hill, up to the sharp bend, over the old railway line, along the straight and turn left onto the farm track. Beyond us, fields of sheep, the auld air-raid shelters – just hints of concrete now, peppered with trees – a few fields more, and the deep North Sea.

Well, here we are Johnny.

And here we are indeed. We drive past half a dozen farm buildings of different age and size, bale stores, a kye byre, the big diesel tank, a couple of derelict, roofless cottages containing unused and ancient ploughs, chickens fleein' aboot unattended, through them all, down a short track and here we are, Stevie's cottage.

Who's were those cheuks?

Ach. Some hippy couple. Pretend farmers, ken, got themselves a big auld Volvo. Dope smokers, no doubt.

He gets out, walks to the back of the car, opens the boot and retrieves my rucksack.

Aye, they asked me o'er a couple o' times when I moved in, but I just thought – fuck that.

I smile.

How?

Well… What would I be to them? A pet wee farmer boy? Ahm no' even farming really, just helping the laird out whilst I'm stopping here. Taking on a few o' my uncle's auld fixing jobs. No – I'm no' sure what I'm doing. Cannae hae them clustering my mind. I mean, say I…

He stops.

Say you what?

Well, say I sell up?

He's never mentioned that. Never mind.

A Brief Shoogle Of Keys

A brief shoogle of keys and we're in. Through the half-glazed, grass-green door, into the narrow entrance, old coats hanging on the rack – *I thought you'd gotten rid of these* – a look – *Aye, you'll be glad I didnae if we're here come winter* – opening the door to Stevie's old room – my room now – single bed, Stevie's old ane though, nothing new, but with clean sheets, I hope. I go in, sit on the bed and Stevie passes me my rucksack, closing the door behind him. Now, the room is quiet. I see the sunlight catching the meandering, floating dust, the window looking smaller and smaller, a patch of damp in the top left corner, this bed just a wee man's bed, not even a full-size adult bed, tiny wee drawers, nae space, nae space. Christ, this is way smaller than I remember it.

It's a fucking prison cell.

I cling to Stevie's words – *Say I sell up.*

Jings, there's a dampness to this room, a real smell. I move over to the window and open it as far as it'll go – a full six inches or so, jamming it open with a book left there, presumably for that very job. It's a bent, sodden, grey-dust drenched book, a curling metallic pink cover, a name I can't make out due to the curl and a title – *The Rose of Enchantment.* Well, that's my evenings sorted.

A knock – *Johnny?*

Aye, come in.

He's in, and the room is full.

You okay in here?

Aye, umm, pretty small, eh?

Aye, but just for sleeping in, ken? The rest of the cottage isn't too bad.

It's barely a cottage. More a bothy. It was a bothy, I'm sure of it. How can I move from a populous city like London to the wide-open spaces of Fife and find myself in a smaller room? Stevie needs to leave the room. Him being in here only accentuates the upturned broom cupboard feel.

You got any tea in?

Aye. Come through.

I follow him. As I do so, we pass another room – *Aye, this is my room* – showing me in, a grand double bed in there, plus – what's that? It's en suite?

You're fucking en suite?

He's laughing, red-faced.

Yer fucking en suite an' I'm in that tiny wee chicken coop? Ya fucking cunt.

Snorting now, body curled, hand up to bright face, tears –

Fucking Stevie!

Both hands, up against him, push him onto the double bed. He rolls over willingly, giggling, speechless, feet in the air, struggling for breath.

Aye, ya prick…

My head's down. I'm smiling, but I'm not happy. My humour is tied.

Johnny…

Johnny…

He's catching his breath.

Aye, well Johnny – you don't have to stay here. Keep it a wee bit. You may like it. I did, ken, growing up. The sunrise is amazing. These fields, the beach – plenty to do here. You won't find yourself alone in that wee room for too lang, I promise you that.

* * *

Cup of tea. Too sweet for me, but happy to have it. I haven't sat in this kitchen for many a year, but it's still the same, ingrained with dust and grease, cooking oils, soot from the Aga cooker. I can tell Stevie's vacuumed the carpet, maybe wiped the windows, maybe had a wee go with the soap on the skirting boards, but I can tell he gave up, too. I can tell the job was too much to take in. I don't blame him. He'll be asking me next, I know that. Fair enough, help pay my way.

So… what happened Stevie? Where've you been? I heard tales of Ireland?

Aye. Well. I was over there a while – finished at agricultural college up Angus way. Three years in all, but easy stuff. I kent it all fine a'ready, but now I've the wee bitty certificate… Then got masel teaching for a college, supposedly, but it wisnae for me. I mean, it helped me be no' so shy – wi' the teaching, but I was just… I was practically just labouring, ken? Running their fucking wee toy farm.

Sip. The cup is clean. There is no oil or dirt, no hair floating on the surface.

Shite, Johnny, I could have been doing that here! Man. I was put up in a tiny wee chalet box caravan thing, in charge of a bunch o' lads a few years younger than me I could hardly understand, them no' listening one bit, just lazy skivers.

I note that the table has been wiped – is clean. There's a fruit bowl, with bananas and an apple. Soon this cleanliness will take over the kitchen. Soon the dirt will be vanquished. I'm sure of it.

Where was it?

Donegal.

As the tea progresses, it gets ever sweeter. Here, towards the end, it tastes like Hieland fudge.

Aye Stevie – mind no sugar for me.

He laughs. *Aye, I mind. Just thought you'd appreciate it this once.*

Ya fud.

So, who were these guys?

Fuck. Aye, well, I was supposed to be learning them a varied farming knowledge – a Foundation in Farming, but Christ in ribbons – I couldnae get a single word in their thick skulls. I stuck at the first year a' teacher and professional like, but then one of them – sip – *one of them I sent out in the tractor – just for some basic tillage, nothing more. But the dowp never came back in. Now, we a' thought – masel and the other instructor gadge – that he'd bunked off, seein' as it was midwinter and cauld. But guess this* – sip – *he'd fucking got stuck in the tractor overnight.*

I laugh.

Eh? How the fuck did he do that?

Well, how indeed? Turns out, next day, we found him, a' hypo – hypo – hypothermic – turns out the tractor had broken down mid-field, its lights aff an a', and he'd been too scared o' the dark to climb out and walk over the field back towards the farm.

So he slept in the cab?

Aye. Nigh on froze, poor wee sod.

My tea is finished. I don't really want any more.

So?

So, well, it turns out, the way they read it – my employers, I mean – that

I was negligent. I should have, it seems, checked he'd come back in, or have telt everyone to take a torch with them in the cab, just in case, ken?

Just in case they break down?

Aye – well no – for me it was mair like, just in case the dowp's scared o' the dark… Christ.

Pause.

Anyhow, he was in hospital for a few days and ended up losing a few toes to frostbite. End result – some doughba' cannae walk onymore and my contract isn't renewed, thank Christ for that.

So you left?

No! I had the end part o' a year to do. Still – the boys listened to me mair after that. I fair toughened up, couldnae be bothered telling them nowt, just treated them as unskilled labourers, helping me run this daft wee farm in the middle o' nowhere. To be honest, I wisnae sure what I was going to do, but then… but then, when ma uncle died, so close after ma aunt – well, it made sense just tae stay back here. Try and work out whit's next.

Not so dissimilar from myself, then. Deaths aside.

So… what is next?

He shakes his head. *I've little idea, Johnny, little idea.*

* * *

It's early evening. I am banjaxed from the journey and the early hours alcohol, spent the afternoon asleep despite the sugary tea, woke up feeling even worse, disconnected, disjointed, fuzzy head, not sure where I was… And now Stevie's got the whisky out. He pours me a mugful, not a glass – he remembers that's my fancy, drinking it from a mug, fine enough.

Cheers Stevie. Great to see you. And thanks.

For the mug?

No, for getting me out. And the mug. Man… I was – running low.

Aye. I bumped into yer auld dear. She said you'd been quiet, finished the college, hadn't found much else.

Troublesome times, Stevie. I sip my whisky. *How did she seem?*

Aye, well. She was keen you came back, I could tell that, what with your Rab bein' away so lang. But, I mean – it was just in Willie Lows I saw her. She was buying a' sorts o' richt posh food I'd ne'er heard of and I was jist standing there listening, haudin' a pair o' roasting tatties.

I smile. Stevie's got the radio on, a Gaelic-speaking station, playing Scottish country dance music. This what his uncle and auntie used to put on and it fits in perfectly, the mood here, seeing Stevie. It's as though the room demanded the familiar bouncing accordion playing to warm it back into life, seep into the carpets and the curtains. I sip at the whisky. It is utterly fantastic, just the right strength, flavour, warmth...

Aye, I wasn't meant to be an artist, I'll tell you that.

Shite! You were a'ways guid. A'ways with the high marks, good pictures – here, mind that picture you did o' auld Mr McKenzie?

I do. But it's not worth mentioning.

Aye but Stevie – you need more than that. I need more than that. Like you – running that wee farm felt false. That's what I was doing. Jumping through hoops to get marks, then when I got to college it was completely different. It's SO fucking dear down there, I was jumping through hoops just to pay the bills. Who'd be an art student? I'll tell you – someone with rich folks or narry a care about a massive overdraft.

He snorts in agreement.

So – What are you going to do?

I finish my whisky. I have very little idea about what I'm going to do. Do I have to decide? Right now? This year even? Maybe I could just drift into something...

Well, I guess I'm going to get a job Stevie boy, gonna get myself a job. But I'm going to have some more whisky first. And then some sleep, I hope.

A Manky Old Toy, Mama

Christ, well no, that was some welcome from ma ain sister. No doubt forgotten a' the times we played as bairns, no wanting me in at a'. "I've got we'ans Mikey, I cannae hae you in" but then letting me in onyway but her fucking husband jist staring at me. "How long's THAT staying? He'd better be out by the weekend and nae drink or drugs in the hoose" and I pull oot ma secret weapon – the saft toy fer the bairn – but there's twa bairns now – how was I tae ken that? But ane's tiny, just a wee baby and the ane I got the toy fer – she didnae want it one bit, pure screwed her nose up "Who's this man? But I don't WANT a manky old toy, Mama" and ma sister like, "She's no' an infant, she willnae want a baby toy, she's at primary next year, she's intae bands and horses and such noo." But me, well, surprised likes, but still too clever about the speed, no' bringing it out at a', even when their dug's sniffing aboot ma bags and the bairn pointing – "What's that smell? What's that smell? It smells like… wee wee" and me laughing – eh, just a bairn eh, she couldnae smell the speed OR the tea, but ma sister's like, "Michael, you are HUMMING, Jesus, you need a shower and wash those claes" but her husband wi' his thundery eyes at me, meeting me in the kitchen and gein it – "You're no settling here pal, I tell you that. What a reeker you are. How dare you? Are there no showers in jeel then? Is that a myth?" But I'm like, I've no' been inside fae a'most a year ya dobber, I've been working the merkit – jist daen my best, ken, daen my best…

But he disnae gie a fuck and ah ken ahm no' wanted. I worked that out quick. Turfed oot by ma own family eh? That disnae sit easy.

All My Trials, Lord

Fucking Jobcentres.

Here we go.

Walk straight up and in. Safely enclosed and hidden. No-one peers in to a Jobcentre from the outside, the aroma, the atmosphere – so off-putting it deters even the most eager rubberneckers. And upon leaving, the joy – the freshness of the air outside, the weight lifted from the shoulders – I don't care who sees me leaving then, as I have left, I am free, the sun will be shining and the crowd welcoming.

I hate these places.

For a while – a short while, but while enough – I'd flirted with a Jobcentre in London, found it a filthy and busy place populated by desperates like myself who were vultured by low value cash-in-hand offers – the day's work handing out flyers, the day filling a skip, the weekend emptying a warehouse, twelve hours on, no hours off. And I did enough of those. You know that man who hands out adverts at tube stations which you politely take then automatically bin? I was that man, for three days, just. And you know that man who turns up unexpected at a building site for a day's labour, but he's wearing his best clothes as he'd hoped to have an interview for an office-y job that morning? I was that man too. My Dr Marten shoes were soon destroyed by the wet grey cement dust coated floors, the nails sticking outside up from planks, the lifting of said planks with my bare, soon-to-be splintered hands, balanced with my feet, keen to avoid injury. I eventually eased off that site due to my proximity to the men who were real men, the easily-herded comedic bullies who'd discovered their strength and safety in numbers.

I discovered that once my name was on the Jobcentre list, once The Dole knew me, had my number, I was theirs to be tormented. It was no easy option for me, this. Once I'd found a way out, I was very happy to stay out.

But I am not out. I have only just arrived. *Oh no.*

Quick scan, get to a safe place before anyone talks to me. Before any officious worker spins their web of fear around me.

Take your time Johnny, dinnae jist go for any old pish. There's nae rent. Mebbe just bills. And food. And the bus – Ahm no' paying you on the bus.

What about my shoes?

Aye. I'll no' buy you shoes either. Best get a job, Johnny. Winks.

Along the walls and standing free-form on easels throughout the room are blue felt boards, lined by white plastic slits. Posted into these slits are many, many declarations of *jobs*. My eyes run along the half-postcard sized notices, each containing their own particular world of opportunity: *Secretary, Care Nurse, PA, Cleaner, Office Temp, Waiter, Clothes Shop, Bar Work…* I do not want more bar work, oh no. I do not need to be serving my old school colleagues, batting away the inevitable question – *What ye up tae?*

Newsagent requires paperboy/adult
All weathers. Must be early starters.
£1 p/h

Jings.

Hotel requires dishwasher
£2.95 p/h
Shift work. No experience needed.

Well, I could do that – and I do have experience. A *maybe.* Let's see what else there is –

Tropical Aquarium Specialist
Must like fish
£3.05 p/h

That sounds okay. I note down the reference number – FFP/162.

Ef – Ef – Pee – one – six – two…

A cough.

Eh?

It's a Jobcentre lady. Putting up new jobs. Standing too close.

Oh, err, nothing. Just mumbling out loud. Sorry.

Can I help you at all? I've not seen you before here have I? Are you registered? You should really register.

I look down at her – and I mean down. She's a wee lassie. But big – wide. But short. A ball, almost. Certainly a snowman-shaped body.

Err – no, I reckon I'll be okay. I've just arrived. I'll see. Thanks. Okay.

I turn and scan the adverts – the new ones she's just placed –

Supermarket check-out assistant
No previous experience required
£2.86 p/h

How about that?

Aye, no. Thanks.

(Go away.)

There's a raspberry smell coming from somewhere. I'm guessing it's her, but I don't want to look. Or smell. I don't want to look as though I'm seeking where the smell is coming from… I mean, it's not *unpleasant* as such, it's just… raspberry.

(Next.)

Kennel Assistant
Must like dogs
£3 p/h

Fuck it. I am ambivalent towards dogs – but it'd be outside, eh? And I could leave this bloody Jobcentre… I could surely do that one. I take the card off the wall and read it again, but this time holding it closer –

Hey – put that back you – there's other people to see that.

She's looking at me, disgusted, as though I've pinched her erse. This close, I suspect that it IS her raspberry aroma. I think it's a perfume, in fact. Or maybe a lip-balm?

Oh – aye. Could you, um, could you mebbe give me the number for these folk?

She smiles. A well-rehearsed, sticky-lipped smile of power.

Put the card back, as I said. Write down the reference number and stand in line.

She points over to a small queue – six people maybe, dejected, heads down, one eyeing towards us, awaiting her return. My back shivers. *Fuck this.* I do a quick calculation – how many dog kennels can be in this area? Four or five? So, that's half-a-dozen short phone calls. Much quicker and more palatable than standing *there* waiting for fragrant ol' *her.*

I look down, taking a second or two to survey and consider my options. The carpet is dark blue, with black and grey threads weaved within, heavy wearing and excellent at hiding spillage and spoilage, chuggy and muck. The walls are off-white and beginning to flake, there's a power socket – power which could be used for all sorts of magnificent and beautiful reasons but here, I suspect, is used solely for the vacuuming. I wonder if she vacuums. If that's part of her responsibilities, or if there's a *someone else,* someone who comes in *just for the vacuuming.* How did they get that job? Was it offered to them here, by her? How could they refuse?

I smile, offer her the slightest of bows, hand the card back and leave.

* * *

And I walk straight into Mikey.

Hey Johnny boy!

I'd forgotten all about him, odd little thing he is. But here he is, real as life in front of me and all too easy to remember. I look him over – he's showing no signs of being cleaned, yet there is sunshine in his step and a broad, genuine smile.

Good to see you Johnny.

He's awaiting my declaration of love and surprise. A small town though, this one – easy to bump into folk – and there's no love there, not from me, anyhow.

What ye daen in there then? You're no' looking fer a job are ye?

He's jabbing towards the Jobcentre and speaking just a little too loud. People are looking at us, together. I am curling up and dying, a snob befriended by a beggar.

Aye, I was, Mikey. I was after a job. What about yourself – are you on your way in?

Eh? No. He peers down the street. *Fuck that. I'm still signed on down in London. I reckon I'll no' be moving ma claim up. No' the noo', anyhoos.*

I'm not making any effort to speak, just vaguely smiling in his direction, awaiting the *goodbye* I crave.

Fancy a quick snifter then, Johnny boy?

It's not yet midday. I do not.

Eh? No. Thanks, but no. I'm trying to get this job thing sorted out, got to make some kind of effort. Stevie…

I stop. I remember to keep as much information as I can to myself.

Stevie, eh? Did that work out with that clown then, eh?

Stevie's the clown? An eyebrow raiser. Mikey continues.

Whereabouts are you, anyhow?

Ach you know – out near Pitlithy.

Too close.

Whit, the houses down there? The wee farm cottages?

Fuck.

Aye.

Fuck.

Mebbe I'll pop down.

Deep breath.

Aye, I wouldn't do that. Stevie wasn't enamoured with you. He's a… he's a private sort of guy.

No flinch.

Ach, we'll win him over, have no worries there, Johnny boy. You know, I could mebbe bide with you twa a bit?

I flinch, visibly. Surely it was visible.

That won't work Mikey. Tiny cottage and Stevie's… Stevie's no' partial tae folk he disnae ken.

He'd get tae ken me though Johnny boy.

I don't reply, I offer no encouragement, no smile, no friendliness. He seems tired, agitated. I tell you though, if he calls me Johnny boy again, I'm going to hit him.

So what now Johnny boy? Spot of lunch and a wee drink?

I don't hit him.

Eh? No, Mikey, no lunch, no drink, I've to phone a few folk, see what they say then get back to the cottage.

Cannae keep Stevie waiting, eh?

He nudges me with his elbow. In my head I call him a *cunt* for three reasons: it was sore, it's unnecessary personal contact and it's embarrassingly public.

What phone box you using?

What? I look at him incredulously.

Eh?

I ken a good phone you could use. Quiet, like.

What? A phone's a phone.

Aye but folk are aye barging in, efter their turn. I ken a right quiet one. Keep your mind focused, Johnny boy.

He's pointing a finger into his skull, kindly and considerately showing me with his actions where my mind lives.

Um...

Aye, c'mon.

And he's off, straight into the road and almost over before I've started moving. I could, of course, have moved in the opposite direction, but I turn, slowly, and follow him. He's waiting at the mouth of a snicket for me to cross the road, whilst I have to negotiate far more cars than he – and he calls out – *C'mon Johnny boy* – waving his arm in a wide, circular movement.

Gaberlunzie

What furry snicket is this? The tarmac has been worn down and taken over by moss, which has in turn been rained and walked on until it's become a shallow soil. I am walking down a narrow, muddy alley with green moss stone walls all to reach the telephone Nirvana. I can smell, and see, that Mikey has lit up a joint and is blowing at the ends, keeping the thing burning. As I approach, he offers it over – *Draw?*

No.

He's still sooking his joint, looking at the glowing end, watching the smoke exit his nostril dramatically. We have stopped.

What the fuck are we doing here? I don't have time to…

Eh? Calm down, I'll just be a minute. I cannae be smoking this in the street eh.

Fuck this. I'm off. Continuing in the same general direction, i.e. deeper into the snicket and not back out. I walk off, looking for the elusive promised phonebox.

I get ten yards then –

Aye, haud on.

And he's off back after me. *Jesus, calm down, Johnny boy.*

The alleyway continues and continues, walls either side looking into grand posh houses, then the university and there – thirty or forty feet away – a phone box. That's the one, like it or not, that is my destination. As I approach I reach into my back pocket for a pencil and a few 10ps, get things started, be prepared. Mikey is behind me, still prattling away about something, but me not really listening –

Fucking, couldn't see the thing at all… had to be there, Christ what a sight.

He was blaming this huge Jamaican fella…

…and that fucking wee dug of his, yelping…

I'm in, door closed. Smells of pish, but of course. There's a Yellow Pages, relatively fresh looking, dry, droop-perched on the shelf, phone numbers scribbled all over the cover, a few pictures of cocks, a promise of *good sex* if I meet *here* at *9pm* on *March 12th…*

Missed it. Damn.

Exhale. Open the fucking phone book. Kennels – under K. Flick, flick, flick.

Nothing there.

Outside, Mikey looking in. Here, with the pish and no kennels under K, easily the more attractive option.

I look again, in the index this time and there, under K, the phone book declares:

For Kennels, look under Dog Boarding Kennels.

Ah. Easy, straight to **B**, nothing there, slight confusion, straight to **D** and I find it. Three. Three numbers to call. Easy – once I've summed up the courage to do the first one, I'm halfway there, almost.

Ten pence in.

Beep beep beep.

Dial the number – no local code needed. I am local. We are local. Tap in the five numbers and wait.

Four rings, then mid-fifth, the phone clicks into life – but it's an answerphone. I slam the receiver down as quick as I can, hoping to retrieve my ten pence, but – no. It's gone.

Fuck. Fuck.

Next number…

Door opens – *Anything wrong?*

No Mikey – well, aye, there was. But c'mon, Mikey – you can see I'm on the phone. Please, oot – I wave him away with my hands, but he shoves past me – *Here, whit number is it yer ringing?* – grasping at the phonebook, mishandling and dropping it onto my feet.

Ah for fuck's sake, Mikey. Fuck off, eh?

I grab the inside of the door and pull it shut, leaving him outside, startled. I retrieve the phone book from the dowp and spittle midden of a floor, find the appropriate page and start again.

Right. Next number. *Fucking cunt. Fuck off.* Here it is –

Ten pence in.

Beep beep beep.

Dial the number, picked up straight-away.

Hello? Balswallie Kennels?

It sounds like an old man. It probably is.

Oh, um, hi there, my name's Johnny. I'm um, just wondering if you've any work going – part-time or full-time or whatever –

Oh – have you any experience of kennels?

Door opens, Mikey in –

Johnny – Just dinnae tell me tae fuck off!

He's not shouting, but he's not far off. Right in the phone box now, up against me – *Dinnae tell me tae fuck off – I fucking found you this fucking phone box! Dinnae forget that – I'm just being friendly, eh? Worried fer you – helping you out –*

He's close in my face, the breath – jings, the breath – what's in there? Hashish, tobacco, uncleaned teeth, a sourness – bits of spit are landing on me – Christ, his eyes are spitting as much as his mouth, all red and wretched. I turn away and from the side of my own mouth –

Mikey, what? I'm on the fucking phone to the fucking kennels for Christ's sake. Go on – fuck off.

He shoves me further up against the wall of the booth – but it's only a two-inch shove, so crammed we are. His arm's up against my neck, leaving me trapped against the window, the thin metal glazing frame touching my neck, me feeling the broken paint as it gently scrapes.

He's looking at me, silent for a bit then: *Dinnae* – shove – *tell* – shove – *me* – shove – *tae* – shove – *fuck* –shove – *off. I've fucking had it the day.*

One last shove then he backs off, straightens up and reverses out of the booth, leaving just me and the *beep beep beep* coming from the receiver – my time wasn't up. The gentleman on the phone had heard the whole affray and decided, quite rightly, to put the phone down. That's that one buggered.

I'm shaken, of course. Wow. We have certainly crossed a line. Right – okay. Quick glance. Mikey's still there. He's still outside. Loveable, huggable, fragrant Mikey is waiting for me, but for what, I don't know. Fuck him. One more number. Dial the number, job done, go home. Get rid of him once and for all.

My heart goes *beat, beat, beat.*

Get my last ten pence, pick up the Yellow Pages from the floor and find the page – one last number then done. Breathe in – Breathe out. This is becoming stressful, but at least I'll be able to tell Stevie all about my efforts.

Stevie – *Did you find any work Johnny?*

Me – *No, but I rang a' the kennels in the book. I'll try something else tomorrow.*

Stevie – *Kennels?*

Ten pence in.

Beep beep beep.

Dial the number, wait, no pick-up, no answerphone, wait some more, Mikey outside still, nowhere to go, may as well wait, wait, wait…

Hello?

Oh, hi – um, is this Dunmoss Kennels?

It is, yes. How may I help?

She's English. Well spoken.

Oh – ah – I was just phoning to see if you need any help? I mean, staff – jobs, you know. Have you got any work available?

My forehead is leaning against the cold plastic of the writing board, directly above the telephone itself. I am concentrating utterly.

Well, yes, as it happens. I DO need someone for the summer months, it's already getting busier. Have YOU any experience with kennels? And I'm sorry, what was your name?

It's Johnny. My name's Johnny. The summer would be great for now. I'm just back up here after being away…

And have you experience, John? In kennels, I mean?

Aye – um, no, but, I've worked in farms all through my teenage years. I ken how to look after animals…

Heh heh – Well, John, it's more the looking after AFTER animals, if you see what I mean, but by all means, come on up and we'll take a look at you.

What sort of time? Quick, Johnny – Ask –

Erm – what sort of time suits you?

Anytime during the day. I should warn you though, the position IS advertised elsewhere.

Okay, erm – I'll come up the now, then?

Fuck. Shouldn't have said *the now*. Sounded common.

Yes John, why don't you do that. And John?

Aha?

Where did you hear about us?

Oh, erm, I'm just looking through the Yellow Pages for work and I was phoning interesting places.

My. That shows initiative. Well John, I'll see you later. My name is Mrs Bradley. Bye now.

And she hangs up, leaving just me and, withering outside, Mikey. I stand, receiver in hand for a few more seconds, happy in the peace, the peace before the troubles. Phone down. Fish in back pocket for paper, find none, attempt to surgically remove the square of Yellow Pages that has her details on but end up ripping the whole page, diagonally, top left to bottom right. I look at what I've got. *Fuck it.* That'll do. Scrumple it into my back pocket, check the telephone for change, find none, turn around open the booth and leave.

Well?

Well what?

He's smiling a put-on, trying smile. Trying to be-friend, to re-friend.

Did you get a joab, Johnny boy?

I *almost* tell him to fuck off. Very close. Instead, I walk away over the mottled car park, away from town, towards the road that I think leads towards the kennels. Mikey calls out –

Where you aff to, then?

I don't stop. I half turn, but continue the walk.

Nowhere, Mikey.

But what about that drink?

Hands in pockets, continue on, quietly – *There's no drink Mikey* – then quicker, purposefully, away.

Whit A Fuckin' Holiday

Well, what can I do now? What can I fucking do? I'm no' chasing him, the mood he's in... I cannae go hame – nae hame, I ken that. Jist... jist a sofa and even that I had tae be aff by breakfast "You can't just lay there smelling the whole room out Michael. We need to eat breakfast. Go on, go on..." Ah Christ that's no' the answer, is it. I'll get tae the bus station, make my way out tae that Stevie's place, he'll be on fine form once I show him how useful ah am. I can fucking do... I don't know. Something. Farm? Aye. I can farm. There've got nae kids, those twa – Stevie and Johnny. No reason to object tae me aince they ken me proper. Ach, Johnny will calm himsel'. I'm a saft lad, deep doon. I jist cannae handle folk haen a rise... Fuck. Was I a bit heated there? Aye, but – ken, I'd ma reasons. I'd ma reasons, he'll ken that. When I tell him anyhoos. Just a day or so when I havenae got a place tae stay – he willnae kick me oot. I'll need tae scoot back tae London come next week anyhoos – got tae sign on and a' that... Disnae seem much fer me here; no' the best gamble, this ane. Whit a fucking holiday! Ach. There's a pub at the bus station eh? Aye, well I've still got a few squid aboot me and mebbe it's time fer a pint. There's always an answer if ye look hard enough and a pint's often enough that answer.

Dugs

A few minutes' walk and I look back – no sign. He took the hint, I hope. And that, I hope, will be that. *Fucking cunt.* What was that all about? The road out to the kennels is a good walk, but it's early still. Lunch can wait – let's get this done.

Aye Stevie, I had an interview today.

He'll be chuffed to hear that – me getting out and getting on. Me too – I'll be chuffed with that. Continue as I mean to continue. Keep out of that fucking dole office, keep the blues off my shoulder. A car passes and I reckon I've only got another mile to walk before I can begin to hitch, before we're suitably on the outskirts of St Andrews. The houses here are grand, big old places, surrounded by high walls and mature evergreens – quite a place to live. I'd live here, for sure, if I could. Maybe there's a flat – maybe I should look. Though Stevie's cool the now...

I pass a tiny newsagent, duck in, steal a Snickers, buy a fake Coca-Cola and leave.

They'll have plenty of business in an area like this. No-one will notice one little Snickers bar gone, I'm sure. It'll be all old grannies and university lecturers using that wee shop. You know, I reckon a wee shop like that must build in a 5% loss of stock for thievery and I doubt they ever make it. Doubt they ever reach their 5%. Really, I'm just helping them out, balancing the books. I open the Cola, taking a sip. It's a rank bad drink, oh yes.

This tastes puir shite.

Past another, lower hedge, ending as I reach the driveway. A late middle-aged couple, him in light pastel colours, her with a startling gold chain round her neck, resting on her dark red and black thick-knitted jumper and ample bosom. She is wearing slacks. Light brown slacks. They are watching me walk open-mouthed, perhaps having heard my bad-Cola directed profanity. I smile at them and then I'm gone – beyond their driveway, out of their sight.

I reckon I'm safe to eat the Snickers now? That's been a while.

Quick look back – no-one there, no crazed storekeeper, no high security guard ducking behind a car – Snickers out, rip wrapping with teeth, pull down, keep on walking, balance Cola, don't fall over.

Between this Cola and the Snickers chocolate/nut/caramel bar, I am consuming so much sugar that the inside of my cheeks are beginning to fur up. I'm making good speed though, alert too, avoiding dog shit and the occasional errant lamppost. I pass by a house I recognise – a modern, retro-build detached villa, probably built in the 50s or 60s but with turrets, Tudor cladding, diamond mine oriel windows… a real uppity mongrel of a house, a maroon-bricked, double-glazed, lovingly cared for folly. Years earlier, Stevie and I had attended a party in this very house – or, more accurately, we'd been in attendance whilst a party had been going on around us. The bravery required to make our way to the gathering was mostly fuelled by alcohol, of course, but said bravery didn't extend to speaking to anyone once we arrived. We had ended up in a sub-room just beyond the kitchen, drinking our vodka, chatting away happily, occasionally stopping completely when someone or other buzzed into the room, opening the door and allowing the murmur of the party, the laughter and jovial happenings to come on in and ridicule our half-in/half-out position. We were like scullery maids, hidden away in the servant's quarters. But no-one asked us to *Join us! Join us!* And we certainly didn't ask them… Come the end of the vodka, our position of half confidence and un-embraced welcome hadn't really changed, so we decided to leave by the back door, if we could find one. On the way out, exiting beyond the washroom, the spin dryer and washing machine, we daftly lifted everything we could see – dust-covered family photos containing relatives relegated to this outer region of the house, a scarf, an umbrella, a bottle of cooking wine, a box of matches, some firelighters…

I'm guessing the bin was their outside bin, but just outside their kitchen door, so most likely for household rubbish and such. It had a cage around it, probably to keep it upright and deter the foxes. The thing about firelighters though, I guess, is they're not keen to go out, just keep on burning, regardless of how initially reluctant their close-proximity bin buddies are. And the cage that kept the whole thing together, of course, as it was burning, the firelighter slowly dropping further and further inside, lighting all around it, plastic mostly, from the smell, but maybe the odd bit of more organic material – cardboard, food, old milk, maybe. We couldn't move it – the bin, I mean – once it was off, the flames were too fierce. Plus it wasn't on wheels – we would have had to actually grab the thing, thus burning our paws. Fuck that. So we hid, hearts racing, in the bushes nearby, the bushes beside the wall to the next house along. We were whispering to each other – *Shall we tell them?* But, it was all *Shall we fuck! We'll get done. No, let's wait. If it catches on the house we'll run back in the back door and rescue everyone – be the brave heroes.* Drink was clouding our judgement, maybe. *Shit, look – here comes some folk* – and a guy came out – the son of the owner, a rugby playing oaf, a bully, a handsome cock, a mid-range intelligence luck-of-birth head honcho. He shouted – *Holy fuck!* And ran back in to raise the troops, soon re-appearing with a dozen or so handsome and pretties, all done up in their fineries. One girl took this moment to vomit, thus drawing some attention her way, the others kept fifteen, twenty feet from the flames. And then we heard –

What about those two who were in the scullery? We should get them out?

Ah, fuck.

Who was it? Those two farm boys? How did they get invited anyhow?

No reply. I was told about it during a maths lesson. Maybe reluctantly and by a bit-part attendee, but I was told and invited, I'm sure. But no-one sang our name, took responsibility for our presence, our, perhaps, *murder*, should we end up burned to the gills in this awful-looking, make-believe dwelling.

But no time for that.

One of the onlookers – a flanker, a wingman, a lieutenant to the house owner's son – skipped back inside this non-burning house, bravely making his way through the perfectly safe rooms, looking for us, shouting so loudly we could all hear him outside.

Ah, shite. They'll know it was us...

I turned to Stevie, but he was away, *Wait there* – crouching down, running alongside the wall, deeper into the garden. I began to follow, but cramp and the draw of the flames kept me where I was, maybe thirty feet from the fire, no more, watching the girls in their shortest of skirts, holding each other's arms, the boys ready to fight in their rolled-up shirt sleeves, some smoking cigarettes with an air of acted nonchalance, being the *cool men,* sipping at their sophisticated white wine. The fire had probably reached its peak and was just then almost beginning to lick the top of the overhanging roof above it. I guess there's a chance, a *slight* chance that the roof could have caught, which wouldn't have been so good. The house would be scarred, regardless, I knew that. There'd be smoke marks on the underside, up the white-washed, genuine Victorian kitchen extension wall…

And then Stevie had appeared, massive shy Stevie, unlikely he'd ever spoken to any of those folk in his puff, but there he was, dragging a garden hose, it spunking out drabs of water as if rudely awoken and not up to full power. The head handsome boy spotted him and rushed to help, but it was only *a garden hose,* not a full strength fireman's effort, needing the strength of many to hold it – and then Stevie spoke, loudly, even I heard it, shaking head boy off – *Don't get the hose, ya dowp, turn the fucking thing on. I couldnae find the tap* – and head boy disappeared, the water spurting, rushing out seconds later, Stevie spreading it all over the bin and then me off, out of sight, running round to the back door, in and through the house, no smoke, no danger other than the fear of bumping into the wingman who'd been dispatched to find us…

And then out of the front, straight into the heart of the party, the adventure and spirit of the blitz. Stevie still washing the bin down with garden hose water, head handsome Harry beside him, occasionally pointing at a dod of rubbish, an escaped flare of paper that had lifted out of the flames a metre or so and dropped.

I find myself beside a most pretty looking girl, one I recognise from school, of course, but do not know. She touches my arm – *Gosh, you were lucky to get out! Where were you?*

I go bright red at the physical contact. The brightest of all the reds. *Erm – I was in the cludgie.*

The what?

Erm – the loo.

She turned to her pal – *Johnny was in the loo. Doing a piss.*

I looked at her friend and smiled. She grinned back – at Me, the pisser. I shivered.

Later that evening, once it'd been declared all clear, this massive adventure had been seen through, Stevie and I had entered the house with the thinned-out crowd, almost in amongst, Stevie talking to Handsome Harry of the House, me with the two girls, occasionally chirping, heart racing with the proximity and the beauty and the perfume. We'd sat around the kitchen table, Stevie the hero, me with some worth, despite no heroics and only an imaginary piss to talk of. Stevie, drunk and sober, was happy to chat, almost, telling people of his farm adventures, how he'd once had to drive out a whole herd of coos from the threat of a fire in a neighbour's byre. There was a noted difference in the speaking, the accents, the speech and questions slowed towards Stevie, but his own accent straightened, vocabulary changed to suit audience. Politer, correct words, no farm slang, no *muckers, doddies* or *hogs* all changed to *spreaders, sheep* and *lambs.* I sat in a haze, smoking the cigarettes offered, listening in, drinking the red wine, speaking when spoken to, then lazily doodling slight images of our dinner party on a newspaper, raising the odd squeal, a smile, a compliment. We were almost the belles of the ball, almost the talk of the town. *Draw Suzy! Draw Suzy!* The bonniest of them all, easy to sketch, over-emphasising her breasts to much notice and humour. *And Steven, draw Steven* – and me looking over to him, sharing a moment, the two of us dowps in amongst the thick of it all, the beautiful people, eye-to-eye, smiling and happy...

* * *

And that was the past, of course. School remained the same, the boundaries of etiquette, class and shyness still there. We laughed, Stevie and I, we laughed at the whole event. *Maybe we should do that at all the parties. Light a fire, get the atmosphere charged, become brave heroes, draw the scene for posterity...*

Sun out, warm on my cheeks, slight breeze on my neck, slight sweat on my back. I look behind me and see a bus approaching, its nametag declaring *Strathkinness.* Aye, that'll do me. Thumb out, bus slows, all aboard.

It's just a wee half-bus. Not even a single decker, a wee half single decker. I pay full fare and sit myself down, back seat, no-one else on board. We sit stationary for a wee half-minute, me perched by myself on the toy bus to teuchter land, then we're off, a shake of the diesel engine, an extra jolt, then easing down the road, the quick route out of town. Soon we're passing fields, country park to our left, entrance to a golf course, farm buildings. The driver shouts out to me – the only passenger – but I can't make out a word over the noise of the engine so move to the front, leaning forward on the barrier at the steps, listening in. He asks – *So where do you want drapped?* I explain *The kennels, please. Ken the auld manse just o'er that big hill coming up? I think that's them,* and then that's him silent, leaving me leaning in towards him like an eejit whilst he gets on with the drive, no doubt a bit perturbed my big heid's popping into his view every time he looks to his left. Good view here at the front though, I can see why the grannies would chose these seats.

I'm dropped off at the foot of a wee drive which leads to the kennels. Tree-enclosed, either side, the path damp with mud and moss and along I go, slow stepping and watchful of the slip, keen not to arrive having slipped but keen to get there all the same, so persevering, looking into the boundary trees, spying a few blackbirds darting about but nothing much else, avoiding the stray branches poking onto the path.

A minute later and I'm there, end of the drive, over the car park towards the house, knock on the door and wait.

I've never been up here. The house itself used to be a manse, I'm told, and some of older folk around still refer to it as such, well, my mother did once, anyhow. An impressive-looking two-storey building, steep black-tiled roofs, ornate but blistered white-painted metal work decorating the upper windows. It is really what the party house we nearly burned down was trying to be – a beautiful old place, characterful and welcoming. I turn from the door and look around – fields, almost just fields, broken up by an occasional shed or stone farm building. There's a shed nearer by, a couple of cars indicating someone is in, despite the lack of answer from my knock suggesting they are out. There's a lot of barking though for sure. Fuck it. I'll walk towards that. Where there's barking there's dugs, after all.

I approach a dilapidated old gate, its hook long since retired and now only remaining closed by the tired nudge of a rusted, browned spring. Sheltered from the sun by the house itself and an imposing hedge, with green fungus and split ridges throughout, I'd guess this gate never really dries, just slowly rots away. I push my way through, smiling, upright, trying to look as unthreatening and personable as possible. It isn't easy. I'm straight onto an overgrown drying green, of sorts, clothes lines draped in spidery angles from old wooden poles. I quickly note this drying green has several incidents of dog shit peppering its finery. Running alongside the overgrown grass is a hastily constructed stone slab path and this seems like the safest route, at least any turd would be highly visible upon the relatively flat grey path. As I wander, the barking slowly gets louder, then some music – choral singing? A church choir, perhaps? Then, I think, a lady's voice – but this lady is no lady. The expletives are very audible, if well presented.

Oh, do be quiet you terrible, terrible dog. Oh, do fuck off. FUCK OFF. I'm trying to clean your mess away.

Then a half-glass door opens and bounding out comes a small black and white mongrel, large floppy ears, wet black nose. And straight to me, and straight up me, over and over again.

Bruno! Bruno! Oh DO get down Bruno. Oh – I'm sorry, so terribly sorry.

She's out herself now, the source of the voice, the same voice I'd heard on the phone, Mrs um… What was it?

Mrs Bradley. Pleased to meet you.

She holds out her hand. It is the definition of filth. Shite upon dust upon paint upon mildew upon…

We shake hands. *Hi. I'm Johnny – I was on the phone earlier?*

She's got her grip on the dog's collar now – *DOWN, Bruno. Stay DOWN. That's it.*

Her clothing is extraordinary: paint-splattered, multiple rips, multiple layers, mismatched shoes, socks too, no doubt, if I could see them beneath her baggiest of stretched and distressed jogging bottoms.

Now off! Off you go! And Bruno is away, running through the too-long grass, first avoiding the mines then stopping to smell them.

Now, there you go. I do enjoy letting them run out, if I have the time, you know.

Piss, leap, lollop; piss, lollop, leap.

We both watch Bruno, for a second, a few seconds more. Slightly awkward but – *So Johnny, let me show you the kennels* – and she's turned and she's off back in, towards the noise of the dogs and the holy warbling. I follow and approach the kennels but am quickly met by a smell, the smell, the *smell.* What on earth…?

She's straight in though. I must follow. Cannot fall at first hurdle. I'm through the first door and hearing a holy choir – I identify the music source straight away, a battered and paint-covered stereo cassette deck, turned up to full volume, the nuns and monks contained within straining at the top of their lungs. It's loud, but that's not the over-riding problem – that'll be the odours.

Beyond everything, anything I've encountered in previous farming years. The wretched stench here is the king of all stench. Okay, the obvious is there – the fresh shite, the piss – but there's more, way more. For a start, and I'm only guessing here, I *think* the over-riding smell is *Old Dog Piss.* An unsubtle, aggressive relation to the fresher of the type. Much else seems slightly more familiar from spreading muck, manure – even the smell of a wet sheep – for I guess the dogs here get damp too and hey, we all know the smell of wet dog. But there's a more overriding damp also, the actual building kindly providing a thick, ever-present stench of its own. What else? A rich, sharp cleaning fluid joining in the nasal assault, bags of musty dog food, fine particles of said food rising and clouding up the already too-choked air. And what the fuck is that on the floor? A pillow case? A yellowing pillow case holding a ball, maybe? I'm staring…

That's tripe.

Of course. Sheep's stomach. Yum.

That's going in with these lads at the bottom – paid extra for a double helping, these big old fellows at the end.

She hoiks up the tripe with a pitch fork and offers it over – *Here, you try.* I'm slightly taken aback but swing into action, grabbing then holding the dinted old fork steadily, watching the tripe intently should it take to leap off the edge.

But it doesn't. It lays as still and easy as an old sheep's stomach.

And then, my trust in the tripe established, the smell taken on board, I begin to notice the dogs either side of me in their identical little cages, five or six feet of run, maybe, four-foot wide if they're lucky, and beyond, at the back a tiny little room – for sleeping perhaps, or the feeling of safety which the relative quiet and dark may bring. On the floor of each cage is an inch or so of wood shavings, absorbing the piss, hiding (a bit) of the shite, turning colour from bright yellow when new to a darker, more caramel-coloured sludge when dampened. The dogs are mostly looking at me, or so it seems, but perhaps it's Mrs Thingy or most likely the tripe, but they're at their doors anyhow, yapping, shaking, pawing, yowling. I think if I were a dog, I'd vote not to be kept in kennels. They may enjoy the smell, mind you. Most dogs I've known have enjoyed a roll in a dead seagull or being nose-deep in a decaying seal.

And here, at the end of the kennels, I myself slow up, head back, ears threatened but more – me threatened, by the volume and anger showing with these two dogs at the back, in opposite cages, guarding, as guard dogs do, furious and hungry, salivating and scaring every living thing in earshot.

Except Mrs... Mrs Bradley. She's not feared at all. She grabs a resting broom, pulls it back and swings it hard into the cage door of the first dog, a large and very hairy Alsatian, shouting *SHUT UP* and *BACK OFF*, then another hit, turning the broom long ways and poking at the dog itself, the dog responding by biting and wrestling with the gnarled broom handle.

Here, John, give it the tripe now, whilst it's distracted.

Cool, I can do that. I make my way over, closer, but there's no obvious way to get the food in... Unless it goes over? Over the door? That must be it. I lean back, tripe almost on the ground, and hoik the tripe into the air. Mrs Bradley looks at me aghast – *What the* – as the tripe lands on the very top of the wire door, out of reach, fragments of it dropping down onto herself, her hair, her shoulders. *Oh, for bloody Nora. John. This stuff... this stuff SMELLS. I DO NOT want it in my hair.*

But the dog has quietened. It's whimpering now, looking up, attempting the odd jump but slipping on the tiles, its thick black claws whipping against the concrete floor, its eyes darting over to us, then back to the food as if to ask, *Ah go on, bring it down now, don't tease...*

And the dog opposite, another Alsatian, has quietened too, similarly confused at this *airing* of its food, perhaps knowing it won't be fed itself until this particular quandary has been settled. With this newfound silence, we can hear the radio, almost clearly. It's still the religious speculators, keeping their peace, calm amongst this midden of noise.

One thing is clear though, it's these twa guard dugs who are providing most of the racket. The other dogs have withdrawn their objections for now, or perhaps are just curious as to why these two have quietened and are giving us a moment's grace as they attempt to work out what's going on, why their world has suddenly, pleasingly, calmed.

Bring the chair.

I look at Mrs Bradley, my eyes perhaps slightly too wide, questioning.

The chair. At the entrance to the kennel. Go on, you'll find it easily enough. Covered in paint. Sturdy.

Okay. I can do that. I stride down towards the door, avoiding slight streams of pish that have escaped the sawdust barricades, catching the glossy black eyes of the other, friendlier dogs as I pass, open the internal door, picking up the chair and walking back towards the end of the kennel, again the dogs following me, their heads slowly turning back again as though watching a lethargic game of tennis.

Right. Now you – you're a young lad – you stand on it and get that tripe down.

I'm silent, but understanding. A slight nod of the head then I'm up on the chair, reaching with my bare fingers –

No! No, you fool – use the fork. Here –

And she's handed me the fork, spikes first, tripe covered spikes first. I grab as far down the shaft as I can, resulting in tripe-wipe upon my jacket arm. Spinning the fork, *debris* dislodges and slips past my mouth by an inch. Too late, but safe, I pull my head back to avoid any more.

Fuck.

Watch your language, John, I don't like swearing, you know. Not in THESE kennels.

I smile. There's a slither of dignity left within her. I wonder how she ended up here, slumming it amongst the shite and stomach. Good pub name that, *The Shite & Stomach.*

Fork up, poke tripe, tripe falls.

And the moment it hits the ground, it's devoured. And the moment it's devoured, the neighbouring guard dog begins to whimper and then to bark and howl, setting the whole damn lot off once more.

Okay, okay, come now John, I'll show you where the tripe is kept.

Great. I climb down. This job may well suck. This may well be a shite job and one to avoid. She's had half a day's work from me already and we haven't even discussed wages. Well, maybe not half a day. Half an hour though, for sure.

Erm – I'm not sure if I can stay…

She carries on walking. Heard me fine, of course, but carries on, out of the kennels and into the fresh air.

Too much for you, is it? This little bit of hard work? She rests the fork on the ground and continues, *Well, I'm not surprised. I've been stuck here myself far too long.* Neck back, head in the air, breathing in the no-longer-in-kennel fresh air. *I DO need help though. Sometimes this all gets a little much, I will admit that.*

Jings, she's well spoken. If I closed my eyes she could be the Queen of England. Or Joan Collins.

No, it's not that, it's just… I have to be somewhere. I reckon – I reckon I may regret this reckon – *I reckon I could come up and help a wee bit. I mean, how much…*

She's straight in –

How much do I pay? Three pounds per hour plus a fifty percent share of all tips. And they can add up, let me tell you.

Tips? That could be good.

Could you begin tomorrow? I could really do with some help tomorrow. This place – she gestures around to the house, the kennels, this shit field grass area we're in, the wooden sheds holding up numerous leaning hand tools and wheelbarrows – *This place could really do with a good tidy.* She looks up and grins at me, almost, *almost* pleading. She wants a Yes, I know that. Fuck it. Why not? That'd impress Stevie, getting work straight away, even though it's a fair hike here from his bit…

What sort of time would you need me?

She's got me. She knows it. She daren't look at me should she blink, or flinch, giving me an out –

8:30am, John, but no earlier. I'm not a strict employer, but I do insist on 8:30am. I will have been up at least two hours by then, so don't think I'm taking advantage. We can break for lunch at midday and then you can leave at 4:30pm.

And then she does look at me – *Is it a deal, John?*

I look around. Jings, there's a lot of stour around here to tidy up. I could do that for a day or two, of course, let her continue with the kennels, the *skilled* work. Maybe that shed could do with a coat of creosote. She could clean these dog keichs up though, fair enough. I don't fancy mowing the lawn here, hitting a shite every few feet, sending it flying in all directions, most likely over me. No, not that, but that aside – and the kennel work, too – aye, I could work here. Give it a week or two anyhow, some money in my pocket, please Stevie...

Aye, fair enough. Now –

Good. Settled. Sorted. She holds out her hand, with a resigned but genuine smile. I offer her my cleaner, softer, less callused hand and we shake. 8:30am? Cripes, that'll be a journey from Stevie's. How am I even going to get home now? I'll hitch, that's how. Sun still high, not a cloud in the sky.

Hame

The hitching is painless. I encounter a man who informs me he's a Military Policeman, on his way to arrest somebody *Absent Without Leave*. I doubt his story, truth be told – would a not-new Vauxhall Astra be a prison vehicle of choice? But I'm happy with the lift and nod along in an interested fashion whilst he spins his tale of bravery. *Aye, this will be an easy one. He knows me, the fella, he'll be expecting me. Knows not to mess with me.*

Me, me, me. It's all about him.

Come St Andrews I jump out at the bus station, wishing him luck and tipping an imaginary hat whilst he roars off importantly. I've missed the four o'clock, but less than an hour to wait until the five. Maybe I'll take a pint in? The bus station pub is welcoming – dark windows, closed door, peace and quiet, I'd hope, at this time... Fuck it. Why not? I'll have the money coming in soon enough, no worries here.

The door has twenty or so thick, mottled glass panels and a long, thin brass handle which I push, stop, then shove open. Stiff. This forcing of the air disturbs the stour inside and quickly I am surrounded by a thin grey haze of cigarette smoke, the smell of sweat, lager and piss. Looking round, I see the gents is right by the exit – I imagine to facilitate other *bus station* but *non-pub* users of said facilities. Judging by the reek, this cludgie is seldom cleaned and I'm guessing that lack of cleaning is similarly for the *non-pub* users of said facilities, though this time the purpose being to put them off. I could do with a piss, but jings, that floating aroma will keep me at bay until I'm a little more desperate.

There's a snooker match on. Lord knows who's playing. Maybe a dozen or so folk watching on – twenty maybe – in different levels of viewing platforms – bar stools, tables, standing – all staring straight at the screen. I hear a quiet, reserved *Oooooorrrrrr* and look up to see a little white man in a dinner suit walking slowly towards a chair. It's not my thing, snooker.

Can I help ye?

Oh – aye – erm – a pint of McEwan's please.

The barman mumbles – *McEwan's is the best buy, the best buy, the best buy…*

And from the snooker choir:

Aaaarrrrrgggh!

Low and orgasmic. One man has his hands on his ears, in a theatrically heightened agony of what he's just seen. My pint arrives and I sup.

You here for the snooker?

It's the barman again.

Eh? No. I'm here for the bus.

He raises his head a little in acknowledgement. He has tight grey hair, a red-veined wrinkled face, buck teeth and a small Hitler moustache. He raises a hand and pinches his small, stubborn nose, pulling it forward, stretching the nostril.

Aye, fuck it. Cannae be bothered with it masel, but keeps the folk in, eh. They get hooked. Somehow.

I look over. The folk are indeed in and they are in respectfully hushed voice:

Oooooooooh.

Low and regretful. A close miss, or a bad thwack, perhaps.

Is this your place, then?

It's the smallest of the talk, almost, but he's being friendly and I have the best part of an hour to kill, so why not. I may be milking this pint, for sure.

Aye, it is that. Well, almost. I've got the lease, ken. How? You after a job?

Eh? My eyes light up, then I remember I have promised my hard-working body to Mrs Bradley. But maybe – well, this place would be easier to get to…

I could do with another pair o' hands. You got any experience? Weekends only, ken. Help collect the glasses, clean the bogs 'n' that.

Fuck. Ugh. No.

Ah, no thanks pal, I've got a job now thanks.

There's a clamp on each shoulder, from behind, hard, firm, shaking me, the McEwan's jumping slightly in its vessel. *A Joab now is it? You're a soft touch, Johnny Boy!*

Ah shite. The smell, the *closeness*, the nerve, the slapping of his shiny black coat… I look at the barman and my expression instantly portrays my thoughts on the situation – anger, embarrassment, fear. He reads my look and nods back, slightly. He must deal with folk like Mikey every single day.

Same again is it, Mikey?

Ah no worries Billy, Johnny Boy here will get me a drink in now he's a working man, won't you Johnny Boy? My my, that was pure quick finding that work. You're letting the side down.

He's drunk. Must have been drinking since I saw him… Will I narry get him another drink. *Ah no – that's me aff* – I look at the clock. My bus isn't for half an hour. Fuck it, I'll walk to the edge of town and get it from there. I raise my glass and sup it down. If I'm drinking, I can't be talking, can barely be listening. Even Mikey will understand that basic rule of pub etiquette.

He grabs my shoulder and I spill a gulp from each side of my mouth, right down my top. What a cunt…

Ah for fuck's sake… Mikey, fucking leave it eh? Will you never fucking learn?

I slam the glass down. There's an actual roar from the snooker fannies:

Aaaaoooooooo.

My jacket is on. I have no belongings to gather. But Mikey's not happy.

Whit's the fucking problem Johnny Boy, eh? Twice in one day yer rude tae me? Fucking posh lad – you're no' better than me, here ye' are, drinking by yersel in the daytime.

He is well cut. Undeniably drunk.

Mikey… I cannae be doing this. Look, it was fine meeting you on the bus, but that's me done. I'm no' a sociable person like you now…

A whit?

A WHIT?

He looks angry. Had he misheard me?

A sociable person. It means…

I ken whit it means. Listen pal…

But I'm not listening. I'm away. I look to the barman – *Aye, cheers Billy* – using his just-learned name, maybe carrying some weight with

Mikey. I turn and I'm gone, but the piss I'm needing hasn't abated and I steer into the toilet, the yellow reek enveloping me, turn the corner stand at the cracked white stone urinal and attempt to proceed.

I make to begin, I get prepared, but before I know it, Mikey's right up behind me, pushing me tight up against the wall. Me, the pisser, am in an uncomfortable position. Although not *pissing*, I am ready, I am *out* where I need to be. I have to stop the first flow, avoid the wall, push my legs back from the urinal, stick my *wang-jang* back in my breeks, deal with Mikey himself.

I'm no' enjoying this Johnny Boy. Every fucking time I see you now you're telling me to fuck off one way or another.

But I'm a big enough lad. I push back with my arms and he falls into the sinks. I'm around, a quick glance and my wee fellow is safely tucked in and I'm off the embarrassment of the leaning on the urinal.

Mikey...

I make to talk, but to say what?

Look – I've got nothing...

But he charges towards me, head down into my chest with an *Opooph.* Fuck. It's actually really sore. I breathe in but the breath halts, I'm winded and backed onto the cludgie once more. Push him off and shout –

Mikey –

But Billy the barman is in, pulling Mikey off me. Roughly, quickly, pulling and pushing Mikey this way and that, not letting him settle, a technique he must have learned *somewhere* for disorientating inebriated ruffians. Collared now, arm up Mikey's back, turns around and marches out. Leaving me with a *Finish your pish* and gone. A fine gift. The gift of finishing my piss. I consider doing just that, but the thought of Mikey leaping back round the corner is too present so I make my way into one of the cubicles and close the door. It locks, thank Christ.

Thank you Christ for this locking door.

There's a loud, and perhaps final, cheer from the snooker crew, followed by a round of applause. I smile, gladdened that someone is happy.

Deep, wretched breath. On the walls, chuggy, stickers, an HIV awareness poster, slime, snot, filth. In the toilet itself – well, you don't want to know. I continue with my business and add to it, finishing up, straightening my clothes, slow my breathing, calming down. Unlock the door and out, wash my hands with the coldest of waters, dry them with a rough blue sodden towel, check my reflection and make my way out.

My path is blocked by an in-stream of snooker fans, talking loudly and animatedly about their experience, their man's win (I'm guessing), who he'll draw in the next round, that evening's plans. I let them pass then pass through myself in the opposite direction. I look over to the bar and Mikey's still there talking to Billy. Billy sees me for a second, nods his head and motions me to leave and looks away. I open the door and walk outside into the remainder of the late afternoon sunshine.

A' Jeely An' Fat

Whit the fuck wiz I daen fichting? Aye, that didnae go sae well. That cannae be the way. I'm no' in the position tae be the man falling oot wi' folk. But whit the fuck wiz Johnny on? I've been nought but friendly wi' him. Christ, his anger eh? No' now… Ah, ma heid man, fucking efternoon drinking, empty stomach, nothing but Billy's microwaved pies tae eat and them pure mingin', cauld insides, a' jeely an' fat… Nae wonder I'm no' at ma best. I need tae get ootae here, straighten up. Oot o' this bar. Too many snooker cunters, that's whit the problem is, fucking nudging past me at the bar… Gie me some space, man. Just some fucking space… Eh? A coffee? Aye Billy, why no' – Nice ane. And Billy? Ane o' those pies an' a' please. Eh? Aye, heat it up. Zap the fucker good an' proper.

Muckle Like Oil

Ah man, what a day.

Stevie looks round – he's cleaning the kitchen, wearing yellow washing-up gloves. Marigolds. He's wearing Marigolds. His face though is flecked with some kind of muck – looks like oil.

Eh? How come. What've YOU been up to?

He's obviously, clearly had a busy enough day himself. Hang on – are those my breakfast dishes he's cleaning? Ah shite, they are.

Listen, Stevie, leave those – I can do them fine –

But they're done. I have acknowledged my lack of the doing though. It's been taken on board. I wonder if he's been doing them for hours, awaiting my arrival, waiting to show me he's not happy to be my skivvy.

Here –

He's facing me know, arms outstretched like a horror film mummy.

What?

Help me get these damn things off.

Ah.

And I'm over, left hand first, peeling the glove off, rolling itself up inside itself – *Make sure you pull that the right way out or it'll never dry* – and same again with his right hand. Underneath the yellow splendour, his hands – his arms – are filthy with oil and dark brown cack. More oil? He should have stuck his hands in the bubbly water. He looks at me and does just that – *No point getting oil on yer dishes, is there Johnny?*

I'm pleased I've something to tell him, pleased I didn't spend the day loping around doing nothing, or drinking, when clearly he's been arm-deep somewhere.

Do you… Would you like a cup of tea?

I would, he says, *I would, whilst you regale me with tales of your adventures as a work-free man in the East Neuk of Fife.*

I mosey to the fridge, pull out the milk, start the kettle, gather the cups, ready the sugar, open the tea caddy, peel out a pair of tea bags, close the caddy, place the bags inside the cups, add the milk, then the freshly boiled water and finally, for him, the sugar.

Aye well, I had an adventure, that's for sure. Where to start? Well, I guess…

I remove the now-watered tea bags and place them carefully in that wee manky box Stevie keeps beside the sink, full of peelings and apple cores and such. And tea-bags.

First bit of news is, I got myself a job, which is pretty good eh? Just for the summer though, but enough for now.

A job? Fucking hell Johnny, quick working! What is it?

He's leaning now, back against the sideboard, mug in hand. I slowly sip at my tea. I am in charge of this situation, and this small rush of power is thrilling me.

Get on with it ya dowp. I need to take a shower.

Ah okay. Aye, no, I eh got a job up at the kennels. Just for the summer, mind.

Aye, you said. Just for the summer. He's staring at me, quiet-like, awaiting more information.

The kennels eh? What, up past Crail way?

No, Dunmoss Kennels at the back of St Andrews. Strathkinness road.

Jings, that'll be some travelling. How are you going to manage that? Are you staying there, likes?

Drink tea. Too hot. Sup tea.

Not sure about the commute – I was going to ask you about the buses…

The buses? How would I ken about the buses to Strathkinness from here? Were you not at the bus station earlier? You should have picked up a leaflet.

Ah –

Ya dowp.

He laughs. My power and majesty have dissolved. *Aye well, time for the shower* – He makes to leave, but before he can – *Oh, and I bumped into that Mikey character again. Not good.* I raise my mug, resting it in my other hand, looking sombre, regaining the conversational upper hand, but Stevie interjects – *He's no' coming here, is he?*

Eh? No. No worries there.

Thank fuck for that.

No he was just… Just causing a bit of trouble. First, he directed me to this daft wee phone box in the middle of nowhere, so I could make a call in the quiet –

Whit, he gave you a hand finding a phone box? Aye, that sounds terrible Johnny. Smirk. *What a tough day you've had.*

Cunter.

No, no, it was worse than that, I mean… Anyway, then he came at me in the bus station bogs…

Stevie laughs, again. *Whit, came at you* – pause – *like a gay lad?*

No, not like that. I'd been taking a drink, he surprised me, I telt him to fuck off and he wasn't happy.

Ah. Never he would be if you told him to fuck off now – I can see that. Never mind. Here – I may have an idea for you, how to get to Strathkinness…

I look up, expectant –

Aye, let me think it through, then I can tell you after my shower. He throws me a dishcloth – clean, this one – *You can get on wi' drying those dishes of yours.*

A Wee Fly, A Root Scootin' Aboot

It's been a fair few days. I've barely had time to reconsider the thoughts that moved me up here, but so far, all seems well, doesn't it? I mean, Mikey aside – but he's just a wee fly, a root scootin' aboot, causing a bit of grief. Stevie's sound. It's great seeing him, great being around him. I'm pleased I've moved things on a bit, got this first job already, coming across well, I hope. I could so easily have slumped into doing *nothing* whilst he worked and worked, then worked and nagged, then nagged and nagged then kicked me out. Drop-kicked me back to London. Back to off-egg sandwiches. But no, it's been cool.

And then I drop a mug, whilst drying it. It falls on the stone cottage floor with a *clanker.*

Fuck it though, it's only a cup, doesn't look special, just from some garage or other I imagine; bend down, pick up the big bits, rest them one inside the other, then the medium bits, cradled, finally any other bit I can manage with my fat fingers. Floor will need brushed, mind, cannae be having china in my foot. Or Stevie's.

He's out of the shower now, I can hear him in his room, singing, *Oh a beggar, a beggar, came o'er the lea...*

One of his auntie's songs. I recognise it well, although I only ever heard that one line, which she'd sing over and over whilst she made us sandwiches or went about her chores, leaving us boys to be boys.

I've got the brush out, easy to find in the obvious cupboard and am slowly but thoroughly getting the rest of the mug up off the floor. Stevie's through. He doesn't notice the mug, just sees me sweeping.

No need, Johnny.

I look up.

No need, though I appreciate the effort. I did it afore you got back.

As calmly and carefully as I can, I top-spring the spring-top bin lid and let it all run off, sleeking into the bin, the chips of the broken mug quietly crunching together. Stevie hears it too – *You broke a mug?* I smile – *Aye, but only one of those wee white anes. It didn't look special.*

He marches over, opens the lid and peeks inside – *Aye fuck it, just ain of them. No worries.*

And then, under his breath, whispered almost, *Pishy wee things.*

Must be odd for him, hard even, being back here by himself. That's surely partly why he called me up. He wipes his face, thick stubble clean from the oil now, staring down at the floor. I'm hoping he hasn't spotted another shard. But no, he's just in his own wee dwam. Then, still quiet – *Fuck it.* And up – loud, looking straight to me – *So Johnny, would ye like tae see how yer going to get tae the kennels the morns?* I smile. *I would, Stevie, I would.* He moves towards the door – *C'mon then, get yer boots on.* My boots are already on. I hope he doesn't notice this flagrant disregard of the house rules.

Outside, still light, warm, comfortable. A slight breeze coming by, but this wee farm house always got a feel from the sea, as nearby as it is. Stevie's walking towards the farm itself, I'm not sure where but I'm after him, jogging to catch up, reaching his side just as we pass the other cottage, the one inhabited by the *hippy couple.* A few chickens can be seen just inside the gate to their garden and Stevie laughs – *I'm amazed they're still aroond, what with the foxes* – but he's not awaiting a reply, soldiering on up the path, me looking back at the few brown hens, ignorant of their fate and pecking away at their fenced landscape.

Here we go, Johnny –

We're at one of the farm sheds, two or three storeys high, pale blue aluminium construction, full of weeds, rusted hand tools, old ploughs, a tractor or two… *I was in here earlier, trying to fix the gearbox of that old Massey, but little luck I had. Maybe tomorrow, but.* He heaves open one of the huge slatted metal gates, just a foot or so, enough for us to get in. I notice straight away there's a couple of dead rats at our feet. *Aye, I got them earlier. I was jist stuck under that tractor, quiet like, and ane of them rushed towards me, me lying on the floor. I jist swung the wrench at it and conked the puir wee bastard.* He certainly did, the head is considerably flattened in. There's a look on the rat's face which suggests it was certainly stunned to have its life ended in such a manner. I ask – *What about the other one?* Stevie looks round – *Eh? Ah – Nah. Just found it. Poison, most likely, the laird had me lay a fair bit down last weekend.* I stare at the two poor buggers but Stevie's off down to the far end of the barn already – *Here you go, Johnny – your carriage awaits.* I follow on, grinning, expectant. Stevie's waiting for me, being uncharacteristically dramatic, holding onto a brown tarpaulin, which is covering something, something – a car maybe? No. Too low, too shallow… He whips it off, well, slowly begins to untie at four of the corners – *wait there Johnny, wait there* – and – *twigged what it is yet?* But I haven't. Judging by the low height, the short, narrow size, I can only presume it's a small horse cart or a large sit-on lawn mower. Neither thought exactly fills me with delight.

And then, starting at the back, he's lifting, carefully, snagged on something first and I can see, creeping into view, the back of two mopeds. Christ – our two wee Honda mopeds from long ago. I begin to laugh, then move over and help out – *Jings, these will never work Stevie, what are they – six years unused?* My old moped – the C50 – appears to have rusted spectacularly, its once proud gleaming silver exhaust now the colour and texture of Weetabix. *Fuck's sake, I polished that – look at the state of it now!* Stevie looks at me. *Once. You polished it once, Johnny and it was a shite, half-hearted polish at that. A bodge polish if there ever was one, in fact –*

Aye, calm down Stevie.

There's a wry look on him now, for sure, that's both bikes uncovered. His, a C90 – bigger than mine, more powerful, but a terrible sky-blue colour, compared to my magnificent bright red. *Aye, that's a lassie's bike, a'ways was.* He's gripping the handles now, pulling it off its stand. *Shut it Johnny, it'll still ride, this one, mark my words. Yours widnae, I ken that. Look at it* – I do. It's upright, rusted, cobwebbed. It seems okay. His isn't much better, just… less Weetabixy. *C'mon, bring yours* – and I follow suit, hoik it down off the stand, begin to wheel it to wherever Stevie's wheeling his. He calls over – *Mind and no' be tempted to start it. If we're to have any chance we should check the oil – change it, really, clean the engine oot, charge the battery, pump the tyres – the whole lot.* Christ. That's a' beyond ma ken. He'll know that though. He does. In fact – *We should just concentrate on the one, mind. Mine, I'm guessing, as yours was shite tae begin with, but we may need to pinch a few parts…*

Cheeky bam. As we wheel them out I look down and see the dunt on the front mud-guard from where I crashed into the tree stump, rusted through completely now, the breach of the paintwork no doubt helping the process.

Stevie's up ahead now, as ever. *Here, Johnny, park it up here.* We're right beside the diesel pump, close reach to all manner of tools, solid concrete floor, no deep mud to sink in to, just slithers of cack. Like a brave, experienced hero I pull the C50 back onto its stand. The easiest of biking jobs. I think I may leave Stevie to it. *I reckon…*

Aye Johnny, you fuck off back inside. Make some tea maybe?

Ah. Cool.

I mind fine you never got on with this stuff. Here – I won't be long. Or I will. One of the two, but I doubt you could swing it either ways. He grins at me.

Okay, cheers. I'll see what food's in…

I'm happy to walk back in, pass the hippy folk with their chickens, the windows of their cottage full of candles and wind-charms, tiny stained glass motifs. The wind's getting colder now and I'm speeding up a little, watching the foam of the waves on the sea in the near distance as I continue down the path. The familiarity of the stones crunching underfoot brings great comfort to me, as if I'd expect Stevie's aunt to be waiting there, buttering some thick white bread and covering it with sugary strawberry jam.

I arrive at the cottage and she's not there. She's lang deid. I sing – *A beggar, a beggar* – and she still doesn't appear. Boots off, but keep jacket on. Not warm, this wee cottage, kitchen aside, the Aga always on. I walk in to the kitchen and look around – what to cook? I'm hoping there'll be something that requires a certain temperature for a certain amount of time – some burgers or something – which I could put along with something that bubbles when ready – tinned soup, perhaps. Or beans. There's nothing though, just tea. Well, there's salt and stuff, plus a few vegetables, but nothing I could use. Only tea. Well, I'll have some tea then, maybe Stevie and I can drive in somewhere and grab a takeaway.

I'm not so sure about this whole bike idea of Stevie's anyhow. I can barely remember riding a bike in the seven or eight years since I hit that tree stump. I was never the best, either, never the most confident or comfortable. I was okay up until second gear, but third – well, there was something about third that worried me a little. Perhaps it was because it was a little bit of an *adult* speed. Not for me, a nervous teenager, back then. Now though – well, I should be okay now, right? With all my life experience? I shouldn't panic on these windy roads, greasy with leaf mulch and angry with cars. I wonder if there's even a helmet for me? Cripes, it better not be that thing I was wearing back then, with the Two-Tone stickers and shoogly wind-shield. That'll not help matters, confidence-wise. And never mind the insurance, the driving licence – although I did have a provisional, back in the day – Maybe that's still valid? Or maybe it's matured into a full licence somehow?

I'm enjoying the tea and the thought of the chip butty. I should really take some tea out to Stevie, he'd appreciate that, especially after the news of the *Nae Food*.

The kettle's boiling again and I'm standing by the work-top, expectant. Although I do have an almost empty mug in one hand, it should be clear that I'm making a second cup, this one for Stevie. He pushes through the front door, just in time – *I cannae smell any food Johnny* – and I pour the not-quite-boiled kettle into his cup, quickly dunk the bag, pull it out and add some sugar and milk, all stirred and prepared in less than fifteen seconds, the time it'll take for him to remove his boots and get through to me. We meet, either side of the door, him looking round my shoulder for evidence of the beginnings of food and me sweetening the disappointment, trying to avert his stove-ward gaze with a cup of lukewarm tea.

Aye, there was no food, Stevie.

He looks at me, dumbfounded. *Aye there is* – opens the fridge and points, pulls out sausages, tomatoes, mushrooms – *What more did you need?*

Aye... what I mean is... I'm no good with the sausage, Stevie. I wouldn't know where to start. I was expecting more... Well, something more... readily prepared.

He smiles and raises an eyebrow.

To be honest, I reckoned we could go for a chip butty...

A fish supper?

Aye, well, no' for me, but you could go for that.

That sounds no' bad. We can take the scooter –

That alarms me – *Eh? Are they working?*

He grins, *Well, no, THEY aren't, but mine will be, I'm pretty sure of that. You can ride, I'll shotgun.*

Fuck. That sounds like a disaster of a plan. How can I steer a bike with that great lummox on it? I nervously rub my chin, questioning. Is he serious? *I'm no' so sure, Stevie…*

Look – tea down – *If you've tae ride tae the kennels the morrow, you'll need the practice. And if that bike breaks doon, I'll need to be there tae fix it, this first ride. Make sense?*

Well, I was kinda thinking… You could drive me to the kennels and I could hitch back home?

He laughs – *No fucking chance… Look, you've got a job, well fucking done, but you've tae ride yersel there. Ahm no' taking you and the bus willnae at that hour, I'm sure of that, unless you set oot the nicht and camp oot at the bus station. Mebbe you'll meet your pal Mikey there.*

He puts over a powerful argument. Fuck it. It's only a wee motor scooter, eh? I'll be okay, take it easy, take it slow. *Here* – and he's off out of the kitchen. I make to follow him, but before I can, he's back in, carrying two full plastic bags. One of them he's unwrapping, layer after layer, newspaper, plastic, then a towel. His prize – his old helmet. Pristine, new-looking. *Is that for me?* I ask, arm out in expectation. *No chance,* he replies, *here's yours* – and he hands me the other bag. I open the bag. No wrapping. No towel. Nothing, just a filthy old helmet. I lift it out and it's full of cobwebs, stour, dirt, sand – *sand?* – the corpses of a few old and transparent spiders, a couple of flies, eggs of some sort and… ants. Feck. Live ants. Stevie's laughing – *Ah ya cunter* – I make to throw it down but he's quick, *Dinnae do that, you'll damage it. You'll just need tae clean it oot. Here* – He points down the corridor – *There's a wee Hoover thing in the hall cupboard. It blaws an' sooks too and you can scoosh the ants oot easily enough. Hey, it'll give you something to do while I'm fixing that bike up.* I look down into the helmet again and there's an ant running onto my hand.

Aye, well, I guess it was down to me to clean it. Stevie's back outside with the bike and I'm crouched over the helmet, Hoover tube in hand, sooking out every last bit of whatever I can find, scraping the helmet itself, getting off old dirt, grit amongst the rubber. Finish up and a quick wipe down then I put it on, engulfing my head and leaving me deaf, temporarily, before my hearing reacts to the sudden yet familiar change in climate. A slight tinnitus is running through my left ear and my head, unsurprisingly, feels rather heavy. I whack the helmet with my drying cloth-covered hand and it makes a satisfying, safe-feeling thud. I smile. I am ready.

I walk outside, helmet off now, not wanting to look the prancing dowp I was in the kitchen, but holding it, presenting it in its clean form to Stevie. It's just beginning to get dark now, the chill and wind picking up a wee bit too. I pass the hippy cottage and inadvertently peer into a window – there they are, at a lang wooden table, eating their evening meal. They look towards me and I pass on, lightly throwing the helmet up and down, feeling its weight in my hands, preparing myself for the evening's ride. Unless Stevie couldn't get it started? That'd be good. I'm sure he'd drive me in this once, or I could even… I could even ask my mother? Tell her I'm home and ask for a lift all in the same sentence? Nah. Not yet. Not just yet…

As I approach Stevie, I hear an old but familiar stutter, the four-stroke engine attempting life. It cuts out but as I turn the corner I can see Stevie trying again, and again, hacking at the kick-start, lightly adjusting the throttle, until finally, with a slow beginning and a mighty puff of who-knows-what, the engine begins to turn over, crawling first, then picking up pace and running, like an angry chainsaw. And my fate is sealed. I wander up to Stevie – *Go on! Well done* – he looks bushed now – *eh? Aye, well there you have it. I'm going inside to get this oil off. Twice in the one day eh. Can you mind how to change the bulbs aye? This front ane is broke. We'll need it so…* he walks over to my bike and switches on the front bulb. The tiny amount of power left in the battery flickers the bulb on, for a second, then off. *So, it's working, your bulb. You get to it – and quick, there's no' much light left here. Then we'll get intae toon and grab a fish supper. And* – He looks up to the sky, admiring, I guess, the warm dark blue above us and the orange hue over in the west – *Maybe we should grab a few beers. Celebrate your job.* Then he's off past me, stopping only to grab at my helmet with his oily hands – *Ah, nice one. Oops, I've made it a bit oily* – He grins, ever eager to wind me up.

How do you replace these bulbs again? I mind them being quite easy – let's face it, Stevie wouldn't leave it to me unless it was so. I lean over it, bending my back, trying to find an easy way in. Ah, there's those two wee screws. I mind them now. I look over to where Stevie had laid his tools and there, on the top of them all, neatly presented, is the screwdriver I need. Cheeky sod, leaving me this wee job to do. I chuckle, walk over and pick it up and then begin, slowly at first, getting the screwdriver to grip, then loosening the screw, out and into my back pocket and onto the next one.

Oh, hello.

I look up. There's a lady standing, maybe six feet away from me, between myself and the path down to the cottages. Long hair. It must be the hippy lady. *Hang on, I'll just…* and luckily this screw comes easily too and is soon deposited in my back pocket.

Hi – Can I help you?

Oh, I live in that cottage there…

She waves her arms vaguely behind her.

…I've seen you passing, just thought I'd say hello.

She's quite bonny, unmade up, thirty-five or so, I'd say. Stevie's description of *Hippy Lady* seems to fit perfectly; loose-fitting Paisley shirt, tight denim jeans. Nice legs, lace-up, battered leather boots. I realise I am staring and move on.

Old Mr McMann's? I ask, presenting myself as a local, someone *safe.*

Yes, that's the one – she shuffles – *although it's ours now. My husband doesn't like it being referred to as Mr McMann's. We've lived here eighteen months, you know.*

Aye well, he lived there fifty years, did he not? You've a while to go. That sounds aggressive. It's not meant to.

Yes, well. Of course. Silence. I'm not so good with the talking, sometimes. I move over to Stevie's bike and begin the same procedure, removing the screws first.

So was that you starting the motor? I'm guessing it was one of these?

Yep, that was me – Almost a boast, then a correction – *Well, not me, but Stevie. Do you know him?*

She shifts her weight from one leg to the other, arms folded. *Well, yes, a little. We got on well with his uncle and aunt, you know.*

I wonder how that was possible. His aunt I always found lovely but jings – his uncle was a curmudgeonly old Masonic bugger. Maybe he'd mellowed in his final few years.

Yes, we brought him some jam, once. He said it was a good jam. We'd made it – she waves her wiry arms towards the path – *using berries we'd picked on the path here down to the beach, and up to the road.* I smile. We used to do that as kids. I move towards her, hand outstretched. She backs off a little before accepting it as an *only a handshake* offering, then seeing, just, in this greying dwam of an evening, that my hands weren't oily filthy. We shake – *I was expecting your hands to be black!* I grin, *No, we're just off into town for some food, just replacing the bulb. Not an oily job.* Although it was a job I hadn't completed yet. *Anyway, I'm Johnny. I'm a pal of Stevie's from way back, from school. Look – if you don't mind, I better get on with this, before it gets any darker.*

Sure, sure. Nice to meet you.

Yep. And a concerted, obvious move back to the bike, back to the beginning of the removal of the headlight. As she wanders away, I jemmy at the light, skiffing my hand under a slice of metal which is slightly protruding from the otherwise smooth headlight. I curse – *Fuck.* She turns – *Sorry?* I suck my finger – *Nothing, oh nothing, good meeting you.* And she's off.

Chups

Bulb changed, awaiting Stevie, staring up into the old barn we'd retrieved the bikes from. We used to play here as kids, chasing rats, hide and seek, building castles in the hay, that sort of thing. The beautiful damp smell of the hay bales still brings back memories of childhood, jemmying our way into other farmers' lofts, exploring ancient old desks, sniffing at the necks of many, many discarded wine bottles, stealing licence plates, knives, tools. At the back of this farm – well, the next farm along – there was a battery chicken place. Seemed ludicrous to us, all this land available and they'd shrunk the individual habitats of the cheuks to the sizes of shoeboxes. Not that we were particularly animal conscious or political, it just seemed – naturally seemed – wrong. Not that we did much about it either, just on occasion letting tyres down, throwing stones from afar at lonesome 4x4s, their driver inside the chicken house, feeding or killing or whatever they did. No-one really seemed to know about that place, or they didn't talk about it anyhow. Once, we found a rook on the road nearby – we'd cycled up there on our BMXs, bored and looking for adventure – and pinned it to the door of the barn, crucifix style. I don't think the unfair world crumbled. I don't think the chickens were freed or mankind progressed. I imagine we made a medium intelligence, low-waged farmer pissed off for thirty seconds or so, whilst he justified his occupation with thoughts of his family and the money that pays for the food that feeds them. *They're only cheuks.*

Stevie's out – *Did ye manage it?*

I did.

Good man. C'mon then. I'll go first, make sure we're a' good.

He ruffles into his helmet, fastening the straps, zipping up his coat, gloves on. How far is he going? Then, sitting astride the C90, he kicks the motor going, it flaring up on second attempt, pumping out stour and smoke, turns the lights on (which work), sends me a mock-salute and powers away making a healthy racket. Within seconds he's out of the farm yard and off up the track to the main road – a road so quiet there's only a car every five minutes or so. We're a long way from civilisation, a long way from St Andrews even. I jog over to the exit and see him skidding this way and that, but basically moving forwards, throwing up dust and stanes left and right, the little red back light jumping up and down with each movement. Before too long it's all I can see, then he turns on to the main road and he's off, just the whine of the engine to be heard. Soon enough and that's gone too and the sound of the wind kicks in, blowing around my ears causing my earring to lightly whistle. Then there's the occasional bleat from the sheep in the nearby field, a rattling door somewhere. I look up – the stars so visible here compared to the always-light environment that is central London. *They do look like cobwebs*, too much to contemplate, all those places, all those possibilities many, many lifetimes away from here. *What's going on that us tiny wee baws don't know about?* There's silence – real, total silence for a second, maybe two, and then I see a light coming along the main road, then hear the motor, slowly getting louder, Stevie returning.

How was it?

Eh? He stops the engine, pulls off his helmet. *Fucking amazing. Forgot how much fun those things are. I may have to buy another – a proper one now.*

What, a new one?

Aye, well, aye, a new-er one. Onyhow, climb on. Your shot. And now, listen – there's no' that much petrol in, so no fucking about. We should just go straight into town.

Umm... do you want to drive? I'm not sure...

Ach, dinnae be saft. You were fine as a bairn. You'll pick it up again before we're out o' the yard. I did – did you see me away?

I did, aye.

Well. That's how easy it is.

But I cannae even start the thing at first. I kick and I kick, then I kick once more and then it lights up. I keep the revs up – Stevie shouting something, but I can't hear what. I sit down, bounce up and down, test the suspension, feel the brake, the clutch. Almost ready to go, tentatively, when Stevie climbs on behind me, slapping his arms tight around my belly. The bike has shrunk what seems like six or seven inches – we're low now, the double weight of me and Stevie pushing the springs down. Fuck it. Here we go, release the clutch and roll away.

At first, my legs panic and slip out either side, as though I'm star-shaped, but it's slowing us and destabilising and before long Stevie calls out *Brrghh ththuu bbh!* and I pull them in, resting them hugging tight against the warmth and vibrations of the engine. We reach the end of the yard and I don't stop – not out of heroics and confidence, but fear of using the brakes – and we're onto the lane leading up to the main road. I try and ride in the middle, avoiding the pot holes and uneven ground, but I'm slipping this way and that, so pull down to the left and do my best to avoid them. There's a shout from behind – *Ghhh foorr ththe oooo* – and suddenly I'm hearing the whine of the engine, still in first gear and I move up to second, then to third and it's calmed down, more comfortable now. I experiment with the brake – on/off/on/off – and Stevie shouts something incomprehensible again. But fuck it, I have to be safe, right? I have to feel safe?

What a racket this thing makes. The light is awful too. I mean, I guess it's the standard light, better, no worse, but it's a dull, coffee-yellow, when I'm longing for an army searchlight or the fog lights of a *Dukes of Hazzard* 4x4. This road isn't the safest, the smoothest, either. It's a C-road, or would be if this council officially had C-roads. I guess it's a B-minor road and as such is afforded very little council funding.

Round the second corner and for the first time I remember to relax, try and enjoy it. I sit back a bit, Stevie moving with me. He removes one arm from around me and pats me twice on the shoulder – encouragement and congratulations – before wrapping it around me again.

We reach the main road, and this time it's the real main road – well, for these parts. I bring the bike to a halt slowly, considered, well enough. Zip up my coat to the neck, turn up the collars, scurry my hands together for warmth. I hear Stevie laughing, then bringing his warm, begloved hands into my view – rubbing it in, rubbing it in. He's always prepared, always ready.

Coming down the deep hill into St Andrews it looks like one beautiful place on this *almost* early summer evening. The juxtaposition of varying aged buildings – medieval cathedral, castle – surrounded by houses far, far newer and a great many in-between, all lit up by the orange lights, all hedged in by and spilling onto the various beaches. Our arrival, chugging downwards, must be audible to all but the deafest of inhabitants, who'll surely be looking up in wonder at this *racket,* this pale yellow light, these two *dafties* riding a bike for one, long since without insurance or licence. Surely we'll be lifted by the polis the moment we pierce the streetlight bubble that covers the tiny city, blurring through my visor like an 80s pop music video. We hadn't discussed *which* chippy, but I know fine which one I prefer – the closest. Sooner we're in, sooner we can get out, into the relative safety of the countryside roads, away from any prying law enforcers, keen to enforce the laws regarding not riding scooters when you're an unschooled, out-of-practise incompetent amateur. We ride past the old city walls, past my old primary, almost to the edge of the town centre itself, then pull in, slowly, easily, into a designated *M/C* slot, parking up beside a far more powerful, far more modern vehicle. Our C90 will be feeling self-conscious. I try to turn the handlebars to the most viewing-awkward position, should anyone be searching for evidence of road tax, switch the engine off, feel Stevie's release and climb off, pull the bike onto its stand and climb off myself, my legs and baws vibrating still, my arms almost numb, my head dizzy from the noise. Helmet off and it's as though someone has allowed me back into reality, the quiet and noise of the street rushing into my ears, my vision cleared, no longer distorted by a scratched, road-soiled visor. *Jings, eh?* Stevie's eyes are wide – *Jings indeed, Johnny, jings indeed. Well done. Now – let's get some food. I'm fucking starving.*

⋆ ⋆ ⋆

We're sitting on the rackety old bench that has been perched high up above the castle, wind blowing still, wrapping, curling around us, but warm compared to the *cauld wind* of the motorbike. Stevie's got fish and chips, myself a chip butty with a pickled onion. *How the fuck do you eat those things?* But they're good for me, slipping and sliding aside. I'm glad I took a few napkins, to clear the vinegar and brown sauce from my fingers once all this is done. The tide's in, we can hear the waves easily enough, not huge, but enough, the sort of waves that'd lull you to sleep or end a summer evening in a beautiful, romantic fashion. Way down below, between us and the castle, there's the small beach, the *Castle Sands*, with its outdoor swimming pools, carved out of the rock and embellished upon, random cracked tiles providing the evidence of a previous town council's commitment to the health of their citizens. There's a bonfire down there, a party going on, no doubt kids from one of the schools, or students, perhaps, their yelps and japes, manly shouts and girly squeals crawling up over the cliff and meeting us, greeting us as we stuff our faces with over-fried chips.

I'm pleased you came up, Johnny boy.

Munch, chew, swallow.

Why, thank you, Miss Stevie. And I appreciate you asking me. I needed to get out of London, for sure. Even if I'm only here for the summer, clearing my head a bit, even if I move back down and try again – well, I'm pleased to be back the now.

Well, you can stay as long as you like. Pause. *I'm enjoying the company.*

Good man.

Here – I met the wifey o' the hippy couple. She seemed fine enough to me. Chatty and such. She said she knew your uncle and aunt?

He looks at me, grinning, shaking his head, chip in hand – *Aye. That's a' she talks about. That an' fucking hedgerow jam.* Chip in mouth.

You can see a few lighthouses from up here, away in the distance, plus the shores of Broughty Ferry, Arbroath, maybe? Their lights twinkling away, vague movement of cars, all blurring into one. Funny, nowadays to drive there from here would take – what, an hour? A little more? But back in the day – I mean, long before my day, back before cars and the bridge and such, a trip over there would take a week or so. Real commitment for a move. I've heard it said that the village where I was born was the most inbred village in Scotland, before the invention of the bicycle. Could be true, I guess. Still a few wazzocks darting about there, for sure.

Here, Johnny – you should go and see your mither.

Aye, I ken that. Give me a chance though. I've only been up a few days. She'll be more pleased to see me once I can tell her I've got some kind of job and that. Maybe get that bike taxed and such too, she's bound to ask about it. Get my provisional licence in order. All takes a week or two…

I'm down to the pickled onion now and it's not a good one. Not pickled enough, too hard and crunchy. Too… oniony.

Christ, Johnny – your breath after eating that thing. I was going to say we should head down to the party, but maybe no' the now.

The skin is tough to chew, slippery, acidic and unforgiving. I have eaten better onions. I force a swallow.

I've still got the hunger Stevie. That didn't do it.

Well, I hope it's not hunger for another onion.

He's staring out over towards the North Carr lighthouse, far in the distance. Between us and there, a half dozen boats of different sizes and types are making their way through the thick water. A tanker, a fishing boat, an oil rig, on its way in or out of Dundee. I wonder how we look to them, if they're spying us through telescopes – perhaps they're coveting my pickled onion? If only they knew the disappointment it had delivered.

Maybe we should go down to the beach? See what's up?

Eh? Aye, mebbe. Mind you've work tomorrow. And that bike isnae locked up.

Aye well, we won't be drinking but…

Mebbe we should get just a couple of beers – we'd look richt rude turning up empty-handed…

Aye, could do – or a bottle o' wine?

Fuck that! I'm no' sharing a bottle o' wine with you and that fucking onion slaver…

I'm no' slaverring! Anyhow – it's almost gone. I lick my lips. My mouth tastes like a hotdog factory floor. Maybe I could buy some mints? Onion, mints, wine – a good, refreshing combination.

* * *

I don't buy wine. I buy two tins of cheap Tennents lager, Stevie buys the other two. A four pack between us. *Three for me mind,* Stevie says. *You cannae be riding us hame drunk now.* I laugh it off, *I won't be drunk on two cans of that pish, on top of my chips and all. Plus, I got that Snickers – the caffeine in that will keep me going.*

Eh? There's no caffeine in a Snickers. It's a chocolate bar, no' a cup o' coffee.

Fuck it, I'll be fine. We won't hang around and I'll drink them quickly.

You'll drink them quickly? Aye, that'll help. How about you stand on yer heid too?

I crack one open regardless, placing the other can in my pocket. *Pssst.* It tastes okay, the alcohol fizzing away at any remnants of onionness.

Still there, but.

We cross the second of the two main St Andrews streets, making our way through the University Gardens, down some unlit concrete steps, taking care, avoiding flowerbeds and rose bushes, not talking, not drawing attention to our light bit of trespassing, eager to avoid a night watchman or park keeper, the embarrassment of being told *Get out of here, this is university land*, an oft-heard rebuke in our younger years. Out onto the lang back street that connects the castle to the golf courses, past the castle and then down the beach path. *See a student fella fell from these cliffs again?* I look up, as though I'm expecting to see him, still tumbling down in slow motion, his light blue shirt flapping. *That's sad.* Crikey, what a way to go. *Aye. Happens though, once every few years.*

The steps to the beach path are far, far older than the outdoor baths, thin and worn, slippy in parts, a rusted-through railing providing a little stability, but all eyes, all concentration, on where your feet are landing. Halfway down, a streetlight is perched, making things momentarily easier, until you're beyond its reach and your eyes have to readjust to the twilight once more. Just as the beach arrives with a pungent seaweed odour, a blonde-haired young girl – fifteen, maybe – bursts out of the half-light and past us, up the stairs, weeping theatrically. We watch her for a moment, then she's pursued, first by a boy – same age, well sculptured hair, good summer-thin shirt – and then another two girls, calling out her name – *Jilly! Jilly!* And, *Oh Gordon, you utter knob!* We stand at the bottom of the stairs smirking, feet just on the sand, eyes barely adjusted to the dark and scan the remaining beach. Three more folk maybe, pals of the runners no doubt, sitting around a too-generous fire. Stevie, watching, takes a sup of his lager, then – *Fuck this Johnny. We're auld men to these lot.* I agree. *Aye. And we'd be richt auld pervos. Let's get going. Get some fuel and get home.*

We walk back via the clifftop path – no real reason, just for the change. Same sort of distance but a different route, overlooking the sea, leaving the castle behind us and slowly approaching the cathedral. When we were schoolkids we'd come up here, here to the muckle-but-broken-down, long-ruined cathedral, find a sheltered spot in amongst its hundreds of graves and scattered mausoleums and begin our vodka experiments or whatever else was on the menu that particular evening. A lot of cigarettes were coughed through, that's for sure. It'd sometimes seem as though the entire underage population of St Andrews and its environs would have the same idea and there'd be pockets of parties in every dank stone neuk, laughing, whispering, drinking. On occasion there'd be a fecht but the dark and the proximity to very real gravestones usually kept the behaviour reasonable. A lot of pisses taken down the auld cathedral well though, sure enough. I wonder if the holy folk did that over in the olden days? After having three too many fortified wines or whatever they tippled back then.

Here, we'll cut through the cathedral, eh?

Once through the wrought iron gate and within the cathedral grounds, it becomes noticeably darker and quieter, for there are no streetlights planted within and the high thick walls block out the sounds of the sea. The passing cars are now just soft purrs, it's womb-like, our senses heightened to what remains – the dark and the quiet. To help ensure the safety of our walk we hush down ourselves, using all our concentration to avoid tripping on the remnants of an inner wall or a collapsed gravestone.

Now and again we hear voices – always seeming a little unnerving in the dark – but for graveyard experts like myself and Stevie there's little fear. After all we were virtually professionals in this very field of stane, once. We know that our hulking darkened figures will be spotted and *Shushed* for, should we be polis or trouble makers, or a couple of the legendary *gays* said to fuck amongst the bushes when the schoolkids went home.

There's one voice I make out. At first I'm thinking nothing of it, just a raised tone, a slight stooshie, a dropped fag, perhaps. Stevie halts though – raising his arm towards me to slow me too, like we're army boys on some night mission.

What is it?

Shhh! Ya dowp.

I'm quiet, I'm still, listening. There's a group of folk – three or maybe – just arguing, but still trying to keep a pretence of kee quiet, so it's pushed, exaggerated whispers. One of the voices – a – seems less controlled, less concerned.

Aye, fucking geeze it, eh – jist geeze a wee fucking scoosh, ahm no' e the lot…

Then a girl, softer voice but anxious – *No, no! Go on, leave us alo*

And another – *Quieten down Jane, keep the noise down…*

They're English, the two girls. Posh-sounding too. From t boarding school, no doubt.

Then – *Fucking just gies a swally then I'll be aff, it's jist a fucking…*

It dawns on me who it is, who it *might be* and Stevie gets it at th exact same time. He turns to me and laughs, quietly – *It's that fuckin jakey cunt you were bumming on the bus.*

I wasn't fucking bumming him and anyhow it's no'…

A girl then, louder now, any fear of being caught by whoever now overtaken by exasperation with their interloper, their situation. *Look, please Michael, thanks for getting us the drink but really, we just want to talk amongst ourselves. Can't you just, can't you…*

Michael is it? Who are YOU? Ma fucking mither? It's fucking Mikey. Mi – key. A' cunt kens that. C'mon, we're pals here, eh…

He doesn't sound angry, more as though he's trying to be charming, but his general demeanour is maybe a little outlandish to these ladies, judging by their received pronunciation.

It's nothing personal Michael, umm, Mikey. I'm sure you're a lovely man but we're clearly not pals – look…

But he's warming up now –

Nah lass, dinnae tell me tae look. YOU look. I get you the swallie like you asked but yer tae fucking snobby tae share, eh? A' fucking nice aforehand, leading me on an' a' that.

What? I was not!

Wi' yer… fucking…

Stevie places his arm on mine. *Fucking hell, whit an erse. I think it's kickin' aff… Mebbe we should –*

Should we fuck. We'll just get dumped with him again.

A scream then, slightly pantomime but female, loud and panicked

– *Get off my bottle, GET OFF ME.*

Ach jist gies a fucking drink, ya cow.

Another female yelp, more serious this one. It's not easy listening. My body stiffens and I look to Stevie – *I think* – but he's way ahead of me. *Ah, fuck it* – Stevie's off towards them, slowly, to avoid kneecapping himself against a gravestone, but determined. I follow, more cautious, but there. The stramash escalates further, there's a bit of shrieking – real screaming, it seems, as though a wee lassie's being manhandled in the dark. In a graveyard, which I guess she is. Stevie stops walking and proceeds to shout – bellow out – as loud as he can – *WHAT THE FUCK IS THIS NOISE? WHO'S THAT FUCKING CUNT CAUSIN' A' THE TROUBLE, EH? FUCK'S GAEN AN?*

And there's silence. He sounded like a man-mountain, deep and low. In a slight flashback I panic and almost drop my remaining can, should the polis arrive and bust us all before I remember I am not a schoolkid anymore.

There's nothing, no reply, then Stevie's off towards them again. *Fucking furryboots you cunts hiding…?*

I hear – and see, vaguely – dispersion. Bodies running this way and that, just one of them still, Mikey I'm guessing. He's quieter now, surprised at the change of events. *Eh? Who the fuck's that? Eh pal?* But the bravado has gone.

I catch Stevie's arm to slow him down and whisper, keen Mikey doesn't get who we are – *Let's get just going Stevie. We cannae be haen this boy with us.*

Stevie turns and I see, I think, just a hint of a grin. *Aye, they've all scarpered. Hang on, jist ane mair* – then louder again – *AH'LL FUCKING BANG YER PUS, YER FUCKING BUNCH O' SHITES* – a parting volley to whoever – to Mikey mostly, but also to get the lassies out of the cathedral grounds, I guess. Then to me, quiet once more – *C'mon Johnny, we'll go out the way we came in. He willnae see us, he'll be keiching his breeks.*

We make to leave, Stevie chortling still – *Aye, he's a puir waste o' space, that boy.*

A Dream: Sheep, Sheep, Don't You Know The Road?

Stevie waiting for me, or perhaps just keeping out of his house, and carrying our two air rifles with him. Well, my father's old air rifle, a' scuffed and bruised, slightly bent barrel, cheap cardboard carrying case – and his own uncle's rifle, polished and perfect and in a camouflaged gun sack. As I approach, he says not a word, just bores his eyes into me and thrusts my Da's rifle into my hands, turns away and heads off, up into the fields.

You okay Stevie? What's up?

He looks back at me.

Aye, ma uncle fair skelped me last nicht when I got home richt enough.

Ah, okay. *Jings,* I say. *How come? It wasn't your fault. How did he know?*

We walk on a bit, then:

He kent fine the moment he saw me, coat all ripped, face scuffed up. Thing is though, Johnny – and he brightens a wee bit, just a tad – *thing is though, he thought I'd had a ficht wi' you!*

And we both laugh, at the thought of us fighting, the thought of me somehow beating him if we had a fight.

Told me I was tae keep away from you, but I telt him it was those boys from the bus and how we'd done nothing wrong at all, but then he's a', "Aye Steven, ye' must hae asked fer it, drinking away, no doubt," and then gaen aff about young Davy Jack frae the village who'd drunk himsel' silly by the age o' twenty, in prison now for daftness, how he'd ruined his life. It was a poor evening Johnny, I tell ye that. He jist went on and on, over and over. In a' my life, I don't need to hear another word about the benefits o' attending agricultural college, that's for sure.

He's not having a good time at home right now, Stevie. He's breaking the seal between being a wee boy under his uncle's glour and guidance and an almost grown-up, an almost equal. He knows it, his uncle knows it. Even I know it and I'm fair deppit at these things. *Jings,* I say, again, full of wisdom, eyebrows raised. Like a coward, I turn away and begin to walk. He'll know everything I was going to say, right? I don't actually need to say anything, do I? I do not. I don't.

Not talking now, but walking, just rootin' oot an' aboot and we end up near the big low field. There are always rabbits and the like hopscotching about, so something to shoot at. We lay down there like army sniper boys, quiet still, mulling things over, waiting for something to pop up for us to shoot down – a crow, maybe, or one of the big nasty sea birds that come up around here. Stevie used to say they were attracted by the sewage pipe which ran close by. Nothing comes though, so out of boredom and no desire to talk, we resort to just shooting randomly at blades of grass and such, just to see the pellets weeshing through the long grass. There are a load of sheep in the field, we know that, but it's such a big lang field – and when we'd laid ourselves down, they were up the other end, gathered around the old broken-down house up there – so we're not paying them any attention.

That is, until one of them strays our way without our seeing and we hit it with a pellet. The field's all ups and downs and wee ditches and such. I don't know how it happened but this poor wee sheepie must have been half-in and half-out of some hole or hidden behind a mound or whatever, but one of us hit it, as sure as eggs, and the day goes from pure silent except the slight wind and the distant waves to some kind of terrible screaming. If you've ever been near a sheep when it's giving birth but the birth's going wrong, you'll know the sound. A real, high, long cry, like a barn owl or a banshee or a poacher in a big old-fashioned gamekeeper's man-trap.

The sheep is blaring away and Stevie and I look at each other, wide-eyed like *What the fuck is that?* We get up and go running over and sure enough, stopping just twenty feet away, a sheep has strayed into our path and one of us has shot it. Could have been either of us, we were both just idling away shooting at the wind. Shooting at the wind and hitting a sheep. Poor shots, both. Stevie's panicking. He knows this flock – it's part of his uncle's responsibility – and Stevie knows it'll be another, far worse run-in with his uncle when this comes out. Stevie's flushed red, panicky red, like when he has to speak in class and he's looking at me accusingly, but only half-heartedly as he knows fine well it could have been him. Probably was him, in fact. Maybe. He rubs his face, like a silent movie actor displaying *dismay*, his big thick leathery hands running from top to bottom, hoping they'll release a face not seeing a sheep in pain, but a sheep running off happy, if shocked. But no, end of face rub, and all's as he left it.

There's a circle of red developing just below the sheep's neck, dripping downwards now, slightly, and it's obvious something is up. It's obvious the sheep's been skelt, maybe we hit one of those big thick vein things. An artery. Stevie looks at me, *Ah Johnny, we're going to have to do something.* I think, *Perhaps, perhaps we could say we found it on some barbed wire?* But Stevie dismisses that, *No way Johnny. No way can I be anywhere near this.* He means there's no way he can be part of the forthcoming drama, the investigation, his uncle explaining to the captain farmer – the laird – just why they've lost a fully grown sheep with a barbed wire wound. Almost unheard of. Sheep aren't that daft – if they hit barbed wire they back off, rather than frottaging to the point of death. *Johnny,* Stevie says, *fuck.*

A minute or so later and we're both right standing by the sheep, the puir dumb sheep, panicking still, and we're leading it – we're leading her – all the way to the upper edge of the field, far away from the sea. She's coming with us, but is starting to struggle a fair bit. Before long we're practically dragging her, she's slowing and getting restless as she's hauled away from the flock, some of whom are watching as we leave, one or two considering following, but just standing there, watching and chewing on the grass. My hand keeps on slipping on her fleece. It's a musty, dirty smell and I've got a thick handful, but the grease and last night's rain is causing my hand to slip. Stevie has a hand on the other side of her neck from the blood, plus one on her back and is edging her forwards, almost lifting her up from the rear end and pushing her along, her slowing even more now as mair blood drips out of her neck and down her front. As we approach the small copse of trees at the top of the field, we both know what we're going to do, but carry on, despite the shiteness of it all.

There's a fence to get over – barbed wire – and we fuck that up considerably, lifting her up haphazardly – she starts pissing everywhere, fear, most likely, all over Stevie's arm and down her own back leg, and I'm lifting her front end, trying to avoid the blood, out at arm's length, my face all screwed-up and held back, like a crap scared Frankenstein monster or whatever. At one point her face gets so close to mine and I get a huge blast of stinking sheep breath, full and foul smelling, old teeth, old grass, fetid tongue. I look at my hand and it's slowly turning salmon pink with a mix of blood and sweat, dew from the grass, grease from her coat.

I'm seeing straight into her eyes, but she's looking beyond me, out to the distance, up into the sky, as if this was the first time she'd ever bothered to look up from the grass that she's spent her forever walking around and eating. As we bungle her over the fence, we drop her, somehow, and she gets caught on the barbed wire, but her fleece is thick enough that she doesn't seem to even notice. Stevie and I get some superhuman strength from somewhere and hulk her right over, leaving her to roll a bit on the other side and come to a dead halt, her injury not allowing her to stand. She bleats an exhausted, defeated cry.

Through the trees, just a few feet, lies our destination. During the Second World War, this whole area was positioned between two airfields – Leuchars and Crail – and was full of dummy aircraft buildings and such to fool the Luftwaffe – but the Ministry Of Defence or whoever it was back then had to build a load of bomb shelters for the farmers and locals – and here we were at one of them. An old bomb shelter. No steps down, just a gaping concrete hole, leading to a fifteen foot drop to old cans of Tennents, rusted old lighter-gas canisters, ripped and sodden scud mags, the odd hopeful spent condom, clothing, remnants of fires long extinguished. The sheep is refusing to budge now, almost as if it knows our plans for it, despite us not really having discussed them ourselves – or maybe the shot and the barbed wire has damaged it more than we thought – but whatever, it's talking, like an individual sheep now, a long way from its flock out of sight and earshot, trying to make us see sense. I wonder about the colouring on its snout and think to myself that the top of its nose is the same shape as a map of Brazil and I'm thinking about God and that big statue of Jesus looking down over all the poor sods in Rio de Janeiro and how I'd love to be there right now and what a fucking easy life those fuckers have. And then we just push and push and the sheep slips, hits its head on the side of the concrete lip around the hole, desperately tries to grab hold with its thin cloven hooves, rests on the edge for a second long eternity and slip-falls into the bomb shelter – is pushed into the bomb shelter – screaming now, its bleat forcing itself out, mouth wide open on the way down and then a crowed silence as we hear the cracking of its neck on the floor below. And then another silence. We look down and there's a small circle of piss coming out underneath the poor wee thing and a rising cloud of whatever the fuck – steam – coming up to us. It stinks. A really nasty, dank, smell. The blood on the neck is hidden, luckily. No prying eyes would see the original wound. A fluke. No skill on our part. Stevie has his hand over his mouth, but not from sickness of whatever, just from disbelief and maybe, maybe just stopping him talking and showing me just how shook up he is.

C'mon the fuck away, I say and head off, sideways, backwards, looking towards the hole and the disturbed leaves all round about it, hitting my head against new shoots of wood on thin branches, catching bits of sap on my jacket and in my hair. Stevie turns around and follows me out, him looking straight at me, walking straight far away from the scene of the crime, his eyes wide and adult.

Tripe

Next morning, by the time I reach the kennels I'm shaken through from the moped. Some journey, especially when nervous and early-morn sleepy. Glad to have an okay night's kip beforehand, glad we didn't drink to excess, glad to make it in one piece. The journey home had been easy; without the nerves of the polis ahead of us – they're barely, if ever, out on the smaller roads – we only had twenty minutes of bone-shattering to contend with. In honesty, I think even Stevie was pleased to get home. The way he hauled himself off the bike, the way he gingerly walked the first few metres after, shaking some feeling back into his arse. I felt pretty good though, I think. I'd managed the first two journeys reasonably well – no crashes, no scrapes – sure, the odd stall, but I was feeling significantly more confident than I would have been if this morning I'd been riding blind – well, not blind obviously, but for the first time in however many years.

As I arrive at the kennels, slowing the scooter to an eventual halt, I see Mrs Bradley, waiting, watching, half bent over, pulling some weeds, bucket in hand. I climb off – *jings, my baws are numbed* – make to brush down my jeans, but really waiting for some blood to return to my legs, my head to acclimatise to the relative quiet. I remove my helmet and am surrounded by the sound of distant barking dogs, birdsong and Mrs Bradley coming towards me, chatting away.

You made it then – I'm impressed. She looks over the Honda, eyes resting on the well-expired tax-disc. She now looks less impressed. *Come, come inside John. Maybe we should start things off with a cup of tea. What do you say?*

That sounds amazing to me. Great. Stuff gloves in bike helmet, rest helmet on bike seat, tie it secure using chin straps and follow, my thighs chafing inside my jeans, worn weary by the vibrations.

Come on, this way – and she pushes open an already ajar wooden door, thick and old, layers of different paints displaying its multi-coloured history, scraping on the floor as it moves. Her wellington boots are kicked off here so I follow suit and follow her through the dingy corridor into the kitchen, where she's pulled out a chair – *Sit yourself down John* – back to me, kettle under tap.

I sit and look around. It's a working kitchen, that's for sure. The floor exhibiting a' sorts of stains, the sideboard buried with bills and papers, ripped cardboard, egg boxes, dead milk cartons. The fridge is covered in dog show rosettes and cheap magnets, gathered from all over – wee green Irish gnomes, a two-tone Mona Lisa, some silver harvest bread broach. Just junk, the same you see sold in tourist shops up and down the country, a lifetime of debris, washing down the side of the fridge, before eventually it'll be unceremoniously discarded and tipped, the enamel magnets still hugging on like barnacles on a whale.

Now John. She presents me with my tea. Should I trust this mug, unaware as I am of its recent history of cleanliness? Perhaps I should. I am thirsty and in need of refreshment and it is right there in front of me and its provider just slightly beyond. A turning down of her fine tea may be seen as rude, as a questioning of her hygiene. I take a sip. It is very good. The milk fresh, the teabag well brewed. Relax.

Now, I hope you don't mind, I shall be popping out for the morning, but back in time for lunch, so I've written you a short list of jobs to be done today. This should all come as second nature to you presently, but just for today, as a memory – she hands me the list, looking away as she does –

Tripe and water to all dogs
Clean out all dogs
Deliver strays to police
Lunch break – make soup
Clean yard
Mow lawn

Okay then. That's quite a list. Hang on, make soup?

Ha. Soup. Where are the tins?

She looks at me, querying – *Oh, there's no tins John, but plenty to find in the cupboards, don't you worry.*

Ah – um – I'm no chef…

She waves me off – *Don't be so silly. Anyone can make soup, surely.*

I survey the kitchen. It's a calamity. Stevie would have a fit in here, lasting a mere minute before strapping on the marigolds. But then, I spot something else – *Um, what's this?* I point at the *Deliver strays to police* sentence.

Well John, it's quite simple. One of the ways I stay afloat – make this business work, if you like – is I take in strays impounded by the council. Now, they stay here first of all, dropped off by the police, and then – Well, after a few days, a week at most, if they haven't been collected, they go off to the larger dog pound in Dundee.

I contemplate.

And what happens there?

Well John – shifting her head, as if to say, it's the way of the world – *Well John, they're either collected, I imagine, or destroyed.*

Ah – *So who's in today?*

You'll see them. They're in the top two cages, I always use those, so as not to get dogs mixed up. Also – She walks to the other side of the kitchen, making a token effort at tidying as she goes – *it keeps them away from the guard dogs. No point making their last few days more stressful than needs be. Anyway* – and she's sat down now – *nothing for us to worry about. Nature takes its course and all that.*

⋆ ⋆ ⋆

Beautiful bright day, plenty of bird song, eyes squinting as I make my way to the large shed where the offal is stored. As I approach, there's a hint of a smell, but nothing too bad – but upon opening the door – sheesh. I'm hit with the inevitable muggy wave of stagnant sheep-stomach-brewed air. Air which has been slowly warmed in the morning sun and boiled into a perfect ball of yeuch. My neck recoils, nose closes, mouth swears before I quickly move back to a safe distance. The shed door's hinges slam it shut. Great.

I find myself a brick, take a deep breath, open the door and wedge it so, let some fresh air back in. Squinting inside I can see the wheelbarrow's in there already, which will save me some time. A' the dust from the straw bales is floating around in the sunlight, thickening the rancid air even more. I just have to do it, I guess, and I do just that. Deep breath, straight to the back of the shed, Mrs Bradley's tripe-gloves on (*not to worry about spiders living within, John*) and arm deep into the tripe barrel. *Aye, ya fucking...* Wee shelves of whatever rub against my bare arm but I'm in and out of the barrel as quickly as I can manage – twelve bits. Tripes? What's the plural of tripe? Mair tripe. Just mair fucking tripe. Then, reversing out with the wheelbarrow, wobbling this side and that, up over the steps, careful now, back into the bright white-yellow sunlight and the fresher air. I don't care what these kennels will smell of now. Don't mind at all how much shit and pish there is to clean up after they're been fed. Any smell at all will be better than the aroma of old, compressed, off, air-dried tripe.

But, the dugs seem to love it. I'm away down towards them and they're barking on, probably hungry, maybe a wee bitty excited at being with a' the other dugs. Open the outer door and they begin to howl and shriek even louder. My head feels as though it's being compressed between two gate posts. *Shut the fuck up.*

A quick glance reveals no dogs are loose, so I skip in front of the wheelbarrow and open the second door – the safety door, then back to where I was and wheel the barrow in. The noise is incredible – all the breezeblock walls acting as a natural echo chamber, the high-pitched yelps, the low, deep growls and barks. I switch the cassette player on with the monks chanting and holy ladies singing most holily. It won't shut the dugs up though, not now, not with breakfast being late and all, the delicious smell of the tripe wafting through to them. Theoretically it's easy, this bit, just got to keep my lips firmly closed for fear of a bit of tripe flying off the pitch fork and into my mouth.

No preferential treatment here, start as I mean to go on. No-one left out or ignored, first I come to, first served, fork into the wheelbarrow and hoiked right over into the kennel, dog number one pouncing on it and running into the corner of the kennel before beginning to devour the food. He'll be finished before I'm back to the top, no doubt. Then the next, a golden Labrador, looking not at me but at the stomach, big lines of spider-web drool coming from his lips. I lift the tripe up and attempt to throw over but not quite – it lands on the floor in front of me – the dug, angry, perplexed, looks at me for a second before straight back to the tripe, then at me, then the tripe. It begins to whimper and pads the floor. Pitchfork down, scrape the tripe off the floor and carefully now, just tip it over the top of the fence. Dog sees food, dog gets food, dog eats food.

All the way down, left to right, until I get to the big bastards at the end, the guard dogs. I look them in their eyes and carefully give them their food. Maybe the eye contact means something, maybe I'll become pack leader or something. Maybe if they escape they won't eat me now. Maybe.

A few scraps of tripe left in the barrow, throw them over to the bigger, fatter, friendlier dogs then leave. I'll be back in an hour or so to clean up.

Pushing the barrow out into the garden and then closing the door is a relief. The stench and the noise behind me – and today – well, today is so beautiful and summery that it's really rather quite pleasant, this short walk back to the tripe bay, avoiding dog turd as I go.

Mrs Bradley had told me I could close all the various gates leading to the kennels, if I didn't mind slobbering hellos, jumping up, the fucking of my legs, biting, barking, sniffing, running. Not the easiest of company. But it's a lovely hot day and I feel like letting a few out, so I do just that. Open the twa doors, wedge them with bricks, let some fresh air into the kennels. From then, it's an experiment, seeing who'll get on and who won't. I'm guessing it's not always the wee dugs you can trust, they can be just as yappy and snappy. The medium-size pets though, the well-fed chaps, they seem mostly okay and I begin with them. The big golden Lab; a young Giant Schnauzer named Jack, bouncy fellow, very friendly; Sammy, some kind of slobbering Bulldog cross. They're out straight away and aff into the garden bit, running as fast as they can, up and down, up and down. Fuck it. Out goes twa wee Blue Rhone Cockers, a Cairn Terrier called Macgregor. Harmless wee dugs, sprinting from one end to the other, the odd yap at the bigger dugs. A huge Springer Spaniel, she can go out too, and straight ignores me for the wide, open spaces of the half-acre garden. I watch them for a wee bit. I think the Springer considers itself to be a young puppy from a far smaller breed, the way she leaps and yelps over the other dogs. Who's left? Well, I'll not be letting the guard dogs out. Fuck that. There's a few creatures I don't feel so confident about – a scruffy black thing, unkempt, mongrel, can't see her eyes, but she's so small and it'd be torture just leaving her in with the others displaying their temporary freedom so flagrantly – so out she goes. We're not supposed to let the council dogs out, but these two wee terriers seem fine and friendly earlier, so I open their cages too. Now the garden is full of the crazed things, drunk on the freedom of the garden and the fresh air. There's a slight breeze, which seems to be coming into the kennels, so even the guard dogs are getting a wee bit of something special. They're still barking though. Jings, they're as ferocious as can be.

I'm supposed to be cleaning now, but the scene outside is too inviting, so I potter out, sit myself down on a rusted once-white iron chair and watch. The animals are having the time of their lives, running this way and that, bounding, nudging balls with their heads then chasing them, snarling at each other then running off, jumping up at the gates, pissing, shitting, sprinting... It's like an extremely unruly Crufts, where the dogs have been fed LSD. I think the Springer would win the prize for most out of control dug, but then one of the wee council terrier things is doing its best to start a fight with whichever animal is closest to it, which is a pretty daft strategy. I get up, fetch a garden hose, turn on the tap and fill up a' the various drinking vessels laying around. Old dog bowls, mostly, obviously, but watering cans, a trough, a plastic tripe bucket, whatever I can see. And the dugs are in them straight away, drinking, splashing, knocking them over and lolloping away. The daft Springer thing wants to drink from the hose and is right up at me, running as close as she can, then turning, back again and away. I put my finger over the end of the hose and spray it right far, creating a wee rainbow, the dugs running in and underneath, trying to drink from the end, rolling on the wet grass underneath, nipping each other, jumping up on me...

John! John!

She's shouting. It's Mrs Bradley.

What on EARTH do you think you're doing?

I stand up, as if standing to attention – *Urm – You said...*

I said to let them out, yes, but not all together. Are you insane? What happens if one of these bitches gets im-preg-nated or bitten? I am not insured for your stupidity, John. Get these dogs back inside at once – starting with that Collie – she is most definitely in heat.

So that's why the others are chasing her, then.

Now. That's me off into town. The police will be here before too long, make sure they give you papers to sign, okay? Otherwise, I don't – we don't – get paid.

Okay, cool. I stand, still smiling.

Go on then – she howls – *get on with it.* Then she's turned and gone.

One by one, I drag the dogs back in on the basis of *who's the most popular?* I don't mind bringing them in. No harm done, I think, and these wee dugs have had a fine run around. And maybe they'll feel more comfortable now they've got to know their neighbours. The last two, of course, are the council dogs. Mrs Bradley is long away so I let them rabbit about a good wee while, jumping in and out of the water, chasing each other.

I hear the approaching polis van easily. There's so little traffic here and despite the noise of the kennel, the diesel engine and creaking suspension are easy to pick out. I make my way over, subconsciously straightening my clothes and checking my pockets for contraband.

Good morning, sir. We're here for (reading) *Two Small Black Mongrels, possible Poodle cross-breed.*

He hands over an A4 blue plastic folder, upon which is fastened an official-looking form. I take it off him and have a quick scan – as if I know what should be there or not. I haven't a clue.

Aye, they're here, of course. So, have you looked for the owners then?

Aye, we have, but no luck.

Full stop.

Great. I look at the floor, kick the muck around for a moment, then ask –

So, what'll happen to these dogs?

Well, once we've taken them away, they'll be rehomed or possibly destroyed, sir.

I look back and see them, oblivious of course, one of them hopping like a kangaroo, the other fighting an imaginary playmate for control over a wee burst plastic baw. We stand and watch, just for a while.

Nice kennels here. I didn't realise you let the dugs out.

Aye, well, not all of them. And we can't have them all out at once, in case of – um – unwanted pregnancy. I sound official, experienced – *Also, the big beasts we leave in the kennels. Guard dogs, you know? Not so friendly.*

I gather the two strays easily enough. They've had their twenty minutes or so, plus their tripe breakfast and now it's time to get put in a tiny wee cage and transported somewhere not too close in the back of a stuffy metal polis van. Not the best part of their day. I doubt I'll hear what happens to them unless I ask, which I won't do. In my mind they'll be adopted by a man with a huge garden and a water hose. In real life they'll probably be injected with a thick red drug and incinerated, maybe together, maybe with a few other lucky playmates. The polis guy takes their leads from me one by one, and lightly pushes them into their new homes. One of the wee blighters has the temerity to look at me as if to say *I could come and live with you and Stevie* – but I'm hardened to such pleads. Cage slams shut, door slams shut. They are now in a dark little place, with only their whimpering and smell for company.

A nod from the polis man and they're off, forms signed, down the driveway, out of my hair.

* * *

It takes me an hour, maybe two, to get the rest of the kennels all cleaned. After Mrs Bradley's bleatings about pregnancy, I'm cautious about letting the dogs out together again, but one by one, well, that's fine for me and the dogs too. They get their extra five minutes run, plus I can squeeze into their tiny wee cages and scoop out rolls of turd that have made their way into the furthest corners. I have no idea how to deal with the guard dogs; their presence and volume inescapable. At first I decide – *I just won't clean them. They'll be fine going one extra day.* But by the time I'm down there, well, I've *almost* acclimatised to their racket. I tell you, having those doors open and cleaning the most recent layers of pish and shite away really does help with the smell, too. Either that or the constant urine reek has eaten away at my ability to smell. Some of those dugs – and not even the small ones – jings, they can pish for Scotland. It's a mighty sight.

Arriving at the guard dogs and despite their volume and their threats, they have my sympathy. For a start, they, like all the other dugs, are locked up. Then, it's their job to bark at things that approach their particular cages. That's what they do – they're guard dogs. So, as far as they're concerned, they're doing what they've been asked to do – scaring the bejesus out of anyone who approaches them.

On top of that sympathy, we have the positioning of their particular domains – at the foot of the kennel, a kennel which seems to have been built, however slightly, on a slope. Just a tiny wee slope right enough, but enough for all the dog pish that escapes the sawdust to slowly, slowly snake its way down into their enclosures. Would you like that? I wouldn't. I too would probably be rather vocal.

The dogs caged beside the guard dogs are purposefully pretty tiny – the Cairn Terrier thing and one of the Cocker Spaniels. Way too small to scale the concrete wall and peak through the upper caging that separates them from the neighbouring guard dogs, or even to get their paws up into the danger zone. They are small and therefore safe dogs to be caged beside such beasts. Cleaning them out is easy and once done I find I have another way of accessing the guard dogs' cage – from the sides.

I get the broom, poke it through the interlinking holes of the wire mesh, *encouraging* the confused under-attack dog to retreat into its tiny enclosed sleeping area at the back of the cage. Then, swing that inner door shut and jam it hard with said broom, I wait, I check, I open the door and run in, locking the sleeping area tight-shut.

I am inside now, mere inches from the guard dog who is barking and scraping furiously at the door. All I can do to justify his imprisonment is to roll his macro turds out, sweep up the sawdust, cover his enclosure with sawdust new, fill up his water bowel, unlock the sleeping area and quickly retreat, locking his cage door behind me.

I dislodge the broom handle and the dog is free. Well, not free exactly, but out of his bed area and into his own main kennel, free of turd and piss, afresh with sawdust. For all those luxuries, he's furious with me, snarling, biting the cage, salivating. An ungrateful beast, but I have cracked the doggy puzzle.

* * *

Finished and walking towards the fresh air, my mind turns to food. It's a surprising thing, that in amongst all this commotion and aroma, an appetite is still developed. A look at my watch and – well, it's almost midday. I suppose I should get started on that soup, maybe leave it to boil away a wee bit, let it cook before Mrs Bradley returns.

The kitchen's unlocked, of course. Not much crime around here, I imagine. And anyway, who'd break into this bric-a-brac kitchen? Someone after a mouldy old crust? I make my way round to the sink and look outside – running down the side of each window there's a thick black mould, green-edged. At the bottom corner it spreads out into a veritable triangle and growing within there a small, child's thumb-sized furry black mould. It's somehow comforting to see, like a child's pet.

I thoroughly, thoroughly wash my hands and scurry for a clean pot. The pot size I'm after is underneath a whole pile of other pots in the sink, it'll mean moving the rest of the buggers, maybe even washing them too. There must be another one? But upon a search, there's not. There won't be. I spy the moulded burnt handle and the puce brown colouring of my quarry, the two wee *once white* lines than run around the rim, suggesting *Sophistication*. The work surface is covered with piles of dirty clothes, crumbs, matchboxes full of dowps, letters unopened and opened, cartons of milk... Aye, Mrs Bradley's not the cleanest of ladies. I decide to place her clothes *dirty pants, socks, track-suit bottoms, a vest or two, a shirt* on top of the fridge and do just that, creating a twelve foot by fourteen foot workspace free, though filthy and sticky looking with rims of tea, more crumbs, smears of butter. I consider wiping it, but the dishcloths look as though they were dooked last winter and have yet to recover, having adopted multiple black skags of burnt toast and who-knows-what-else. Dirty pots on dirty sideboard? That's fine. I get to my pot and using a sharp knife begin to scrape away most of the dirtage, using my hands to ensure it's smooth and clean. Before long it's coming out nicely, even the Go Faster stripes running underneath its rim beginning to gleam white again. Ready to go. I place it on the cooker and turn the heat up underneath it – just to kill any lingering germs – fill the kettle to the brim and set it going. Vegetable time. Yee-ha.

My improvised recipe is as follows: wash the potatoes, scrub 'em thoroughly (being raised beside a field often used for growing tatties, I know not to want to eat the muck they're grown in), chop 'em up into tiny wee bits, chuck them in the pot and cover with boiling water. Add loads of salt and pepper and then see what else is around. Open the fridge. Leeks. Leeks are around. What else. Milk? Nah. Cheese?

Nah. You can't put cheese in soup, can you? Nothing else. Some old bacon. Fuck bacon, not interested in that. Leeks it is. Pull that top layer off, chop them into double two pence pieces and pop them in the pot. I have made potato and leek soup. I've heard of that, haven't you? It's a real soup, for sure.

Take the first wee taste – it tastes of *nothing* – add a further whack of pepper and a load more salt. That'll help it. Right. I'll leave it to simmer away a wee bit.

I head outside, Mrs B's provided wellington boots slopping back on easily, and look for the next part of the days' work – the lawn mower, for cutting down the grass-furnished canine lavatory. I wonder how the auld dried poo will react when hit by the rotor blades of the mower? I walk to the tool shed, enjoying the hot morning sun on my neck, feeling good to be working, away from London, busy, occupied. Within the shed there's no mower though – so where could it be? I spy a gate, open it and walk around through a thin snicket to the back of the house, which, unsurprisingly, is just as slipshod and calamitous as the front – watering cans, sodden unidentifiable clothing, burst baws, washing lines, a couple of smaller sheds, pots, grow bags, split concrete paths... And there, at the end of this section of lush botanic greenery, awaits the mower. It's a sit-down mower, like a wee baby tractor. I smile. I've driven a few tractors, never one of these things, but compared to a moped with threadbare tyres it has to be easy. In my head, the raised position I'll be from the ground can only be a good thing when it comes to avoiding fast-flying, recently disturbed turd debris.

The keys are in the ignition. I have no idea about petrol, what it takes even – would a wee thing like this be diesel? Maybe. We'll see.

I turn the ignition – nothing. And again? Nothing. Okay.

I climb off and look around the mower, examining wheel rims, looking for a clue. If there's no fuel, if that's the problem, I'm fucked, really, as I don't know where the fuel would be stored – or even what type of fuel it takes. Is there a kick-start? Ah – here look – a pull-start thing, like on a normal petrol mower. Their equivalent of a kick-start in fact. These are buggers to get going, I'm aware of that, I'm also aware that there's sometimes an element of black magic required – hold the clutch whilst depressing the brake whilst pulling the pull-start whilst reciting the Lord's Prayer backwards.

The first pull is exploratory, really. Just to see how much give there is, how much energy I'm going to use. The mower barely growls in response. I am going to have to do better than that.

The second pull is a real pull, I guess, but I wasn't really expecting it to work, if I were being honest. And it didn't. The mower growled this time, yep, but soon quietened again.

By the third pull I'm looking around me, seeing if any farmer nearby is laughing at my efforts. There's no-one in sight. I limber up, flex the pull-grip a couple of times and then – *Holy Mother of God* – I yank the pully beast as hard as I can, inviting a feeling of near-shoulder-dislocation and a shallow burn down my arm. The mower shakes slowly, considers starting, but gives up, happy to sit in peace.

Four and five I experiment with clutch and key position, accelerator usage, that sort of area. Technical things. Blind guesses.

And number six, the engine starts and continues. It's diesel; the suffocating thick grey-blue stour emanating from the stunted exhaust tells me that. And jings and cripes, let me tell you, if I thought the dogs were loud, they are nothing compared to this. There's a constant roaring in my ears, an initially terrifying barrage of inescapable volume. Such is my surprise I expect a neighbour to come rushing to complain – even though there are no neighbours for at least a half-mile – and berate me with a perplexing – *How fucking loud is that? It's loud as fuck!* – But there is no neighbour, just me, and I've got to drive this thing, this vast, vibrating, howling and angry wasp.

I have an idea. I skip through to the front of the building, retrieve my scooter helmet and return wearing said helmet. The volume is cut by 50% and I am extremely grateful of my slither of inspiration. For just a moment longer I watch the mechanical beast shake away to itself, then take the plunge, bite the bullet – mount the mower.

My teeth are shaking. My ear drums are complaining. My shoulder is benefiting from the massage, but my buttocks are numbing and my baws – well, my baws are curdling. I catch sight of myself, reflected in a window and spy a very foolish-looking fellow indeed, wearing a crash helmet whilst riding a mower. As though I am *pretending* to be a racing car driver, in high pursuit of *pole position* or am zipping away out-front, keeping all and sundry behind me as I streak to victory. I am neither. I am merely riding a small garden sit-down mower. Mow, mow, mow.

Gear selected, trundle forwards. I'd say we're at a fast walking pace. I attempt to turn – a good, tight turning circle – then I'm facing the correct way and am veering towards the path to the dogshits' rest. En route, I inadvertently pass over the garden hose, causing a rubber-wretching from below. *What's that?* Carry on, look back – *Ah.* The grass cutter is on. I've been cutting as I ride, mistakenly of course, and now I have multi-lacerated the no-doubt prized garden hose. Well, at least it wasn't a snake, a foot or a dug. Engine off. Helmet off. Deep breath, take stock. Within those few moments, I have sweated into the helmet rather profusely. Maybe a break is needed.

Back inside, back into the kitchen and relax. Deep breath, free of the noise of the mower, the stench of the dogs. I approach the soup and it looks okay, somehow. Almost soup-like, in that the potato has dissolved a wee bitty and made the water cloudy, like soup. However, I taste it and it's not good, there's a real lack of flavour going on which I could get criticised for. I check the cupboards to see whatever there is – mustard – that's like chilli, right? That'll do, a teaspoon, stirred in. Beef stock cubes – stock cubes! I should have thought of this earlier – but a quick rummage reveals no vegetable stock and I won't be eating a powdered cow, if I can help it.

Fucking potato, leek and mustard soup it'll have to be. As a gamble, a hope, I grind in yet more salt and pepper. Time to leave it. Somehow it may fix itself, I guess.

Outside in the rare Fife sun, the barking of dogs is distant, the smell of the kennels a mere memory. It is, after all, a beautiful early summer's day. There's a haze, bird song, the smell of the countryside – this could be a good job, riding up here on my wee scooter, given free reign of the place, these tips Mrs Bradley mentioned...

Until I turn a corner and see the blasted mower once more.

And again – helmet on, my old sweat chilling my forehead, curling around my ears and dripping down my neck. Visor up, so some contact with the outdoor world, but my hearing diminished. Approach the mower, remember the secret hand/foot signals of accelerator/clutch/yank – and pull-start the damned muckle thing.

First time. I love it. Man conquers machine. Sit astride, handbrake off, away we go.

I doddle around the corner, bumbling, wobbling, shaking, unsure but moving, through the opened gate, turn the corner and approach the dog run, lower the cutter and off we go.

It's good. It's easy – fun almost. There's a wee thick hessian sack at the back of the mower and after a minute the engine's noise changes – to a more high-pitched whine – to signify the sack is full. I pause, raise the blades, turn the engine off – such is my confidence with the restart – and make to release the grass. I know where it goes, I think, there's a large pile of probably *last year's* grass beside one of the sheds. This lot can just go on top.

There's a latch, then another, then a third and then we're free. I can't help but look – grass mostly, with narrow slices of dried dog poo. Lorne sausage. What was I expecting? Onto the pile it goes.

The grass takes an hour. Just as I finish, and am emptying a sack of cack onto the pile, Mrs Bradley returns. I am wearing my helmet, but have grown into *the look*; I am no longer self-conscious, I am now at one with my tools. She peers round the corner, spies the shortened grass – not well cut, not accurate, but far better than what was there before – and wanders over to me. *What on earth is that on your head?* I smile and remove the helmet, sweat dripping on me, red-faced upon contact with the fresh air, my ears reacquainting themselves with relative cool of the *outside* and the lack of roaring mower.

Ah, it's just for my ears. That mower... I make to point.

Yes, yes, I know all about that mower. Now, do you know what I do for it?

I don't. Of course not. I await the information –

I tie a damp towel around my head.

Arms folded and triumphant. She has discovered China, invented the wheel, cultivated a much-sought yeast.

We sit inside, hungry both, awaiting the soup. I've almost forgotten how gnadgered it was, forgotten it was going to be awful. My hope has somehow made it delicious, savoury, wholesome... I don't break the bubble of imagination. I merely stir the concoction one final time and prepare a bowl for her and a bowl for me. I grab a couple of saucers and place a slightly stale piece of white bread on each. She takes her glasses off, pulls her bowl over and says *Thanks John, I've been waiting on this all morning.* Spoon in, she takes a big load, straight into her mouth. Spoon out, instantly. She gulps and then she squirms. *Oh, John.* Spoon down. *This really is something rotten.*

⋆ ⋆ ⋆

We're fine, Mrs Bradley and I. She came up with some apples and cheese and we had those with the stale bread. Better than nothing and now she knows for sure I can't cook, she's resigned to it. She'll do the cooking, she says, leave me to do the scampering and cleaning; the outside work. I'm happy with that. We've been laughing away at the whole soup situation, how badly it'd come out, the soup I mean, the duff mistakes I'd made. She even showed me where there were more ingredients – a freezer full of peas and sweetcorn that *Would have made all the difference* although I can't see how. It's black magic to me, it seems, soup making. How can that be? I know not.

She was happy with *everything else* though. She'd been meaning to mow that lawn *forever.* She was dreading the police, she hates handing over the strays. *Sometimes I just hide when the police arrive. Keep them another week, see. Doesn't cost me too much extra and sometimes they'll cover it.* An auld safty, is Mrs B.

And how did you manage the guard dogs? A smile, a challenge. I think she'd expected me to not bother, or to get eaten alive. *Did you find the neck harnesses?* The neck harnesses? No-one told me about those… *Eh? No. Where are those? No, I, um, encouraged them into their back-pens, then swept out the front bits.*

Just their front runs?

Accusing look.

Aye, I'm afraid so.

A snort – *Yes my lad, I bet you WERE afraid. Never mind, tomorrow I'll show you where the neck harnesses are.*

They sound even worse. What the fuck is a neck harness? I bet it's one of those things you see on the telly when the polis take away out-of-control dogs. I'm not sure my dog shepherding skills are at that level just yet.

But when it's time to go, we're all friendly, she's happy – asking, even, if I'd like an *advance* but no, me with a few pound in my pockets yet, the pleasures of landing on Stevie cushioning any financial woes I would otherwise have encountered. I tell Mrs Bradley, *Well, I'm going to see my mother, tell her I'm back up here, see how she is.* And Mrs Bradley seems surprised that I haven't done so yet, but *I've only been up a few days* and *I wanted to have a job, be settled, not another worry for her* – and she smiled at that, a considerate lad, me, it seems. *Well John, I'll see you tomorrow morning, we'll have it all to do again, no doubt I can find some additional work – maybe you could start creosoting the sheds, they surely need done.* I glance over and see the thin brown peelings, just hanging off the sun-bleached rain-rotted sheds. They need done, sure enough. At least I'll be outside the sheds and not within, with their cobwebs and tripe. I kick-start the moped, not first time, not second, but third, none too shabby. Compared to the mower, this is the epitome of quiet, reserved transport.

Do Ye Ken The Way Frae San Andres?

Well Christ above, I've been abandoned tae the masses. And a ticket hame? Nae bother – I thought. But the fucking cheap tickets are three days in advance, so twa mair days stuck here in Scootchland San Andres. I'd be hame the noo if it weren't fer that… Fucking cunters judge ye though, eh? See my wee sis – see her? Aye, we were aye close but now… Wouldnae even let me in last night, until the last minute, when she opened the door and called me in, like a dug – "Mikey, you can come in now, abody's in bed" and "Frank kens yer staying, but he's fine so lang as yer oot by 7am so he can get breakfast in peace". 7am? Eight whole hours of warmth. But, better than nowt, so I'm in and trying tae chat wi' baby sis, asking aboot the we'ans – her feeding ane o' them on the pap richt there in front o' me, a' brazen like, me puir red and staring the ither way – then ma sis getting a wee laugh when I mind her o' that time we put worms in Da's work sarnies and him eating them a' the same, or no' telling on anyhoos. But then me fucking up again – offering her the speed, ken, well, no really offering, but telling her I'd bought it up for her – then she's aff – "Michael, I'm breastfeeding, I cannae be passing drugs through to my children, they'll get taken intae care like we did and how much fun was THAT eh?" then "You have to grow up now Michael, your life's going the wrong way." And fuck, doesn't she just sound like the Queen of England herself now, her and Frank with this house and the mortgage. Aye, I say, Aye, I wisnae offering ye it – I didnae ken you'd hae a bairn on yer pap, I jist… "Don't say pap, Michael. It's revolting." Christ, everything I say, every little word, just wrang, pure wrang. 7am here I come, up and out, up and out. When's that fucking bus again? It's like that sang – mind it? But back tae front – De ye ken the way away frae San Andres? I got nae cunt looking oot fae me, in San Andres…

Ma

For the first few years after my father flitted we'd receive presents at Christmas and a week or so after our birthdays, but they became less reliable and more reliably token; an Oxfam charity calendar one year – every eight-year-old boy's dream – a Parker Pen another. He became reliably duff. I don't know if it was my mother who'd driven him out of Fife or the Fife weather itself, but out he'd gone and I'd not seen him in living memory and not heard from him since I was fifteen. The last contact, the final letter, containing a five pound note and a photograph of him, sitting, it seemed, on a yacht, thick black hair, abundant moustache. Who was he smiling at in the photo? I don't know.

It wasn't me though.

I still have the picture somewhere. It's bent, but flat. Crumpled but clear. Brittle. As is the way with photographs printed in a certain era, the colours are slowly fading, the details blurring, the picture dissolving. The irony isn't lost on me – this thing, this one thing that is all I have, this loved and hated ridiculous moustached thing – it too is slowly deserting me.

My mother, bless her, had done her best and she'd done well enough, not using our reduced circumstances as an excuse to give up on teaching me about art, poetry, music. Not that I took to any of it, of course. Or at least, I didn't think I did, then. It was just boring crud, especially when compared to the bales outside, the sea close by...

She'd been pleased I'd gone down the Art College route, worried maybe I'd struggle to survive with it as a trade, but she had kept that worry almost hidden, offered me as much support as she could and the little money she had. I took not a penny. I was keen and I am keen to not be another loved one pulling her down.

From the outside, her cottage, our cottage, looks exactly the same. There's been no work put into these outside window frames since the last time I painted, which must be seven years ago now. At the time I thought – *this paint job will last three years and the next one will only need a top-up* – but the top-up has never come, and now they're just as scraffy as before. I think if we'd been in a village, or by any neighbours similarly concerned, Ma would have had the place spruced up by now, done it herself maybe, but here, a hundred yards from the main road, sheltered by trees, hidden by the gullying of the fields – here, the cottage is slowly being left to rot. Maybe if I'd been back here more often I could have gotten them done. Maybe that's what she was waiting for. I imagine that when she dies, when my mother dies, then the landlord may have them looked at, replaced with these horror plastic windows that are cropping up all over, ruining yet warming cottages such as these.

The bathroom window is but a thin mottled slit, never letting much light in, distorting views, preserving privacy for those inside – hidden from the prying eyes of passing bovine. I can make out bottles – shampoo, conditioner – sat in the window, further cluttering the eyeline, darkening the room. Beyond to the next room and it's my old bedroom and here there is nothing but a couple of books to see – thick, damp-padded novels leaning against the window – open curtains and then black, the view inside curtailed by this brightness outside.

She would have heard the moped, of course. I doubt she'll think it's me though, more likely an underage village lad earning his spurs, whoring up and down the lane on his untaxed, uninsured moped. She'd not be half-wrong, but this lad should know better. *Tomorrow, tomorrow.* Stevie reckons we could get the thing MOT'd overnight, almost. *The man who does the tractors stays next farm along, he'd run it through wi' them. The laird wouldnae notice the extra wee cost.* Sounds nice and easy. I wonder who'd get into the most grief if I were caught riding this thing? Stevie, the owner, or me, the rider? Me, of course. I know that. I'm just playing for time, occupying my mind before I reach the front door.

And here it is. Pillar box red. It's been painted – new paint – badly though, thick, shiny, greasy paint, splattered down the stonework, unsmooth, gloopy, bubbles and drips all too visible. I'm almost hesitant to knock, should it still be wet. *Is this metal paint? For vehicles and such…*

And the door opens and there she is, smiling. *Well, hello John. I've been expecting you.* She's beaming. Thick grey hair, thick bottle glasses, wide, open grin. I can't help but smile back – and why shouldn't I? She's aged, but not too much. When was I last here? Christmas before last? Not too far. Sixteen months, perhaps. Have I aged? She grabs at my hands – affectionate, I think – but no, she's checking, looking – and then another smile – *Ah. You've stopped smoking. Good lad. Come inside now.*

The yellow giveaway stains that once bedecked my wiry fingers have now gone. Not through good sense or devotion or the power of the maternal nag, but through the government's desire to price me out of the tobacco industry and my own desire to stop giving money to people who experiment on beagles. No matter though, same end achieved. Healthy young son appears home, home to the midden.

Though a very different midden to Mrs B's scattershot affair. My mother's environment is mostly shared with old clothing, coats upon coats taking up half the space in the narrow doorway, a hundred pairs of shoes are frozen stiff on the floor, as if caught mid-scuffle, mid-rammy. Piles of *unsuitable for farmland* footwear, half a dozen wellington boots and – *are those my primary school pumps?* They are, they will be. I dwell no more, pass them by. After all, who am I to judge? It's only a few thousand yesterdays since I last wore them. Laying along the floor, like draught excluders, but up against the walls, not doors, are unidentifiable long black fabrics – leggings, maybe, or scarves – as if dropped and in time scuffled to the edges by passing feet.

She's up ahead of me, squeezed into the polite and tidy kitchen bearing many small framed sketches on the wall, mostly by herself, mostly of the immediate area, one or two of the view outside. I note there's a long, grey plastic pot, speckled with multi-colours of paint, housing half a dozen different-sized paint brushes. Ah good, she's painting again.

Tea? After your journey?

I will.

I start to well-up, just a little – just from the *being back here* I guess, turn around and subtly wipe my eyes, look some more at the pictures, returning to a mid-air tea cup, floating directly in front of me.

There you go. As you like it. Pause. *As you liked it.*

Aye – sorry I haven't been back for a while…

She's pawing the air and shaking her head – *No matter, no matter. Here, come on through,* and through we go, beyond the kitchen, more coats on doors, a half-dozen aprons, thick woollen socks discarded in a pile, for *the mending* no doubt, the darning, getting them ready for the next winter. *Take those shoes off,* but they're off already, at the edge of the kitchen and into the living room, the sitting room, with its deep, white-grey sheep's wool carpet, fluffy at the edges, worn in the middle and the pathways, once a haven of adventures for a younger me, driving cars through the snow, adventures with plastic play figures, undiscovered planets. Later, in teenage years, I remember scrubbing the damn thing clean for hours on end after scurrying, rolling through the carpet hunting for and extinguishing lost bits of dope that had jumped from the end of a badly rolled joint and threatened to set the whole house ablaze.

So, you're back.

I nod.

I am. I'm...

Staying with Steven? I thought you would be.

Of course she knew. She'd have been telt by someone – *That's your boy back. Staying with Steven McGillycuddy, I see. What's going on there? How come he's not been to see you? I spotted him in town, with some tramp. Is that him now? A druggy? Has he been seeing his father?*

I slurp my tea.

Aye, staying with Steven. Just for now, likes.

Don't say "likes".

I slurp my tea and purse my lips.

Funny thing, he got in touch. I hadn't bothered – you know, when you told me about his uncle and auntie – but he bothered. He got in touch with me.

The Paisley pattern on the arm of this armchair is almost worn through. A lovely Japanese blue, maybe. A deep, navy, silk feel. A good chair. I pick at it.

Don't pick the chair, John, it's on its last legs already.

I grin. It's been on its last legs since I was a we'an. It is now on the memory of the ghost of its last legs. I cease to pick though.

So, how have you been? The house looks...

Full? Yes, it is. The more I keep, the warmer it keeps. Keeps the wind from rushing through, keeps the cold from killing me off. For another year, at least.

Ever the melodrama.

I see you had the door painted? Looks good. It doesn't and she knows it. She snorts. *I think the laird had his dog do it, by the look of things. Or his blind cousin. His blind, daft, colour blind, weakling cousin.*

I laugh. *Is it tractor paint?*

You know, I think it is. Her humour reined in. She's angered by it. *What a clot that man is. I should have done it myself. And now – get this John – now, he's threatening to have the same oaf do the entire house – the windows, the inside and everything. And all in that frightful colour! John – I think he's wanting rid of me.*

There's no way they'd paint the inside of the house with red tractor paint. That'd be the actions of an insane man.

I don't believe you, Mother. The outside, maybe. The windows DO need painted, after all.

She looks at me and shuffles in her seat. *Well. YOU'RE here now, John. You and Steven could paint these windows in an afternoon. There's only – what – five of them? And that bathroom doesn't count. More of a crack than a window.*

We could, we could. Steven's helping out just at the farm...

And you?

She'll know already, somehow. Somebody would have told someone who bumped into someone.

Well, I've just started...

She watches, expectant.

I've just started at the kennels up beyond Strathkinness. Mind them?

Don't say "mind".

I rub my chin. Stubble. Not much.

Aye, with Mrs Bradley. Perhaps you know her?

She nods.

I do. Queer woman. You know, it was her that had that dog escape a year or so back. Ran out onto the road and got killed by that woman from Strathmiglo who runs the Post Office there. Pregnant, she was.

What, the dog?

No! She puts her cup down, emphasising the importance of the matter. *No. The woman from Strathmiglo.*

I focus my eyes, trying to look concerned. *And was she... was the baby… okay?*

She looks disappointed.

Perfectly normal birth.

Her story is somewhat deflated. Then –

Is that what the stink is John? I do hope so. I do hope you haven't lost control of your functions just yet.

Cheeky. *No, no. None of the piss smell is my piss and none of the shit either. The sweat though, well that…*

John! Do not use those words.

I remember her saying far, far worse. Just the once, but once is enough. On a shopping trip to Edinburgh – a good two-hour journey of bendy roads, traffic jams and bad weather – struggling to find a parking space, losing our tempers, frustrated at our combined lack of Edinburgh knowledge, snapping at one another, finding a space eventually only for us to be gazumped by a quicker, more city-wise driver. My mother had leant out of the window and shouted *YOU FUCKING CUNT.*

Have you spoken to Steven, John?

Eh? Of course I have. How?

She tuts at my language. *And don't say "how", John, it's an awful expression. What I meant was, have you spoken to him about his uncle and auntie? About how they died? It wasn't pleasant you know.*

I shift, awkwardly. *Um, no. Well, a wee bit. But no.*

Well – I'd been looking after them, practically – then a quick look, to see if I'm going to question her, which I don't – *They'd both had the big cancer scares you know, him with his lungs, her with her* – another glance my way – *you know, her insides – and they'd been given the all-clear, or at least I think they were. That's what they had told me, anyhow, when I was around there, which was often enough but probably not as often as I could, if I was being honest – but anyway, it came back – of course it did, as that's how they died, but first her and then him, but then them both of course. They'd gotten terribly thin, you know the way they do, the cancer folk, and –*

Jings, they both died of cancer?

Another look, this one less sympathetic, annoyed I'd broken her trail of thought.

Yes, are you not listening? Well, that's what I'm telling you and, well, it was up to me to help Steven because I'd seen him at his aunt's funeral, you see – Jeannie, that was her name, his aunt Jeannie, lovely woman – and gotten talking to him there, and he asked about you and I said, well, I can't remember ALL I said, but I said I hadn't seen you and it'd be good to see you soon and maybe Steven should contact you, but of course, he had his own problems with his uncle being so ill at the time – Oscar, that was it – queer name for a Scot, Oscar, but that was him. Maybe he was an immigrant, but I don't think so –

He was a Mason, you know?

Was he? What's that got to do with it? She looks perplexed. *Are you saying Oscar is a Masonic name? That doesn't sound right to me.*

Umm…

She shakes her head – *But anyway, I said if I could help with Oscar I would – he looked right frail at the funeral, and upset of course, but also quiet and dignified – you know the way people who are SO sick become, as if they're mentally preparing for the next step, the big drop…*

She tails off, quiet now.

I speak, but it's nothing – just trite talk. Balloon talk; talk for the sake of talking – *Aye, well. A shame, but. And no, I haven't spoken to Stevie. Not about that. Not at any length.*

I'm just tired, hungry and my body is aching from a short day's manual labour. It's easier to think of other things. Any other things. Time to move things on.

So… do you actually know Mrs Bradley? Have you met her?

Her eyes divert from mine, are they a wee bit teary? She's looking eastward, out towards the window.

Well, no. But I know of her and sometimes that is enough.

And quiet, again.

At that moment, in the peace and the solemn atmosphere, my stomach lets out a dramatic gurgle, declaring its empty state. I snort, lightly, in humour and it brings a small smile to her lips. I look round to the kitchen – *Is there…?*

She nods. *Help yourself John, anything you fancy.*

She's up now, slow walking to the kitchen, not in a race, but lifting my mug as she passes. *I'll help you. Things have been moved.*

Again, there it is. The slight grind, slight nag at my absence. Things'll not have been moved at all, I know that. In fact, from passing through earlier, I'm sure I recognised the very same peanut butter pot from my last visit.

Aye well, I'm up now, so I can come round more often.

And do the windows?

What? Is this why she wanted me up?

She turns and grins a wry look, which says, *That's what you told me a few years ago, that you'd be up and round more often.*

She opens a drawer – the same drawer as ever – picks two very-silver bits of cutlery and flat-palms them onto the work surface, then a cupboard above, inside and a plate I recognise well, placed firmly with both hands beside the tablespoon and fork.

The bread's in the bin –

And there it is. The new addition, a cream tin hollow declaring *BREAD* in faux lino-print lettering. I'd never've found that, for sure. She clatters away at it, pulling at the rim, somehow trying to close it even further – surely, she must know it opens upwards?

So... Have you heard from Rab at all?

She turns, having opened the bread bin, surprising herself, and retrieved a slice of thick white bread, flapping it onto my plate.

Robert? Oh yes. I hear from him a lot. He's doing very well now, you know. Working – he's got his own boating company in Mexico. He renovates boats for the rich, retired Americans. Some very big vessels, not like the fishing boats you see round here, no – some have cars inside, can you imagine that? For when they dock somewhere new and need to get around...

This is her tourist spiel. This is the nonsense she tells her buddies, and maybe herself, maybe.

Oh yes, Robert's doing very well. He called me just last week to say they'd gotten a big contract and were just about to buy their second home, plus...

She's in a dwam, an autopilot response much used and no doubt pleased to be off the cancer talk. I interrupt –

And how about John? How's he doing these days?

She looks at me. *What, you? Don't be so daft and so rude.*

Silence.

Butter out of the fridge but not passed towards me. *Help yourself. You know where everything is.* And then she's off, squeezing by me, back away from the sitting room, towards the bedrooms. I hear her door open then close, clicked shut.

Just me now, me and the kitchen and the view. Endless brown field, beyond that the sea, over to the right a good proper farm steading, far in the distance. In her pictures, the one she's painted, she's bought in details I cannot see, summer flowers breaking up the harsh/shite brown, birds hovering, tractor working. An amalgamation of the best bits. *The Hits of the Fields, Volume One.* I remember this house used to stink to high heaven when they'd fertilise that field – using the fish fertiliser mixed with farm manure. Christ, those were long days, the aroma folding over you like a wet duvet. Inescapable, unable to wash clothes for the fear of the drying amongst the thick insult, fear of attending school smelling like a fishwife who'd fallen deep into a slurry pit. My toast pops up.

Ma doesn't return and I'm anxious to leave, get to Stevie's whilst proper food is still on the agenda. Hope he's bought something in, or maybe planning on us going into town. Whatever though, I'm keen to get over there. Habit, and laziness, but mostly habit, means I discard my plate and cutlery beside the sink, no effort to clean it. I do put the butter back in the fridge and – just as I am about to leave – I straighten up the butter knife and the sticky-with-red silver jam spoon. Neat. Dirty, but neat.

Okay ma, that's me away.

Silence.

I knock on her door – *Ma? That's me away. I'll pop by through the week. Okay?*

A shuffle. *Okay, John.* And then the door opens. *Through the week. Good. But not on Tuesday, okay?* Why not Tuesday? *And not Thursday, either.* Okay, not Tuesday or Thursday. *But Wednesday is fine.* Okay, sorted. I have a dinner date with my ma on Wednesday night. *Oh, and John* – I'm still here, have barely moved – *Bring Stevie. I want to thank him.* She's got me there – *Thank him?* She takes my right hand in her right hand and pats it with her left. *For bringing you back up, John.*

I can feel the tears building behind my eyes, know not what to do so nod a thank you – as you would to a foreign shop-keeper who'd served you a cheap biscuit – release my hand and make my way out, turning just to say *Cheers, Ma.* And – *Have a think about what colour you'd like the windows?*

John – John – Forget about the windows will you, just for a minute.

She's watching, watching me as I put on the helmet, pull up my (Stevie's) gloves, sit astride the moped. One chance, switch on, clutch in, kick-start, first attempt, and sit, bouncing up and down, ready to go. Too troublesome to dismount now, to turn even, but do my best, halfway round, wave a *goodbye,* then off, scuttling and bouncing along the narrow yellow lane.

Clarty Chairty Shops

Well, these are no' the days, these are no' the moments I wis looking forwards to, this has just become a drag, a battle frae 7am until midday, when I can drink a lager doon without appearing like a drunkard. I've found a good wee café mind, offering a fu' fry-up, char an' a'. Sharing ma table with tramps though, ken – real tramps, pish-stinking – plus cooncil workies, skiving aff, signing in 7am, straight tae breakfast at 7:05am. I'm neither one nor t'other, biding ma time, wishing it wis warmer up here, wishing I had a book or a paper, wishing things were different, wishing the tea didnae race through me causing me tae pish a' morning. And these shops – Christ man, San Andres has nae shops at a' but clarty chairty shops and see me? I dinnae shop in chairty shops. Even in London I keep well awa frae the chairty shops, making sure I'm a lang way fae ma hoose afore I visit them, so nae cunt sees me being a scabby second-hander, fucking judging me an' that. No' that I ken anyone here it seems, ken? I've rapped on a few doors, rang a few numbers... nuhin. Naebody aboot. A few mithers, no' seeming so pleased tae see me "Aye Mikey, no, Davey boy's awa' in Glenrothes now, da'en the roads eh" and that sort o' pish. Ach. I cannae walk aroond a' day looking fae folk, I'm no' some Olympian, fucking Daley Thompson eh and I'm no' desperate either – I'm ma own man. Found masel a good wee bookies for the efternoons – free coffee, ken? Keeps me alert, fresh. I've worked it out tae – they dinnae want ye hanging aroond unless ye bet, so I place bets on horses an 'oor away. They cannae kick me oot, ken I'm waiting an' a' the time, me drinking free coffee and pissing, mair coffee, mair piss afore ma supper and the call o' the food returns, intae the pub, a pint tae relax me, tak the edge of a' that cheap pishy freebie coffee, then see what the evening brings up, eh? That reminds me, I'll hae tae check those bets the morns' – mebbe I'll be a rich man, get a hotel room... Mebbe no' though, eh. Mebbe no'. I tell ye, they get a' sorts in the bookies up here richt enough, deft auld guys, a' white-bearded, deppit young folk, just ootae school, nae fucking clue aboot life – a few women, big women, barmaids maybe, way past their prime, pocky skin, bulging tracky bottoms, too much makeup, slobbed on claes – and listen – I'm sure I spotted ain o' ma auld teachers fae school. Fair hid his face but, when he saw me. Who was it? Mr Broon? Mr Smart? Aye, something daft like that. Funny tae see him though, all auld an' creepin' aboot, secret agent-like in the bookies. Whit a duffer that boy is eh, no' so smart now, sharing air space wi' a' the rest o' them free coffee chumps. Aye, this is no' the life fae me. I'll be hame soon an' glad. Ach – ken what? Mebbe I'll just head up tae those kennels, see if Johnny's in – see if he's calmed down yet. Aye. That's it. I'll just sup the rest o' this pint down…

Muckers

I get back to the cottage and Stevie's standing right there at the doorway like an auld wifey, awaiting my return.

Hey.

A' right ya cunt. How was yer work?

Ach. Aye, it was fine. Follow him inside, gloves off. Kick at my boots, get them loose, finally my jacket. *Saw my Ma too.*

Oh aye?

Aye.

'Bout time.

'Bout time, Stevie.

How was she?

Hang the jacket up, helmet too, kick-scoosh the boots to one side. *She seemed pleased to see me... She likes you, I can tell you that.*

Aye well, I'm richt likeable.

Aye, you're a richt likeable catch for an auld dear, Stevie boy.

Ha. And you're a cheeky bam. Hey – have you eaten? At your mither's, I mean?

Eh? No' really. I'm famished.

Aye well, guid – as I've cooked food. A wee meal for us baith.

Ah ya beauty. I was hoping...

Aye. Well, don't hope for too much. It'll beat chips though, I reckon. Now, you're puir honking, so get in the shower. And be quick, as I've been waiting on you coming back before I ate masel and am no' waiting much longer.

* * *

I'm sat down, waiting, shower water still cauld on my lugs. There are two chairs opposite each other at the old kitchen table, where ten, fifteen years earlier Stevie's aunt would have served me white bread with butter and strawberry jam, pleased her wee nephew had a friend round, happy to see us bouncing round the farmyard.

Did your mither pile in tae you for no' seeing her then?

Stevie's opened a couple of Tennant's and I'm enjoying the peace, the rest.

Aye, a wee bit... It wisnae easy, but good to see her all the same. I said we'd mebbe see her next week.

Perhaps, aye.

He places a large pot of steaming pasta in front of us – there's way too much for two.

Jings, you like your pasta.

So it seems. Grows that stuff, eh. Expands. Jist a wee bag I put in.

I help myself, a reasonable portion then a little more, the pasta mountain shrinking briefly before popcorning back into shape.

Wow.

And then another pot, this one a crimson liquid, still bubbling, tiny specks of tomato leaping out of the top, freckling my white-with-brown-edging plate.

Is this soup? Soup with pasta?

Is it fuck. It's a fucking vegetable sauce thing. Dinnae ask me. I'd normally put diced lamb in, ken, but whit with you no' eating beasts – well. I put another tin of tomatoes in. That'll dae.

I look at the surface of the concoction, air bubbles still appearing as if through lava.

Plenty hot though.

Then he's back to the grill and removes two massive, steaming steaks.

And these beauties are for me.

He sits down, his eyes focused on the spitting meat the whole journey. Ladles a spoon of pasta, then the sauce, but these are clearly mere colourings to his dish, a little variation. We are left with enough pasta and sauce to feed a family of pigs.

Aye, there's some vegetables in there too.

I sink the ladle in – once, twice – no vegetables, just the pot of stage-blood.

They'll be doon the bottom.

I scoop, I scoop, I scoop. There is nothing. And then –

A mushroom?

Aye, that's ane of them. I put anither in an' a'. That's fer me mind, if ye find it.

He's laughing, then straight into cutting his meat.

Well, thanks for cooking anyhow. Kind of. I was pretty hungry, I tell you.

He looks up from his feast –

Aye, I'm no' a vegetable... a whit is it? A vegetarian chef. You'll hae tae learn that bit.

Ach, I've cooked plenty in London. I can look after myself, no worries.

Stevie winks – *Aye, I'm sure ye can, Johnny boy.*

* * *

So – do you ever think about your faither still?

Of course. I miss him... I mean – he may still turn up one day. Mebbe... Ach. How come? Why do you ask?

Ach – it's just... I think aboot ma folks often enough. Especially now... A' the way through though, I was always telt that I widnae miss them and that I couldnae possibly mind them at a', but I can. I could. Christ.

Aye. My mother wasn't keen to have my da' mentioned at a'... I just have that one picture.

You still got that? I suppose you would. I mind when that arrived, you were like seeing a spook. A phantom. Fucking grinning oot at us.

Aye. Worst Christmas o' my life, that ane. My mother was – well, in tears. I had this daft picture to look at, talk to. Ne'er fucking talked back to me though.

Here – check this oot then...

What is it?

Haud on, ah'll just find it in the kist... there – there ye go.

Oh aye. Fuck. Wow. Is that your uncle, then? Some flares on 'im. Is that your auntie? Nah, that's no...

Nah. You're richt, it's no' her. It's ma folks. Ma REAL folks. Ma mither and faither.

What? Fucking hell. No... and – and that bairn...

Aye. I guess that's me. Here – gies it.

How...

Well, my auntie it was, I think. She was the main ane. She... she just figured I'd be better forgetting, eh. I didnae though. And when my uncle

– when he was on his way oot… Well. He telt me. He said – "There's a photae o' ma brother. Yer da'. Hidden somewhere aboot". I thought he was a' daft wi' the drugs, put it tae the back o' my mind…I mean – I couldnae look then, could I? How'd it seem tae him on his last legs, me scurrying aboot fer someone else…

But then, when he died, efter he was taken awa', efter the funeral – I minded and I looked. And I found them, back o' a drawer in a wee wooden box.

Stevie stares at the picture for a moment, then he's back up and bringing over another two lagers. He opens them and then takes a swig from both –

Hey haud up…

Haud up yerself, ya dowp – here –

He places the cans on the table, then he's back into the kist, opening the wider lower doors this time, retrieving a bottle of single malt – a Macallan. He pops the already-loose cork and drops a dram or two into each of the Tennants.

Here, gie it a minute tae settle.

High class, Stevie.

Aye. High class. That's me.

⋆ ⋆ ⋆

So, did you – have you met anyone, since school?

Eh? Loads o' folk.

No, I mean – lassies.

He pushes the meat around his plate.

Nah. Well – nah. Kind of. There was this one lassie o'er in Ireland. She was local, ken, worked at the college.

A tutor?

Nah. A dinner lady.

A dinner lady? What, an auld wifey?

No. She wisnae auld at a'. Same age as me in fact. I guess…

Oh aye. So…

Aye, well – She was as shy as masel. The twa o' us gaen beetroot red whenever we saw ane anither. Christ, I could barely ask for ma peas…

Heh.

The sloppy pasta is over-cooked but the sauce is good, despite its lonesome nature. I'm saving the mushroom until last.

So, what happened?

Aye well – she – um – we… Ach. Nothing. Kind of.

He looks up at me, utensils temporarily ceasing their work – *We got drunk one night – staff Christmas party. But I was with a' the other tutors and she was at the other side o' the hall, wi' a' her pals. Daft. I didnae get on with the other folk much, so was just watching her dance and such…*

And is that it? You didn't even talk to her?

Och – I… We bumped into each other on the way tae the cludgie and I said "Aye".

Wow.

And?

And, then efter – well, I didnae exactly dance.

I grin at the thought.

But I… she came and took ma hand and – well, I was pretty steamboat by then – I kind o' – I kind o' shoogled a wee bit beside her…

And we're both laughing now.

And she had ma hand – tiny wee fingers she had, a'most like a we'an, but richt lovely eyes, bonny red hair –

Ginger?

Aye – but Irish ginger, somehow.

Eh?

Aye, fuck. She looked mighty.

So…

Well…

He takes a sup.

Christmas came and I was back here – he gesticulates around, his eyes falling and resting on cupboards, doorways, perhaps remembering them when the house was fuller, slowing his story, distracting him – *and then… and then, when I retuned – Well, she wisnae in that first week and then I saw her one day and… well that was when that wee daftie lost his toes. That very nicht. Well, my standing in the college went doon wi' the tutors a wee bit. I ne'er got on with them, really, but efter that – I couldnae be ersed. I stopped ga'en tae lunch, brung ma own sarnies. Barely saw her again, ne'er to speak tae.* He shakes his head. *Whit a loon I was. Shan times.*

There's a minute of near silence, just the clatter of the knives and forks, the munching of the remainder of the food, the lifting and returning of drinks.

And yerself? How about you?

Aye, there was one or two. I did okay, I guess. Different though, we were all flung in together. And at the start – well, a'body was keen to be best pals wi' a'body else. I think the accent helped. I was with one richt crazy doughba'. That was Charlie…

Charlie?

Aye.

Lassie?

Aye. Charlie the lassie. She was Canadian. Paid a fortune to be o'er in London, or her folks did. But she was just as shite at it as me.

You wereny shite! Ya dowp.

Ach – I don't mean shite – I meant… she was just as distracted as me. Jings, she was well worse, even. Richt intae speed and…

Speed?

Aye – speed, you know. Whizz. Whatever. I hated it. Made my heart go fruity loops and stuff. I think that was it, she was doon there seemingly just to burn out and that's what she did, pretty much. I only lasted a few weeks with her afore she lept aff with someone else. A guy from a different course.

Sorry about that.

I'm no'. She was a richt head fuck.

And we're quiet. Stevie's looking at me curiously, then –

But… fruity loops? How do ye mean?

Ach… it just made me feel as if I was… as if I was dying for a shite.

And now he's laughing, spitting out a slither o' meat. *Aye, some fucking drug that sounds, Johnny boy. Mind an' no' gi' me ony.*

* * *

Aye, ma uncle was… Thin. Way too thin. Cheekbones oot, eyes sunken, hair a' short and spiked. He wanted to be here, ken, no' inside hospital. No' in Dundee. Christ, he hated that toon. He telt me he'd rather live twa days less and die at hame then spend twa days in a fucking ward wi' o'er dying folk. So – that was it. They bought him big fluffy pillows so he could sit up, a walking tray so he could get his ain tea and biscuits, get tae the cludgie... Gave him these health drinks to power him back up, but he hated them. Telt me they tasted o' nothing. He'd jist lie there, listening tae the teuchter music on the radio, then he'd ask for the telly on for the sheep dug trials or the weather – jist the weather, no' the news. He kent the news, the news was he was dying soon enough. I put yon Archers programme on aince, my aunt used to tune in, ken, but he was like – "It's jist posh actor folk talking shite, it's no' fer me". Aye... A few other folk came up but he wisnae interested in them. Visitors, ken. Frae the village. Maybe the vicar would get in a'fore shootin' the craw as soon as he could, aff tae the next puir auld sod... The nurses were guid, mind. Gave him aye plenty o' painkillers. Local doctor too. Hey – mind Susy Hopkins? Aye ye do. The heid lassie at school when we first went up? Showed us a' aroond school that first day? Well – she was there, she was the doctor who came in. Ken whit she telt me? She said – "It's his last days Steven, you do know that, right? Be careful with the painkillers, they'll get him in the end" but she'd hand me the whole lot – way too much fer the dose he was on... Christ, she'd be bent over tae inject him and I'd catch masel no wanting tae look at ma uncle or the needle and puir staring at her erse – but no' like, no' in a pervy way, jist ma eyes no' kenning whaur tae look and ma uncle – well, he had water in his eyes but he's peering up at me checking her oot and he smiles. I'm no' sure if it was the drugs like, or his spying me, but, well, he smiled. He was pleased I was there, mebbe. Pleased I was hame.

* * *

That's me beat, Stevie. I'm going to turn in.

Aye? Well. I might jist take another dram. Sit up a while.

No' in a lager again though, eh? I smile. *That was awfy.*

He gives me a tired grin. *Aye, that was awfy enough.*

He's sitting stock-still, just slowly wafting that picture of his folks back and forth.

Well... G'night Stevie.

Aye. G'nicht Johnny boy.

Cam' O'er The Lea

Stevie's up first, slams doors, coughs in the shower, rattles the frying pan, wakes me up. The moment, the second he's out the front door, I'm up myself, not bothering with the shower, but filling up with tea, toast and jam. A slight caffeine nudge and quick sugar rush just enough to get me dressed, off and out of the door, then back in immediately to retrieve the bike keys, picking up the helmet as I pass and lazily brushing out the dust and sand contained within as I make my way outside.

Good weather. An early morning spring sun, low, burning the fields, mist rising off them; a breeze coming off the sea, bringing with it the smells of the beach and beyond; songbirds happily outnumbering the more cumbersome rackety seagulls. It's almost a crime to put this scraggy, battered crashhelmet on, muting my senses and eventually delivering me to less fragrant climes, but off I am, starting the motor third time, out down the path, through the farmyard onto the track and away to work.

I had considered stopping en route at a supermarket. Buy a sandwich, perhaps, and avoid the soup scenario, but the vibrating of the Honda unfocusses my mind somewhat and I feel my meagre breakfast slowly churning, deadening any thoughts of future food. Also, my hangover – if that is what it is – is being exacerbated by the volume and *brain shake* of this damned bike ride. I was a fool to take on this job, a fool to agree to the scooter, a fool to drink last night, a fool to fill up this morning with fizzy jam on toast. But here I am, sugar crashing on a moped with a throbbing head and awkward stomach, pondering my lot. When Stevie and I were kids, it never seemed this way around. I mean, it never seemed as though Stevie would be the one helping me out. I had, I thought, the intelligence over him, the ideas, the ability to see the hypocrisy and daftness of everyday situations. But looking at it now, I was just lazy. Stevie though – well, he's worked. And he's worked at being able to work some more. Even now – between proper work – he's doing more solid hours in a day than I achieved all week in London and I doubt I'll suddenly discover a taste for sweeping up dog keich that'll spin me all a-flutter with excitement. I need to find something. Anything.

The kennels arrive and as I trundle up the hill I spy Mrs Bradley and curse my lack of tax disc and insurance once more. This afternoon, I shall sort it out, somehow. I shall deliver the bike to Stevie's pal for a quick 'n' easy farm financed MOT. The tyres, I must say, are looking a little suspect, but with the dry weather the slight flecks of white rubber that are nudging through aren't too much of a concern. Only if I were stopped by the polis would they cause my heart to race, but then they'd just be one further tiny foul-up, one more MOT fail, one extra reason to be fined amongst a no doubt whole heap of niggling, worn-out parts.

She's not smiling, Mrs B, as I approach, but I'm taking that as her usual early morn disposition. I mean, I may not be early, but I'm not late, surely. It can't be ten past the hour yet, if that. I'll be in amongst the howling beasts in moments – it's not as though this job requires any preparation. I bring the bike to a halt alongside the tripe shed, facing it away from Mrs Bradley and well tucked in, out of sight of any tax conscientious, visiting dog-owners. Engine off, shoulders down, breathe in, remove the helmet, dismount, wipe my forehead, hoik the bike onto its stand, gloves off and walk over to Mrs B. I'm smiling, bringing the joys of the early summer morn with me. She is scowling, most definitely scowling.

Well. You've got a nerve.

Sorry? Am I late? Have I come at the wrong time? Did I yesterday inadvertently mount a dog with the mower, shred it into a thousand pieces and not notice? My face must display my confusion, as that is all there is.

Oh don't come that with me. You know full well what I mean.

I look around for a clue – but there's nothing. Just the same cluttered yard there was yesterday. My clothes are pretty skanky compared to yesterday, but that's not a reason to complain, is it? I mean, it's not as though I'm…

Your brother was up.

Well, that takes me by surprise. *My brother? What – Rab?*

Rab?

Oh, um – Robert you mean? He's in Mexico.

She looks at me as though I am not just extremely daft but extremely irritating too. I am well assured that I am missing the point.

No. Not Rab, not Robert, not from Mexico. Your other brother.

I shake my head – *I don't have another brother.*

She shifts her bodyweight and I notice for the first time that she's holding a pair of hedge trimmers, worn rubber handles, foot-long rusted blades jutting slightly towards me. *I mean your brother Michael.*

Eh? I don't have a brother called Michael... but I momentarily close my eyes and a vision of Mikey appears, sneering at me, raising a finger.

Fuck. Do you mean... Mikey?

Aha. She grins a self-satisfied and smug grin, as though she'd somehow tricked me into confessing – *Yes I do. Now, I should tell you right now, since this seems to be the first you know of it, that the police have been informed and are on the look-out for him right now.*

What did he... Look, I'm sorry ...

And so you should be – sharp now, angry – *he's a devil that boy. Frightened the life out of me.* Stamps feet. *How DARE you say he could sleep up here? What right of that was yours? I barely know you. I had to chase the little villain out of my own house.*

No, no – I mean –

And he stole some money, John, which I guess was your plan all along, right? To find out how much of a soft touch I was? Well, congratulations. You've hoodwinked me good and proper, but you'll be paying for it now John.

And she storms off, back inside, slamming the door shut and audibly clicking the lock tight. I'm shaken, the adrenalin running through me, the accused with no chance to reply. I look around me and nothing seems terribly broken or smashed up – what did he do? Mikey, I mean? Steal a few quid? How did he get up here anyhow? I walk to the door and knock.

Listen, he's not my brother. I barely know him –

No reply. I knock more, harder – bam, bam, bam.

Mrs Bradley – I don't know him. Well, barely. I barely know him. But he's not my brother...

Fuck. Cunt. That cunt Mikey. What's he been up to?

I straighten up and look around me once more – there's a slight wind in the trees and it seems to be pushing my nerves further, my inability to think straight. Should I go?

I knock again – *It is nothing to do with me. I don't know the guy. He's just a guy I met on a bus, I can't help it if he…*

And the door opens. Not quick, but the lock is thrown back and then the door hauled inwards. She's there, Mrs B, the same hedge cutters held aloft –

Well now, we'll see. I called the police when I heard your – your stupid moped and they'll be up any minute. They were half expecting you or your brother would turn back up. I'm sure you can tell them all about it.

I stand back, I display my empty hands, I raise my eyebrows, I shake my head – *He's not my brother.*

She jabs forward with the shears – *Brother or not is beside the point. Whoever it is, whoever you set me up with, you're a little… bastard, John, I tell you. I got NO sleep last night whatsoever, imagining he was still here, in amongst the trees. Did you ever think about that? About what problems your little game may cause? I am exhausted.*

I think she's been crying. There's no answer. I've said it all before. I look to the ground – *Look –*

No. YOU look. You're in serious trouble, John, conspiracy to burgle, threatening with a deadly weapon…

What?

And I tell you one more thing – if you think you're getting away with ANYTHING – that blasted old scooter of yours is the first to be reported. How dare you, John? How DARE you?

And the door slams shut.

What can I do? I can't run. I have nothing to run from. Running would implicate guilt. Isn't that what we're told? But hang on – deadly weapon?

Mrs Bradley – Mrs Bradley – what was the deadly weapon? Mrs Bradley?

There's no answer. I place my hands in my hair and run them down, through onto my face, pinching my nose and trying to work out what just happened. One thing I do know though, the polis will be up and I'll be here too – and no doubt suspected of some crime or other. And that fucking bike – I could do without that.

I look over and see the exhaust pedal, the ancient number plate, the foam-spilling seat. If I saw this moped, sitting where it is behind a stinking little shed, I'd presume it off-road. But maybe I should help things along?

I walk over to the bike and feel the engine, but I don't even need to. The heat's coming off it still, quite clearly. So, she called, what, five minutes ago? They'll be here any time. It'll still be warm then, the evidence will still be glowing. I look around for somewhere to hide it, but, well, unless I take it far away… Maybe I could hide it behind the back of the house? It just needs to be out of Mrs Bradley's vision. I chug it off its stand and begin to wheel it, bringing out from beside the shed. I can hear a vehicle though so I wait, still, listening and – yep – they're slowing down. It sounds diesel, they're heading up here – it's a polis van. Fuck this. I open the door to the shed and quickly, roughly wheel the moped in. It hops down the small ramp, front wheel complaining, turns right and rides into the wall. Out of sight and out of mind. I hope. Back out, close the door, move away, stand my ground and wait.

Polis

One, then two. Close their doors, hats on, standing in front of the van. Anonymous uniforms, lack of acknowledgement or recognition, adjusting shirts and coats. I note that one of them is wearing trainers. White trainers, the type one'd wear for squash, or running. He looks a little *Michael Jackson,* in this smart-casual approach. Maybe it's dress-down day at work? I stand and watch, nervously awaiting whatever should occur.

Fellow number one approaches. He is wearing normal polis issue footwear.

Mr McHugh? John McHugh?

I nod, strangely relieved of the contact. It has begun, after all – *Aye, that's me, but listen –*

I'm afraid we're going to have to place you under caution Mr McHugh. Do you understand what that means?

He is still walking towards me. I panic. The blood rushes to my feet – *Aye, of course, but listen –*

You are not obliged to say anything but anything you do say…

I was just, I was just –

Polis fellow number two begins his approach, taking a wider path in his soft white shoes, but still loping towards me.

But anything you DO say…

Both stopping a mere three feet from me now. Crowding me. More sweat upon the sweat of the journey, the sweat of the hangover.

…will be noted down and used in evidence.

Okay.

Right – can I talk now?

Polis man number one is looking all around him, surveying the detritus a kennel kicks up, listening to the dogs, perhaps looking for Mrs Bradley. Then – *So you know why we're up here, Mr McHugh? Suspected burglary, possible assault?*

Aye, but…

Well, first of all – would you mind telling me what you're doing here right now?

Sure, yeah – I came to work. I mean, I only started yesterday but…

Bit of a coincidence, is it not? He's still not looking at me, he's playing all aloof.

Eh? What's that?

Then he looks at me, straight into my eyes.

You starting work here one day and that very night old Mrs Bradley here being visited by someone claiming to be your brother…

Aye, but he's NOT my brother, you see –

We know that, Mr McHugh. We're the polis. We're no' daft. Mrs Bradley gave us your name and we saw your mother this morning – she was out last night – At a Bridge game with the local priest, apparently – but this morning she confirmed that you had ONE brother and that he was in – pause – *Mexico – and that you, quite clearly, didn't fit the description of the suspect.*

Well, that's good, but – *You visited my mother?*

Aye. Normal procedure. It was your last known address up here. I tell you, it looks pretty suspicious, you starting work one day, this Michael character arriving that evening and noising up Mrs Bradley…

Aye. I can see that, but, it's all explainable. It's all – just nonsense…

But that's no explanation.

So, you'll be keen to tell us where – WHO – this brother Michael of yours is then?

Well, um… Am I going to be a *grass*? I guess I am. Easy decision. My loyalty to Mikey has barely been stretched, seeing as I had no loyalty to him whatsoever. But first, a minor attempt at learning the lay of the land, before I actually stake Mikey to it – *Could you, um, could you tell me what happened here last night?*

No. Emphatic. *Mr McHugh, you tell us what you know. That's for the best.*

A lock shifts, handle turns and door opens, Mrs Bradley emerging, hedge trimmers still in hand. She's peering, listening, but not getting involved. She better not mention that moped. Maybe if I get in first…

Right. Okay. The guy, who I presume came up here yesterday – Michael, or Mikey, as I know him –

So you know him then, Mr McHugh?

Polis fellow No.2. I stop and look at him as if he's daft, perhaps a wee warning in my eyes of *Not to interrupt me again or suffer the consequences* – but he shifts on his foot an inch towards me and I back off – *Aye, well, I tell you what, how about I tell you all about it?*

You do that Mr McHugh. He's grinning an irritating, smug, powerful grin. I have decided this man is a cock. His ridiculous footwear has merely confirmed it. I wonder who he was at school? A bullied wee ferret, no doubt.

I met Mikey on the bus up from London. Never seen him before, don't know where he is now, don't know anything about him. He's no' pal, I'm no' his accomplice, I came here fair and square for work and if he's done something daft, it's on his heid, no' mine.

The polis man smiles. His demeanour is winding me up, causing me to lose patience and talk. He is winning this slightest of battles – but then, I have nothing to hide, do I? I'm happy to talk.

He told me he had a sister up here? And he did know my brother Rab – so maybe he was at school with him? But Rab's in Mexico...

We're aware of that, Mr McHugh.

Aye, he's well clever this one. I continue –

And that's it. Last few times I saw him, in fact, we fell out. I told him to fuck off. We didn't exactly part on good terms...

Goodness! It's Mrs Bradley, though she hasn't moved her position, she's just letting us know she's around, part of the drama.

So, if that's true, Mr McHugh, how did this Michael character come up here? And how did he know you had been here? It all sounds very unlikely to me.

I shake my head. *Well, I don't know HOW he came here, but I'd guess a bus, or by foot or* – don't say moped – *who knows, but he knew I was coming up here as I'd told him I was calling kennels and there's only three in the book –*

Why were you calling kennels, Mr McHugh?

Come on. I was looking for work. Look – you spoke to my ma. You'll ken I'm just back up and have been looking for work. You ken I've found a place to bide and I hope you'll have looked up my record and seen I've got no previous. You must know that no-one would be so daft to come and clean up dog shecht for a day just so their buddy can come up and steal a tenner or whatever? I mean...

I leave it. I have declared my innocence, I think.

Aye, fair enough, Mr McHugh. We know all that. So. What we don't know is, who this Michael – Mikey – character is. Though from the description Mrs Bradley gave, we have an idea. Is there anything else you could offer to help us out?

Fuck it. Shop him in and get this over with. The little cunt that he is. But with what?

I don't – I can't add much more. Wee guy. Black greasy hair. Stinks. Got a sister up here. I guess… late twenties?

Hang on – No.1 reaches in his black leather folder and hands me over a copy of a pencil sketch – *Does this look like him?*

It's an artist's impression. It's shite. Really bad. A spider sitting astride a potato. However, I can sense the essence of Mikey in there – somehow, it just looks manky enough. It carries enough of his general *mealworm* demeanour.

Aye, that's him… although…

I leave a gap, a rest, I am now in control of the situation – or this moment, at least –

You know, I could do a better picture of him, if it'd help? I, umm – I do folks' portraits, ken?

The polis folk seem surprised, although I'm sure Ma told them I was an artist – it would have been her opening gambit, practically, assuring them that this *kennel cleaning* was only temporary – but artists aside, I guess this offer of a more accurate sketch isn't something they're usually offered. No.2 speaks – *Could you now?* He nods his head with a slow, exaggerated gurn. No.1 moves his hat back a tad, friendlier-seeming. *Well, that certainly may help, Mr McHugh. It'd count in your favour, too.*

I am just about to say *I haven't done a single thing wrong, polis man number two* when I remember the moped. I bite my tongue, change my tack. *Well, if I can do anything to help you catch the bad man, I'm happy to.*

Sketchy

We're inside Mrs Bradley's and I'm sat at the kitchen table, paper and pen (provided by the polis) in hand. Directly in my line of vision is the pot I'd used to create the soup that had Mrs Bradley dancing with delight. I wonder if it's still full? She wouldn't have eaten it. Maybe the dogs got it? Maybe the council used it to euthanise their strays. Mrs Bradley is in the room, she heard what I'd said, my explanation, but she's still wary of me, annoyed I've been allowed back in her house, to sit at her table. I use the time to talk, put over my side of the story.

Aye, no, I barely knew him. Sat by me on the bus, leeched on to me. I was at the Art College down there, you know –

I start with a nose. Anyone's nose. Noses all look the same, right? Except for the big ones. Or the small ones. Or the broken ones, too. They look different. I give this Mikey an average nose.

He had me right scared in that phonebox. And did I tell you he had a go at me in the Station Arms too? Aye, I've got plenty of witnesses to that. A match was on – snooker, you know. The barman will remember it fine, he pulled Mikey off me.

Hendry?

Polisman No.2. Our Lord of the Surprising Trainers.

Eh? I couldn't say. I didn't catch his surname…

No, I mean, was Steven Hendry playing?

Ah right – no idea. Cannae abide snooker. Some wee lad playing some fat lad with an auld guy refereeing.

Aye, Hendry that would have been. I saw it on the telly. Good match. That Hendry boy is something else.

He looks at me for a response, but I believe I have made my thoughts on snooker clear. He continues –

Would you be willing to report this – incident – Johnny?

Um, aye, sure. I could tell you exactly what happened and up to you to go on with it or not. Honestly, I doubt you'd get a conviction for a wee scuffle in a pub cludgie, but you never know.

You leave that to us, Mr McHugh.

He removes his hat completely.

As a potential victim, it's not for you to worry about that sort of thing.

I note his textbook sympathy.

Mrs B ventures my way and looks over my shoulder. It's taking an age this picture, and my hands are still shaking from the adrenalin and shock of it all, but she reckons she can recognise something – *Yes, yes, that's him. That's the man who was here.*

I've only drawn a nose. Shall I leave it there? Let them plaster pictures of a nose all over St Andrews?

No.1 asks – *You're shaking something awfy. Would you go a cup of tea? Calm things down?*

You know, that'd be amazing. I'd love one – *Aye. That'd be braw. Thank you.* He looks over to trainer cop and nods him into action. Ach, a little disappointing. Between these two, I suspect trainer cop will be the lesser skilled of the tea makers. Never mind though, good to see him doing something for me anyhows, that'll do.

An ear, an ear, start on an ear. Hidden behind a black fuzz of hair. Should I do an outline of the head first? I don't want to look like an amateur, but similarly I don't want the picture to be as bad as the original sketch. I need to reclaim some credibility here, both for my job's sake and my own chance of being cleared.

Did have an earring? I can't even remember. He must have. He did.

He didn't.

Mrs Bradley?

She's over with the kettle but her eyes dart to me, surprised I've spoken to her, broken the barrier between accused and accuser. She's not sure how to react, what to say.

Erm – was he wearing an earring last night?

What? An earring? Well... Yes. No. I'm not sure. Yes, he was.

That's cleared things up. I give him an earring. A mid-sized, pirate-style earring, then I add a pearl drop to it, making it look slightly *effeminate.* That'll learn him, should he ever see it.

My tea arrives. It's not bad. *Thank you,* I say.

No worries. How long will this take? The trainers boaby is talking.

Oh. Fuck – are we in a hurry?

I've been dragging this, due to the shakes and the importance, I guess. The nerves. *I could speed things up?*

Ah, no but – it's just – I had ma breakfast at the back o' seven this morn and it's near enough eleven now. I could eat. Shall we leave you here and come back fer the picture?

Mrs Bradley exclaims, *No!*

I'd be fine with that...

No!

Well, I didnae bring ony sarnies...

But Mrs Bradley's not happy.

You can't leave me. You simply can't... What if this Mikey character returns?

He won't. But right enough, they could get into a' sorts of shite if he comes back and murders us both. Me bleating about my moped would be small beans then.

What was this deadly weapon you mentioned, Mrs Bradley?

Concentrates the mind, a well-placed mention of a deadly weapon. Both the polis twitch our way, curious what the reply will be – *You never mentioned that to US Mrs Bradley, did you? Is there something you left out, perhaps?* Then adding, softly, remembering their training perhaps – *What with the stress of the occasion?*

She looks ashen-faced. Hands down, she adjusts some cutlery on the table, before quietly, whispering, *He had that chain he'd found outside. Do you remember? I did mention it.*

What – the dug lead?

Well, yes. It was a dog lead, but all the same...

Ach, that's no' deadly weapon.

He chuckles.

But what if he'd choked me with it? He could have, you know?

I butt in, keen to hear what exactly went on – *So what happened? How did he get here? Why did he say he was my brother?*

She exhales deeply, perhaps pleased to be off the dog lead story – *Well then* – and sits, scraping the chair on the floor as she moves it.

I've been over this already with these two – She waves her hand in the polis folks' direction. *What happened was this.* She's thinking, stacking her thoughts carefully before continuing. *Well. The first I heard was the knocking at the door and I thought – "Who's that knock-knock-knocking at my door?" – Well, you know, you would and even though I'm a kennels – a business, you know – I still don't expect people to roll up at THAT hour, unless it's been pre-arranged, of course, in which case it's usually fine, but no, not this time, not last night, last night I had just checked the boarding kennels – which reminds me, John, we'll have to clean them as soon as you've done that –*

Ah. It turns out I'm re-hired.

And there I was, back inside I was, making a sandwich, I think, ham and pickle, yes, ham and pickle…

Mrs Bradley?

It's polis man No.2. I suspect I know what he's going to ask.

Would there be any chance… Would there be any chance, madam, I could have one of those ham and pickle sarnies now? I wouldn't ask, it's just…

I know, I know, you left your sandwiches at home. You told us. You poor man. No. I'm afraid not. I finished the bread this morning. My nerves had made me hungry, you see.

We ponder with wonder her marvellous, appetite-accelerating nerves. But I have an idea –

Mrs Bradley?

Yes?

Is there any of that soup left? You know, the soup I made?

What? She looks surprised I'd bring it up. *But that soup…* Then, a realisation – *Yes. You could try the soup that John here made. It was a little…tart for my pleasure, but you may well find it suits you. Here* – she passes by him and places her hand on the saucepan lid – *be sure and warm it first.*

Ah grand, thanks. Should I warm the whole lot, or just take a portion and warm that?

His colleague is shaking his head, bemused. *Eating on the job? Not on, Wullie, not on.*

So. His name's Wullie. Good to put a name to a pair of shoes.

And how about you sir? Would you like some also? But he's not going for it. *No thank you, madam, I'll eat when we get back to the station, thank you very much.*

John?

I don't reply. I smirk a little and draw an eyelash. Then I raise my right eyebrow and gently, slowly shake my head, *No.*

We'll both be arrested for poisoning a police officer. Assaulting his taste buds. He lights the gas under the soup and allows it to slowly warm. How I long for its wholesome aroma to fill the kitchen.

But anyway, when I opened the door it was the horrible little ratty man that John is drawing now. Now, my FIRST thought was that he was a customer, so of course I was friendly, as I would be, a businesswoman, but no, he wasn't after a dog at all – it turns out he was looking for Johnny. Now of course, John wasn't here and I had no intention of letting him in until he told me he was in fact John's brother...

I look nothing like him – he's a wee dowp –

...so in he came, regardless of me saying I couldn't help and he was asking when John would be back, you know, that sort of thing. I told him it wouldn't be that evening, of course, as John had finished work for the day but I offered him a drink – a cup of tea, I meant –

Have you a bowl for this soup?

I'm sorry?

Oh – it's just this soup, Mrs Bradley. Have you a bowl for it? It seems... warm now.

Well, warm's half the battle.

Oh, just eat from the pan. We don't stand on ceremony here, do we John? She grins. *No-one else will be having that soup now, I'm sure.*

Result. Ya beauty. I'm pure dead starving.

He lifts a soiled spoon from the sideboard and rinses it, rubbing any debris with his thumb. All eyes on Wullie. The soup pot lid comes off, delicately placed behind the taps, and the spoon goes in, haphazardly, no respect for the soup, then out again, piled high, spare soup tilting back into the pan. Slower now, careful not to spill any more and then in – straight into his mouth. His eyes pull back into his head, his head jutting back further. A swallow, a large, ungainly swallow – and another – a secondary, cautionary swallow – then he looks back into the soup bucket, as if he's curious of who the culprit was, whosoever had tainted that mouthful of his imaginary delicious soup so. Then, once more, one more spoonful – and it's just as bad, but this time – this time – his head juts back slightly less and the look of confusion on his face is more tempered. He licks his lips.

Is this Japanese?

Eh?

Is this a Japanese soup? I had one like this before – o'er in Gauldry.

Oh – aye – it's a Japanese soup. Well, a Japanese recipe.

He takes another spoonful, forcing it down – *Aye, richt queer folk, those Japanese.*

A Tail Dragger

Aye well, that wisnae what I had attempted tae happen afore it happened. That wisnae the prerequisite fae success, was it Mikey boy? From the fucking knock-knock-knocking onwards – disaster. That woman, though – she could've listened, she must be loaded wi' that big hoose o' hers and a' those yappy dugs. I mean, I wiz only efter Johnny, really, then she's a' friendly and such, ge'in it, "OOoo DOO come in for a CUP of TEA" and a' the hoaty-toaty pish and then, efter a' that, Johnny's no' there, so – well? Whit the fuck wiz I supposed to dae? Chatting away – I reckon I said we were LIKE brothers, but she thought I said… Ach, ne'ermind – but well, I guess, mebbe, I shouldnae hae asked if I could kip o'er until Johnny returns – but, ken, she was so friendly, I jist thought…

Aye but it wisnae just that, she didnae like the auld "cunter" word either, then she's like sniffing me – or the air aroond me, the deft auld bird she is, ge'in it – "Oh, you'll HAVE to LEAVE now" an' a' – "DO get going young man or I'll CALL the POLICE" ushering me oot, flapping her arms, me knocking her bag doon – by accident, ken – then picking it up and her still at me "Leave IT! Leave IT! Get your HANDS off my purse!" So I throw it on the table but the wifey's still efter me, close now, pushing me? Ahm quick outside, grab a chain fae the wa' and swinging it at her, telling her GET TAE FUCK, YE AULD HAG but, well, that did it – fuck, the look on her puss, eh? Whit a sight.

But then there's me reckoning, Christ, she'd mebbe o' called the polis, so I'm no risking the road and thinking – I cannae go tae ma sister's, no' wi' the polis mebbe arriving. So I'm just taking ma time, walking through the woods aside her, then the road beyond, down tae Cupar, the polis willnae suspect me doon there, a' sorts o' dobbers in Cupar eftera', then, well, fuck – it's nicht afore I ken it – no' even making it halfway tae Cupar – and I end up kipping in a wee farmer's barn I found, empty, just a few totty bags, big blue oil cans, that sort o' thing, me sweeping the floor wi' ane o' the bags, then laying down, but nae sleep, nae comfort, so whit tae dae but gub ma sister's speed… Fuck, if the polis found me it'd no' do me good haen it anyhoo, plus ma sis didnae want it… And that's the life richt there, me speeding oot ma tree in a freezin' tiny wee shed, butt end o' nowhere, hungry like the wolf. No' what I'd planned for, I tell you that.

So I guess now I should get tae Johnny's gaff. I can crash there easy fer ma last nicht, sure enough, afore the bus hame tae London. Hame tae London – there's the truth richt there. Fuck San Andres. Johnny'll be cool, aye, just for the one nicht. Whit've I got tae lose?

Kiech And Wazz

Mrs Bradley had put on a good luncheon spread as soon as the polis men departed and I was well fed for the journey home. We were late with the dogs, of course, I'm not sure they're so aware of specific times, but it did mean that when a few folk arrived to pick up their little treasures, said little treasures were stuck in a concrete box surrounded by their own kiech and wazz. People have to learn these things maybe. Kennels aren't holidays for dogs, they're prisons – tiny wee stinking noisy frightening filthy prisons.

But never me mind, it's a job and this slight Mikey hitch aside, myself and Mrs Bradley seem to be settling in, getting along quite nicely. I'm pleased to be working, pleased to be outside, pleased to be away from town and not doing anything *too* menial. I mean, I know, I'm cleaning up shite, rolling the turds in sawdust, how more menial could it get? But I'd rather be doing this than – well, shop work? Bar work? Hotel work? Ach. I'd do it all, I reckon, if needs be. I *have* done it all.

The sky's been threatening most of the afternoon and just before it's time for me to leave, the rain begins, just a spit at first, narry a drop and those that did reach me just good and cooling. By the time I've retrieved the moped from the wretch of the tripe shed it's coming down harder and I'm pleased; the rain will hopefully clean off any tripe stench that may have settled on the handlebars or worked its way into the black leather seat. I leave it to stand getting wet, then head into the house to say my goodbyes.

Aye well, thanks Mrs B. I'm sorry about all that Mikey business. I'm glad you could see through it.

Well, I'm glad that you're here to help. The situation is of mutual benefit. I just hope that he doesn't return, that's all.

She's asking me, hoping for reassurance, her eyes reading my reaction.

Ach, you know – I don't think he will. You chased him off. He's a cowardly guy, I reckon, not so much going on upstairs, maybe. He'll know you called the police. He won't want any bother. Probably halfway down to London by now.

That does it. She smiles and hands me a filthy dish towel. A gift of such magnitude – well, I'm not sure how to respond.

To dry your seat.

Ah.

Grand. Thanks.

Keep it. You may need it to wipe your visor.

By now, the rain is coming down stronger, fairly audible in the kitchen, bouncing off the lintels onto the window panes, dancing in the scattered abandoned dog bowls, providing fresh water for tomorrow's brief escapees.

Right. I better get going. See you the morns.

Okay, yes – and John? Do get the tax done on that moped, will you? I'm not even going to ask you if it's MOT'd.

Caught.

I will. I will. It's all in hand. One thing after the other.

And off and out.

* * *

Riding an uninsured, elderly moped on single-track farm roads through a heavy rain storm after a long day's stress of work and accusation isn't the most relaxing experience. I find myself struggling along; 20mph at times, even slower around the bends, my visor impenetrable though the flowing water cascading in front of my eyes so pitched up now, catching the wind and causing my face to get soaked, my eyes barely open, reacting shut against directs hits from the rain. My jacket is zipped shut, of course, but even then the wet is dribbling down my chin onto my neck and down, down through my jacket and onto my chest, my chest which is freezing now due to that soaked jacket being pushed upon it by the journey and again, the rain. My back feels as though it is under a cold shower and the wet is dripping down my breeks, causing uncomfortable wet-nappy feelings and chafing around my waist, my calves, my thighs, my buttocks. Stevie better be a mind-reader – a considerate, thoughtful mind-reader, well experienced with building hot fires and running deep baths, making thick tomato soup and providing well-earned spirits.

My headlamp is on, full-forward, warning people of the approaching unfortunate, and as cars come towards me on this one berth road, moving slightly to their left so we both have space, I can imagine their warmth and enjoyable adventure, tucked up in their Vauxhalls or whatever. As they edge me *too close* towards the verge, I curse them, wishing them leaky roofs, broken heating, empty petrol tanks. They've seen me, for sure, the young lummox, getting nicely soaked through on a no-luck journey to wherever. My once faded-blue jeans now as dark as the sea, puddles forming within the turn-ups, dripping through into my sodden canvas trainers. Steer past a downed branch – what a hero – try and avoid the puddles, but the whole road is soaked now, so try and avoid the *deeper* puddles, whichever ones they may be. Mostly I gamble right, but on occasion the front wheel of my transport will dip worryingly into the unknown – although only a few inches, and barely noticeable in a car or usually even a moped at this terrifyingly un-worrying speed – but with the water hiding the depth and the fear of falling off – who'd pick me up? The polis? That wouldn't do me much good. I'd have to abandon the bike behind a wall and walk/hitch home. And who on earth would pick up a man sodden from face to foot such as me?

Field by field, turn by turn, the cottage gets closer. Barely noticing now the splashes of clay-coloured muck that leaps onto my trousers, my jacket, the bike, every time I go through the smallest of puddles. There's a light on in the cottage and I can see Stevie's auld car – he's home. It must have taken me – what, an hour? An hour to ride fifteen miles? The twist and turns, the buffeting wind, the fear of the skid. But now, home is upon me. Good ol' Stevie will be standing, laughing at me no doubt, but smiling, grinning at my misfortune. He's bound to say I deserved it, for whatever reason. I pull in, halt the engine, revel in the relative silence for a second and then stand, straight-legged, and dismount, my jeans ribbing my inner thighs, pulling the skin down and off. I'll be bright red. Jings, can barely walk, but on my way, then break into a jog, an actually more pleasing experience, some blood returning to the numbness of my legs, the effects of the vibrations of the engine slowly subduing. Down the lane, past the hippy folk, a wee bit further along and there I am. Stand under the wee postie shelter, remove my helmet to discover my hair just as soaked as the rest of me – possibly from the rain somehow creeping up from my neck, possibly from the sweat of the journey. I peel my jacket off, moaning slightly, sure Stevie can hear, so over-acting, over-egging, swearing away – *fucking hell* – my shirt just as wet, but leave that on. The laces of my trainers soaked together, seemingly fused together in the wet, impossible to simply *pull and release* now, no, now it's a sit down and examine job, work out just *who* goes *where,* then gently teasing it out, trying not to lose my patience and worsen the situation, finally one shoe off, then the other, one sock off, then the last – and in the door, unlocked, into the dry, me dripping everywhere, from everywhere.

Stevie! Stevie!

Aye Johnny, ahm in here.

He doesn't sound too grand. Wait until he sees me, that'll cheer him up. *Hang on* – and I detour via the bathroom, leaving, for now just, my shoes, socks, jacket and helmet in the bath itself. Let them drip-dry there.

Man, what a journey – talking loudly, so he can hear in the different room – *never seen rain like that for a long time* – struggling to open my fly and relieve myself, the water foaming from my breeks as I undo the zip – *and you'll never guess what happened? Fucking hell man* – finish up, zip up, wash hands in the water provided by the tap, lukewarm, but heavenly in comparison. Then drying my hair, my face, my arms… Through I go, trying not to drip any further. I walk in – *That cunt…*

And Stevie is sitting, staring at me, a large wrench in his hand and a face like thunder. There, on the floor between us, is Mikey. He's not moving and there's a large, protruding red mark on the back of his neck, looking like a balancing and too-red fish-finger.

Christ. Fuck… Is that…?

It is. It's that Mikey cunt. And Johnny – you're going to have to help me here. He's pure dead as fuck and I pure kelt him.

Pure Dead As Fuck

I'm staring. And dripping. My legs are throbbing with the cold and wet of the journey, my head's feeling light – and there, still on the floor, still *pure dead as fuck* – is Mikey. Mikey's legs are curled round one another at an unnatural angle and one of his hands is pointing up at me – almost as though he's awaiting a handshake. The other hand is crumpled under his belly. That stinking black jacket of his is still on. Probably more water resistant than my own, but no use to him now. He hasn't moved, but then – he can't, can he? Being dead and all. Fucking hell. I need to sit down. I make to do just that.

Hey Johnny, dinnae sit down there – yer soaking wet. And here – yer dripping all over the carpet. Get a towel or whatever, c'mon.

What? A fucking towel for my drips? Fucking hell, Stevie – Can you no' see Mikey there? There's a big fucking drip right there.

I collapse into a chair and regret it at once, the water of my jeans and shirt pushing against me, frozen cold. *Ah, fuck it.* Straight back up, staring, all the time at the red welt on Mikey's neck. But I've got to get out of these clothes. But there's a dead body in front of me. You know, I'm just pleased I took that piss.

This is too much Stevie. Let me get dressed, then I'll come through. Okay?

He's silent, white-faced now, staring at Mikey. I'm out of the door and almost running to my room, as if that'd help. Everything seems more complex, fitting through the doorway, closing the door, the silence of the room, ripping these drenched trousers off, clarty scants and shirt. Find a towel and rub away, up and down, but careful, aware that there'll be stench and sweat in amongst that moisture, so maybe I should have a shower but *There's a dead body in the living room* and I just need to run away or go and find out what happened or whatever the fuck and before I can decide or do anything other than rip on a new pair of bleach-white cotton scants, I'm back in the living room, staring at Mikey, then at Stevie, then at Mikey.

He looks up. Stevie, I mean. No' Mikey – he's deid.

Yer breeks should be dry. Hung on the pulley in the kitchen.

Here I am, standing pasty-white, Scottish-blue naked, save for a pair of Ys. I am Captain Scotland, muscle-free idiot, arriving just too late to save the cunter. I become aware of my nakedness and make my way back to the kitchen, jumping and heaving my clean breeks down, pulling them on there and then, returning to my room and grabbing a clean t-shirt. My trousers were still wet, it seems, or maybe it's just transference of moisture from my not-quite-dry legs. Whatever, the slight chafe of the walk has become less so and I'm warming up – enough for me. I re-enter the room. THE room. The room of the body.

It's still there.

So…

Christ, what a day.

I grin – *Aye, me too. Though maybe you've JUST had it worse.*

Stevie looks up. No smile – *What the fuck are we going to do?*

We. We, we, we. Umm…

I'm not sure, Stevie. What… what happened?

Och – this fucking… dullard. That's what happened.

Even in death, Stevie is not too fond of Mikey. Extinguishing his very being hasn't been quite enough, it seems.

Man. Why couldn't he just…

He gestures, throwing his hands in the air –

Take NO for an answer? What a fucking prick. And now…

He gestures again, fanning the air in front of Mikey –

And now he's dead as fuck. Cluttering up ma floor.

A giggle. A snortle, then slight tears in his eyes, but quickly pulled in, sniffed away. *Well, Johnny, I have to ask – are you going to help here? Or am I gonna have to do it masel?*

I can feel my heart beating in my head. I can hear the beats, quickening. I need to sit down and do just that.

Do what, Stevie?

But he's not meeting my eye, he's got his muckle big hand over his mouth and is looking any which where other than Mikey or me. Examining the sideboard still cluttered with his family effects, despite his proclaimed de-cluttering. There's one old framed photograph of his uncle and aunt, his uncle's thick arms wrapped around her waist and his coarse face, deep, wrinkled, land-scorched features smiling over her own softer face, but with a light in her eyes that showed she had real love for that man and real happiness, at least for just that one fraction of a second. There's a clock, Edwardian, I guess, always wound and ticking when I visited here as a child, but now dead silent and still, a thin layer of dirty white dust snowed on top. Leaning against it is Stevie's newly found picture of himself with his parents, perhaps on their way into a frame themselves. All these beloved faces, looking on.

I was just – I was trying to work. I got up early, a little hungover, but okay. Trying to fix that damn baling machine again – as if the laird cannae afford a new one – but onyway. A wipe of his hands, pulling them deep down, over his face once more. *Then the laird himsel' pops up and gies it – "You still not fixed that, Stevie lad? You've not got your uncle's way with machines, that's for sure" then he fucks off laughing, leaving me even more frustrated with this auld heap o' junk, the bolts a' rusted on, that's whit's causing the trouble, no' me, I've got to re-weld a whole section, just making sure it's safe on HIS farm. Anyhow. I get on with it and by – what, one o'clock? Half-by? Something like that, it's a'most done, but jings, I'm exhausted and ma heid's throbbing still, so I call it time for lunch and walk back, fair sweating and tired, frustrated with the bolts and hot from the welder cutting out of the plate I needed switched. Anyway.* And he looks up, to see how I'm listening – judging? Ignoring? I'm just listening. My eyes are all on Stevie, the peripheral vision refusing to even acknowledge the hunk of black clothing, laying between us like an enormous black crow. *And then that Caroline wifey sees me and spies I'm on ma way back, so she's like, "Yoohoo! Steven!" and a' that, but I just want away, so I wave and say hello but she's ootae her wee garden bit and then asking me "as a gerdner" what she should do with her winter perennials and ahm thinking – "We're a'most on summer" – but anyhow, I couldnae help, I kent that, but she asked me intae the garden and I'm too polite...*

And silence. This isn't going to hold up in any court of law. He was tired from talking to the bonny lassie about plants, so he killed Mikey. There must be more than that. *Erm... Should we not call the polis or something? You know, this guy was round up at the kennels causing grief last night – the polis ken a' about him. How did... I mean, how...*

I fucking walloped him, that's how.

Right. He's said it.

Aye, I know, I mean, I guessed – but, I mean – how? How, as in why?

Stevie shakes his head. *He was the last fucking thing I needed to see. I finished – what, four o'clock? A' day it took tae fix that fucking plate into place under the thresher. I'm wiped oot and it's pishing with rain a' aroond. And then – that cunt* – he points at Mikey – *That cunt's boots appear underneath – I can see his boots, ken, but nothing else, wi' me deep inside that machine. I ken his voice richt aff – "Johnny! Johnny! Is that you, Johnny?" And ahm like – all polite and such – "No, he's no' here, he'll be at his work, some o' us work, try up at the kennels mebbe." And he tells me – "Ach it's you, I'll just wait" and that's him quiet, me squeezing oot from underneath and there he is, smoking a tab richt close to the diesel pump, like a fucking dowp o' the boy he is.*

Was.

Aye, was. So ahm like – "Fucking put that out, ya dowp, yer richt aside the diesel pump" and he looks at me like AHM the daftie, no' moving or onyhing, so I'm richt o'er and tak it oot o' his hands, throwing it tae the ground awa frae the pump, then he's up and at me, but I raise ma fist and the wee cheuk backs richt doon. Gies it – "Ah'll just wait for Johnny".

As though I'm to blame.

Then he's like – "Aye, I wiz up at Johnny's work, chatting wi' the posh lady there" and a' that pish, me thinking how the fuck did he ken where you were anyhoo?

He was right behind me when I called up. I mean – practically in the phone box. Not hard to work it out.

Well, anyways, I'm aff inside, walking as quick as I can, no sign of that Caroline to waste ma time, thank fuck, but this dowp boy following me, talking shite about a' sorts, just rambling on and on about nothing at a'. And I tell ye – he looked a total fucking wreck.

Smirk. Smirking at the dead man. That'll learn him. I take the luxury of a good stare – if a stare at a dead man can be called *good.* He had thin, old hands, Mikey. And thick hair. I wonder what's in those pockets of his? Maybe we should rifle through them, like in the movies. I can't see his face though. Stevie can. Stevie's looking right at it. You know, I don't want to see it. Not one bit.

And then he's following me through the rain, following me inside, me no' being quick enough to close the door and keen for a proper warm shower, but that cunt in the hoose so no' trusting him – him asking fer "A wee bit o' food – just a slice o'bread – Johnny's bread'll dae."

Johnny's bread?

Aha.

I haven't got any bread.

Aye. And I telt him – there's nae food for you here – but he's non-stop, "I need tae eat man, I've nae slept" and a' that. Fucking daein ma heid in.

So – when was this? About…

Aboot an hour ago, just. He gesticulates – *He'll – he'll still be warm. Just.*

I look again at Still-Warm Mikey. When does the *rigor mortis* kick in?

And then Stevie is quickly, spectacularly sick, right beside himself, careful not to hit the corpse, I guess. Then again, and once more. Waves of sick, becoming smaller and less frequent. Stevie's heid's down and he tries to sit back upright, but the strings of sick are still in his mouth and he's spluttering, coughing onto the floor. Slowly, slowly, he raises his head.

Hey Johnny, quit staring and get me a towel, eh?

Which one?

What? Any fucking one. Your one. I don't care. A big fucking one, for a big fucking boak of sick.

I walk into the corridor, my stomach bubbling and pushing up to my throat, it too quite keen to dispel the remainder of my lunch. A big towel. His towel – that's the towel. Into the bathroom and straight back out. When I return, Stevie's wiping his mouth with his sleeve over and over and staring at Mikey. I hand over the towel and wait – what am I supposed to do here?

So, should we… call the polis?

No fucking way.

How no'?

Cause I killed him. I'll get jailed. I'm no' after that, not one bit.

But you could say…

Say what? I just fucking whacked him Johnny. He was smoking in here – in this room – and he picked up that photo of my mither and faither – and guess what he said? Guess?

I have no idea whatsoever.

He said – "Who are these teuchters?" and that was it. I was carrying that spanner I'd been working with and I just hit the cunt as hard as I could on the back o' the neck and he fell down straight away, nae crying, nae noise, nothing, just… deid.

You killed him because he called your folks "teuchters"? That's a little…

Exactly. I'll be jailed tae fuck. Fir fucking life.

But… why?

I was fucking exhausted, Johnny. And YOU ken I didnae like that cunt. He shouldnae o' been here. I didnae mean tae kill him though, jist… get the fucker oot o' my evening, that's a. Ootae ma hoose.

Well.

Remind me never to call you a teuchter, Stevie.

He laughs, a tiny, short laugh, then looks back down at Mikey.

So, we've got to get rid o' him.

What? Listen – we could still tell the polis something…

Aye. No Johnny. I've thought it through. I cannae lie for shit. You know that. If I said it were an accident, or I fought him off, or he came at me – they'd ken I was talking shecht. I mean – I got him from behind, they'll be able to see that, that big fucking welt on his neck. No. That's not an option. It can't be.

But even then, it's no murder Stevie, it's mair, umm – culpable homicide. You'd be out in, what, six years?

Stevie looks up, directly at me. *I'm no' doing any years if I can help it – six or twelve, baith a michty lang haul from where I'm sitting, especially when there's still a guid chance I can do nae years at a'. You help me here, no fucking harm done. If it goes wrang and we're caught, I'll fess up, tell them I killed him and threatened you tae help me, or you weren't there at a' – Whitever – you won't be guilty. I promise you on everything I have, every bit of time we've shared throughout our lives, every fucking moment, every favour I've done you and you me, every fecht we've had, every secret kept. I swear on a' that – I'll no' let you go down, if it goes wrang. But I need you now, Johnny. I've fucked up and I need you.*

No' So Braw, No' So Bricht

We wait until dark, of course. Meantime, Stevie cleans the sick up, puts his big devilish spanner back up at the farm – *I want no fucking reminder when we return* – scrubs the carpet with detergent, hoping there won't be an everlasting *sick patch* from here on in. Then we close the living room door and have showers; long, hot showers. I have a hunger, but everything seems to remind me of the welt on Mikey's neck, despite them both being well out of sight. Pasta? *Welt.* Bread? *Welt.* I cannot eat. Yet I am aware how hungry I am so I attempt to fool myself – I begin to clean the kitchen and as I go, I quickly snatch an oat cake and wolf it down before my imagination considers it a *welt cake.* Then, wiping the top of the cooker, dead vegetables, slices of ham or whatever, pulled away with a kitchen roll and binned – looking away as I distribute the rubbish, the site of the rotting food looking all the more like – you guessed it. But a banana won't do any harm. I look out of the window, the rain off now, dusk settling, me searching for distraction and finding the hippy wifey, Caroline, walking up the path. She turns and smiles, waves. I wave back, being as cool and as *There's no cadaver in here, madam* as I can imagine. I continue to munch the banana, but looking away from her now, further down the path, giving her no *in* to a conversation, no chance of her wanting to visit, to discuss early winter perennials or whatever the rot it was Stevie got caught with. Then she's off out of my sight.

Soon, Stevie's back, back in the room. I half tense, as though he's going to whack me next, but he doesn't, he just sits down facing me, looking wet-headed, red-faced. He's been greetin' for Scotland, I ken that.

So. What's it to be, Johnny?

I try and look sympathetic. *Whatever you want, Stevie, whatever you want.*

Okay.

He's examining his hands, biting his forefinger, still not making eye contact.

Well. Thank you…

I've no' done anything yet – hey, I'm no' cutting him up. Fuck that.

He smiles. *No need. No need. I've got it worked out. C'mon, it's getting dark. Get things ready and prepared. We've got to run this through, make no mistakes. Here, I've got this old duvet cover we can use.*

Use for what?

Tae move him, ya dowp. Tae move him.

Stevie…

Aha?

We're not feeding him to the dogs, are we?

A laugh. Short, more a release of tension. *No. But that's not a bad idea.*

It is. It is a bad idea.

The moment I touch the body, I am an accessory. The moment I move him, I join the corpse waltz.

Stevie opens the living room door and Mikey's still there, unmoved.

C'mon. This isnae going tae get easier.

Stevie crouches down and lays the duvet cover beside Mikey, on the floor. The cover itself is patterned with roses, which I find quite apt – usually coffins have flowers on board, right? Well, this one does too. Printed on, but there – season-proof and almost everlasting, just slightly dulling with each wash. Stevie flattens the duvet, straightening it, getting rid of any creases.

He'll appreciate that Stevie.

Eh? Aye, I ken. First fucking uncreased bit o' clothing the cunt's e'er worn.

But he's going overboard, pulling and adjusting, getting it just right – as if it could be just right. I don't think duvets are sold with instructions for wrapping up bodies. Stevie's just putting it off, the moment he has to touch – the moment *we* have to touch Mikey. I wonder – could I kick Mikey over onto the duvet? With my eyes shut?

It's flat. Flat and ready. Stevie sits back. *C'mon Johnny – time to do this.* Stevie's down on his knees, facing Mikey's back. That means the only space for me is in front, facing his face.

C'mon Johnny, we've got to get on.

I… Is – are his eyes open?

Whispers – *No Johnny, they are not.*

And I make my way over. His face is normal, closed, asleep. His lips may be hanging slightly, but maybe I'm imagining that. Maybe they're just as they always have been. Do lips even hang after death? I've never heard of the *death-lip-hang.* His eyes are closed though, thankfully. Christ, though – it's Mikey. Right here, right dead.

Okay Johnny, now, roll him over.

What? Me? How me?

No, we'll both do it. Here – you push his legs, I'll grab his shoulders.

Thank fuck for that. I don't want to be anywhere near that head when it lollops over. It'll be like that scene in Jaws. I move down to his legs and can't help but to catch the whiff of sweat and urine from his crotch. *Jings this boy never got clean, did he? Poor lad.* And then I push the legs, before Stevie's ready, causing a half-turn of Mikey's body.

Wait, wait! I've got tae move this cover…

And then, with a slight hoik from Stevie, the trunk of the body rolls on top of the duvet cover, its head edging, rolling towards Stevie's thigh and finally resting, nestled up against Stevie's jeans, like a lover awaiting a stroke from a caring hand. Stevie moves back *Fucking…* before pulling, ripping the duvet all the way under Stevie and imploring me to do the same – *C'mon ya cunt!* Who's the cunt? Me? The duvet? Mikey? Who knows, but I pull away, easier on my side, the weight of the legs nothing in comparison. And then it's the tucking in, the pulling up of the duvet cover, wrapping around the legs, the boots, the revolting crotch. Mummification. Stevie gets the body, tucks in the arms, all done at arm's length, hides the head and then begins tying the edges of the duvet cover together – *Should we not just, um, tape him up?* Stevie looks at me, halting, then continues – *No. We need to be able to release him.* Release him where? *Where's he going Stevie?*

I just figured we'd… I just figured we'd get him in the tide. Let the sea sort him out?

What? That's your idea?

Aye. It is – folk go missing the whole time off this coast, you ken that. One mair body. Who's tae ken the difference? Plus, it'd wash away any forensics stuff, eh – like this fucking carpet. Wha' kens? He couldae – he couldae gone fer a walk on the beach, slipped and broken his neck. Got taken out tae sea. Let's be honest – nae cunt's gonna miss this cunt, are they? Nae cunt's gonnae start a big enquiry?

I guess not. Okay, that's the plan. It doesn't involve any saws and dogs, so it's good for me.

* * *

Mikey's wrapped up, ready to go. *Get your jacket on, I'm going to make sure there's naebody about.* Stevie opens the front door, looks both ways, suspicious, walks up to the farm. A usual occurrence. I await his return – just me and house-guest Mikey. Maybe I should put on some music? Would he like a bit of radio? A cup of tea… I catch sight of myself in the mirror, an almost-starring role in this bizarre occurrence. I need a shave. I look old. Not too old, just… older than I used to. Prime of my life. Just the right age to be disposing of bodies. I walk back into the living room and see Mikey there, all wrapped up like a rose-printed, giant Cornish pasty. The silence in the room, the shared space, the still air – I think I may move away from here; from this cottage. I wonder if Stevie will? He doesn't seem too keen on the laird, that's sure enough. Or his neighbours. And now – well now he has some new memories to be forgotten. This house is full of dead bodies; his uncle in the bedroom, Mikey in here – who else we don't know about? These auld farm cottages. Some story – some history.

Stevie returns and finds me. *Okay, cool. Nice evening, actually, now that rain has passed. The hippy folk seem oot, lights aff – better for us – so we should get moving. This time o' nicht, there should be nae-one anywhere around here. Let's get to it. Here – I'll grab the big end – my rubbish we're disposing of efter all.* A smirk. What's he smirking at? Maybe at getting this over with, maybe just the ludicrousness of the situation. *Ready?* No, but yes. Yes, but no. I nod. *Yep.*

Okay, one, two three – up!

And he's pretty light, at first. Okay, that's okay. Hard to carry him by these knots though, that becomes apparent soon enough, Stevie struggling too, the material thinning, pulling through his hands – *okay, put him down.*

That didn't last long.

We're going to have tae lift him. Like, proper. By his body. Like a carpet, maybe. That cover willnae hold lang.

Okay, that sounds fine to me. I mean, I'll only have his legs, right? Protected by two layers of duvet and his jeans. It'll be like carrying a Christmas tree that's been wrapped in a duvet cover. Two Christmas trees, maybe – or, two legs. Wearing shoes.

Fuck. It'll be like carrying a dead guy.

Okay? Take hold – come on, worse for me than you, I've got the dowp's heid bouncing about.

He gets hold of the shoulders and I move gingerly towards the lower legs.

Okay – one, two three –

We try – we *do* try, but the body slips inside the duvet and Stevie's left holding the sheets, nothing more. Mikey doesn't roll out, but he does appear to crouch, to slip down inside his chrysalis, shoogling even closer towards me. I'm sure I can smell him through the duvet. He smells like an old folks' home. A portable, compact, old folks' home.

Ah, fuck this Johnny. You know...

And I look to him, curious about what I know.

I'll just fucking fireman's lift. In for a penny, eh? He winks at me. *Give me a hand* – and Stevie crouches down, arms around the main bulk of the body. I grab the duvet and attempt to help shift the body onto Stevie's shoulders, then adjust and actually hold the body, through the sheets, ready for Stevie's stand. *Okay, here we go.* And he rises like a weightlifter, straight up. I attempt to help but really I'm just knocking Stevie off balance. Nae bother though, he's up standing, straight finally and seemingly reasonably secure. *Right. Let's get going. Johnny – you handle the doors, then dot out in front of me to make sure the coast's still clear.*

Sure thing. I smile – *I'll ensure the coast's clear, a' the way to the coast, where we shall jettison our bounty.*

Some fucking bounty, Johnny lad. Let's get going. He's not getting any lighter.

⋆ ⋆ ⋆

There is nobody around, just a darkening, cloudy evening, speckles of rain but nowhere near as heavy as it was earlier. I wait for a moment, but Stevie overtakes me and trudges off down the lane, directly to the beach, maybe just 250 yards away. I'm not sure what to do, as the watchman, but close the door, look behind us, up the lane towards the farm and the hippies' place. All quiet. Turning back and already Stevie's a good twenty feet away from me, he's got a shift on, moving quick. I hurry down to catch up, my eyes adjusting to the gloom, a pale blue light emerging, guiding my feet but not so well as they catch puddle after puddle, thin, sandy mud and whatever other sludge and stour the rain has exposed.

Jings, you're quick enough. Is he heavy?

Heavy enough.

I can see from his walking that the weight's taking a strain. Stevie's legs are straightening, as if the act of walking, the bending and unbending of his legs, is too exhausting. He's coming across a little Douglas Bader. You know, if Stevie's having trouble with the lift, I'll not last ten yards. He's got twice the strength of me. Maybe we should get the moped?

Shall I get the bike?

Eh?

Shall I get the bike?

What? No, don't be fucking daft. Here – take Mikey.

And Stevie lunges towards me, lifting and turning Mikey all in one, heading towards me, my arms involuntarily outstretch and I make to carry, to hold, as though I were being handed a baby – Stevie and mine's very own baby – but it's not a baby it's a huge ol' sack o' totties, stinking, knee-jarring, head-avoiding, wretch-inducing bag o' totties. And Christ alive, he nearly flattens me right there. *Help ma fucking boab* – upon impact my legs buckle, their muscles screaming, my lower back reminding me of an injury long since forgotten – leaping out of a haystack at the age of six and landing awkwardly – Six! Six years old and here's the damn pain right back now. Somehow though, somehow I manage to straighten, just, keeping my eye on the horizon to help balance, remind myself of my bearings and my task. And as soon as I can, I begin the slow stagger forwards. He is heavy. I thought he was light, but no – he is heavy. Or I am weak. One foot forward, follow; one foot forward, follow. I am walking, a treacle, unsteady lurch, but walking. I'm minded of the fellows in the trenches of World War One. There's no way I'd've been able to carry Stevie or any other big fella should they have been injured. I am lucky. My only experience, thus far, of carrying a dead human's body is this one and there's no blood, no gun fire, no noise, only...

(Whispers) *Shit, what the fuck's that?*

A moment's silence then Stevie shoves me off the side of the road and straight into the ditch. I collapse down, my hands and knees deep in the fresh-from-the-afternoon ditch water and soaked through in an instant, Mikey launching forwards off me like a rocket pack loosened from a 1960s Sci-Fi spaceman. *What the fuck?*

But Stevie's down beside me – *Shut the fuck up, I saw someone. Wait there.* Then he's up, leaving me pondering my lot, Mikey's lot. I can feel the cold water slowly creeping up my jeans, making its way over my crotch, slowly crawling over and torturing my testicles. I am used to this feeling, having swum in the North Sea many, many times, but it is never a feeling to enjoy or look forward to and is usually accompanied with screams of *Oosh Ya Cunt!* Today though, this evening, it is borne in silence, my eyes widening and watering in sympathy, slowly watching Mikey sinking, sinking into the bog, the ditch, the trapped air of the duvet cover slightly keeping afloat before that too is almost gone. He'll be mucky now, for sure. And that duvet cover will need washed.

Stevie grabs me. *C'mon, o'er the wall – quiet* – He wrenches me out – I'm soaked, but no matter, no concern – *Where's Mikey?*

He's in the sheuch.

(Whispered, hurriedly) *Where? Where? I can't see him –*

He's sank.

Sank?

Aye, sank – look –

But there's nothing to see. He's sank.

Okay, over –

And Stevie practically throws me over the wall.

Now, I've never been particularly lucky, but then wasn't my most fortuitous of moments. I rolled down, caught my arm and my cheek – ma fucking cheek! – on the barbed wire and carried on down, through the long grass of the sodden siding, coming to rest, I think, in some sheep shit. I grab my face, instantly, but can't feel a thing, other than wet – but the rain's been getting slowly, slowly harder and it could just be rain or ditch water – but then why does it sting? I sit up, on my knees, just.

Get down and shut up.

Stevie crawls over. *Someone's coming.*

Aye, I gathered that. Who?

How the fuck would I ken? They're a way off. Almost at the beach.

Shall we get Mikey?

What? And ask him what to do? Dinnae be saft. If you couldnae see him, they'll no' see him.

They?

Aye, well – whoever it is.

Was is two folk?

I havenae a Jimny. Too far.

So… What do we do?

We wait. Wait and see.

And that's what we do. I slowly, quietly, get into a more dignified position. I attempt to wipe the sheep shit off me – in my ear? – certainly on my elbows, my forearms. My cheek is stinging, but there's no way of knowing or checking in this dark. There's a slight throb there too, which doesn't seem good. Stevie's breathing heavy – probably from the excitement and the carrying of Mikey. He's very audible though and sounds how I would imagine a pervert hiding in the bushes would sound – fast, deep breaths, working himself up to climax, or in this case, I hope, down to quiet.

I whisper, then I whisper slightly louder: *Stevie – STEVIE.*

He turns and exaggerates a shushing action, his white teeth visible and his lips curl open, his forefinger pointing up towards his nose: *SHHH!*

I reply – *You're breathing too heavy. Keep it down.*

But he's angry –

Aye and you're fucking cunting too heavy.

What? What does that even mean?

Just fucking keep it down yourself – listen – they're coming.

And if we closed our eyes and concentrated, which we did, we could just hear the beginning of the approaching footsteps, quiet at first, of course, and slowly, gradually louder. But taking an age. A torture. My heart giving a loud pumping, then I'm feeling sick, then I need to shit, I feel dizzy. I shorten my breaths as much as I can, I lower my neck and look down to the ground, finally bringing my face to a patch of grass and allowing myself some good long breaths, quiet though, not quite panicking yet.

Slow, unrushed, undramatic footfall.

There can only be one person there, for sure. And it has to be Caroline, back from a walk. Why didn't I tell Stevie I'd seen her earlier? What a fud. And she, if it is her, she takes an age, the tapping, squelching of her walk getting closer, the slight echo of her footfall on the path confusing us to where exactly she is and the rain – it's not helping, with splashes, drips, a constant, slow hiss, the hiss that probably stopped her hearing our calamitous departure from the path. I tell you what, if Stevie and I go to prison for thirty-seven years because of Caroline, I won't be telling Stevie that I'd seen Caroline out of the kitchen window just a few minutes before we were arrested.

And then the walking stops. Or is it just so far away we can no longer hear it? We lay still, quiet, ears eager for the tapping to return, but no such luck. The continuous rain is now dripping off my nose onto the grass below. At least, I assume, it'll be slowly rinsing any sheep shit off my cheek and clothing. I consider the wall – was it tall enough for me to now sit up without being spotted? Is someone watching me right now, wondering what on earth I'm doing curled up in a sheep field, getting pissed on by the rain?

I wait. Wait, wait, wait. Nothing, no sound but the rain and an occasional bleating sheep. Then, rustling – but close, very close. It's either a sheep or a Stevie. I look up – Stevie, God bless him. He whispers, *extremely* quietly, *Stay down.*

But fuck that. I look up, just for my back's sake as much as anything else; curved over, cold and soaked like this, it is beginning to scream a little...

Stevie's walking on his knees, approaching the wall, slowly peeking over. His head is just over, half-coconut style, looking this way and that, then braver, up a little and looking for Mikey, along the path and back down to me, before coming back my way.

I think they've gone. What the fuck are we going to do though? We cannae risk hauling him doon tae the sea now – wha' kens whit's up? – they may be having a barbeque – they've not gone oot efter a – if it's that Caroline.

They won't be having a barbeque. It's raining.

Shall we just wait here? Wait until it's later?

No. No – fuck, we cannae risk it. What if someone walks up again and that fucking duvet cover's sprang off and they see Mikey there? What if they SAW Mikey and are aff tae call the polis? No – we have to move him. And now.

Where?

I don't know… Fucking – I don't know.

Here, in the dark, the grey, the wet, the gloom, I can just see Stevie's eyes, looking at me for an answer.

Umm, you know what we could do?

What's that?

Dump him down that air raid shelter. It's overgrown as fuck there now, no-one will ever find him and if they did – maybe they'd think he was looking for shelter, fell in and broke his neck.

Do you reckon?

I don't know. Maybe?

Stevie's silent. This can't be the best idea though, dumping him like an old mattress, shitting on our own doorstep. I'd not sleep, I know that, I'd be having dreams about Mikey climbing out and tapping on my window. We should just tell the polis what happened, there's still time surely, maybe change it around – say I was there and Mikey was coming at me with a knife and Stevie had no choice, or maybe he fell off the moped – we were going to sell him it – or…

No. I'm no' having him down that hole, just waiting tae be found. That time – that time with yon sheep down there… Jings, I couldnae sleep, feart of it being found, me getting the blame, a' that rot. Nah. Imagine that, ten-fold wi' Mikey, jist waiting fer the day some wee fellas from the village go exploring and find him, or his skeleton or fucking just next week ain o' the farmer boys awa fer a fly fag – I cannae be ha'en that hanging o'er me. We need this quick and totally believable. That water – the sea – it's still the best bet. We jist… we jist hae tae take him o'er the fields, so naebody sees us on the lane by accident or otherwise. If the polis come we'll spy their cars, sure enough, their lights creeping across, but they willnae hae dugs or any shite like that, these wee Fife polis, they'd just be a couple o' plods who'd fuck off as quick as they came.

Then, turning to Mikey – *The sea it is.*

I nod. *You're right, you're right.* But it's not. I don't know what is though, right now. I do know if the polis came and found him either with us phoning them or them just arriving – they'd not believe any accident story, the state he's in now, dumped in a waterlogged ditch.

Okay. Here's what – I'll jump over, fish Mikey oot and hoik him o'er the wall. Then, fer speed, we'll get him ootae that shitey quilt and carry him, the twa o' us, o'er the field and down beyond to the beach – but we'll take him richt far along, awa' frae the cottages – cool?

Cool.

Okay. Good.

And he's off, pushing through the barbed wire, stomach resting against the wall and then leaping over. It's not cool though, really. It's pretty shonky, to say the least. Dumping a body at sea? I stand up, my knees creaking, soaked trousers sticking to my legs. Hands on knees, taking some deep breaths, getting ready for the toil ahead.

I can hear Stevie struggling in the ditch so I hold the wire down and peek over, glancing all ways for any movement, any sign of commotion. Nothing. Looking down, longer, allowing my eyes to settle and Stevie's there, struggling with Mikey, now significantly heavier I guess due to the weight of the water his clothing's absorbed, the duvet cover's absorbed, plus the pull and suction of the mud and the ditch.

Do you need a hand?

Whit?

DO YOU NEED A HAND?

All whispered.

AYE. TAE FUCK. C'MON.

And I perch over, my jeans catching as I vault. In this darkness, I am perfectly dressed, but upon returning to a lightened room, I strongly suspect I'll need showered, if not bleached. The warm numbness of my cheek is very present, topped off with a light, irritating twitch, as though a small fly has become trapped inside my skin and is exploring ways to escape by kicking with its legs. Stevie is in the ditch, stood at Mikey's head, arms around, I guess, where Mikey's arms would be.

Johnny, we have to untie this duvet cover right now, as quick as we can. He's no' coming out sooked in like that.

But untying mud-sodden duvet covers in the near pitch black isn't easy; I struggle with every knot, the water having expanded the material and now acting as a glue. It's not working. It won't work.

Fuck it. I'll get a knife.

Johnny – don't be daft—

What, Stevie? I live here. I'm allowed to be here. Nothing bad can happen with me being here. Hoik back over the wall if you're worried. I'll be quick as fuck.

And I turn and jog, settling into an easy rhythm, feeling my knees' surprise at the sudden leg movement, my back's pleasure with the stretching, body heaving up and down, feet occasionally skidding in the mire, up to the cottages, the light from the hippy couple's place and my own front door. Not locked, turn the handle and in.

Sheesh. Is there time for a breather, a stock-take? I switch the light on and make my way into the kitchen, marvelling at my soiled breeks and the water dripping off every item of clothing. I get a large pair of scissors, then consider anything else I'll need – a knife? No good, plus it would look dodgy if we were caught carrying a knife... but not as dodgy as if we were caught carrying Mikey. The knife would be the least of our worries. No. Fuck the knife. The knife's staying here.

Lolloping out of the kitchen in my dramatic hurry, I spy myself in the hall mirror; my face mud-patched and bloody, the barbed wire scratch on my cheek a *medium* wound, neither a scratch nor serious. It will not scar but it will not heal by bedtime. Tomorrow, at work, I will have a noticeable cut to explain. *I had a fight with Stevie/I cut masel shaving/I slipped onto a milk bottle/I crashed into some barbed wire whilst disposing of a body...*

That'll not do. No time to wash my face and little point in doing it now – just get outside. Hall light off, door open, quick glance for potential menace, then off back down the road, slow jog, quiet as I can.

I approach, the slight arc of spilling light from the cottage kitchen diminishing the further I get, the closer I am to Stevie. *Hey. It's me.*

Aye, I ken that ya dowp – what did you bring?

These big scissors – here – I hand them over. They're real scissors, you know, muckle handled, for the cutting of thick material – curtains and such, I guess, originally, but now Stevie uses them for the cooking – cutting meat and the like. They'll be perfect.

You should have bought a knife! These are fucking hopeless things. Ach well, I'll give it a go.

In the darkness, I doubt Stevie can see my face, reddening with anger and embarrassment at my scissor failure. Who's helping who here? Who was the eejit that killed Mikey in the first place? As I feel my body tense, the rush of blood to my head pulsates through my cheek, throbbing and clipping with each heartbeat. I keep schtum. I do not say a word. By the sound of things and by the occasional light flashes of the scissor blades, I can only presume that they're actually working fine.

Snip, snip, snip.

Aye, no, they're fine actually. Here, you go from the feet up—

And he hands them back, allowing me time to bend once more towards the corpse. But I cannot reach from the luxury of the roadside. Oh no, I have to clamour back into the sheuch and begin the cut from there. *Watch you don't get his claes* – but of course, of course, my hands submerged in the mire, the fresh cold yeuch swamping my shoes and creeping up once more up my barely dried but slightly warmed trousers. Here, in the water, my hands silently batter away all debris in their quest to *cut*, what I'm hoping are twigs, leaves and mulch, but could easily be beasts, bugs or keich. I discover the beginning of the material – the source, the explorer's gold – and begin my duties, carefully but quickly. This duvet is fucked now, it shall not be used again except, maybe, as rags, though I suspect Stevie will dispose of it as soon as he can, eager to lose any evidence that may nibble on his conscience.

Cut one, cut two, straighten the cloth and cut some more. Easy territory once over the gatherings, comfortable, straight duvet, splitting apart gracefully at the request of the blades. Up we go, past the knee, pulling the roses as far from the crotch as I can manage, snip, snip, almost at Stevie's mark, reached and pulled aside, as if gutting a fish, skinning a lamb, a crooked caesarean. And here within lies Mikey, sodden, soaking, puir dead Mikey, in a shallow bath of filth and rainwater. *Okay – Let's try again* – I look to Stevie and he's got his arms wrapped around Mikey's armpits, Mikey's head resting awkwardly against Stevie's stomach – *C'mon man! Get a move on. This is real, we need to move.*

I always was a dreamer, it seems.

I place the scissors by the side of the road and gather Mikey's legs, inadvertently pushing him further up towards Stevie, Mikey's hair surely now tickling Stevie's chin – *Ah for Christ's sake... Okay, ready, lift after three – one, two...*

And there's a car coming. Not along our track yet, but definitely on the B-road that connects to it. Stevie's up with Mikey – *Up now Johnny* – and I'm shaken into action, legs complaining as I lift Mikey's lower half, my own thin body and the sponged weight of my breeks, scants and shirt. We're up now, the three of us, and the car's only getting closer – *Throw him. Now* – and before I can talk of barbed wire or caution, Stevie's heaving Mikey upwards, shunting him over the wall, a higher wall for us, submerged as we are in the drainage. Up, up and away, I follow suit, pushing, dropping, moving my hands onto Mikey's *thighs* and then his *arse,* heaving him over the wall. Done. Mikey hurries from my grip like a fleeing sheep. *And oursels* – Stevie does the scramble, then the leap and he's over. I can see the car lights, clearly their arc shows they're coming our way. Someone visiting the hippy couple? The polis? Who knows? I'm just about to jump myself when I spy the scissors, lying clearly on the main drag. I make to grab them, collapsing back into the muddy pool on all fours and stretching, reaching, just arriving and pulling them in. And the car is here now, at the cottages, a mere thirty metres away from where I am. I have no choice, I turn and semi-submerge, pulling down all traces of duvet I can see, pocket the potential glint of the scissors and lie, quiet.

There's no sound from the other side of the wall. Stevie must have guessed what I'm doing.

The car stops. I'd suggest, by the distance I could estimate, it has parked outside our cottage – but maybe, potentially, the hippies' place. Let's see.

The quiet revealed when the engine is cut is broken by the metallic sound of a car door opening, a wait, some still and then closed with a *clunk.* My senses are rather compromised, the cold of the ditch eating away at me, the fear propelling my heart oh too quickly, the darkness provided by the grassy mossy walls only emphasising the coffin feeling of my situation, as I stare straight up into the clouds, consistent scatterings of rain still falling upon me. Through those, through the rain and the clouds, there's the occasional view straight to the stars, way beyond a measurable distance, but watching, unjudging, curious of my next move.

Rat-a-tat-tat.

Someone is knocking on our cottage door. It's too close to be the hippies' place.

Rat-a-tat-tat.

Christ. This wasn't what we needed.

Be They Beasties Or Be They Twigs

John! John! Are you in, John?

And it's my mother. Did I lock the door? I didn't. Is she going to go inside? She will. If there's no answer. Can I answer her? Definitely not. So, she'll go inside. What's been left? What evidence? None, surely? There was no blood, Stevie wiped away his vomit... Maybe just my muddy foot prints? No harm there. It's a cottage at a farm.

RAT-A-TAT-TAT

John! Steven! Hello?

Another door opens, further along the road. There's an unintelligible voice, quiet, but most definitely female; Caroline, of course. She'll be out to see what's what. Well, she'll enjoy meeting my mother, that's for sure. They can extract information and talk together quite wonderfully, I imagine. The hubbub is still occurring, the two voices quieter now, my mother's slightly more *horned* accent poking through a little more successfully than Caroline's. I make out a few words, but nothing vital – *Anyway... Well... As I was saying... Steven...*

Fucking hurry up and go away. I'm fair freezing in here, the cold reaching right through me, no longer consigned to the arms and legs, the small of the back and neck.

But they don't, they mumble and they rhubarb. I pray for the rain to thicken, to push them apart or drive them inside. I, after all, am already thoroughly soaked through, I have nothing to lose, no dry patch of shirt or hair to protect. I am well and truly dooked, feeling my testicles slowly, slowly shrinking and all manner of objects brushing my neck.

I wonder of Stevie, what he's thinking, of his position. Of course, he'll have the relative warmth of the field, the cauld wind freezing further his no-doubt equally watered clothing. Maybe he will have landed awkwardly on Mikey, or is using his belly as a cushion and is resting, dreaming of more innocent times.

Voices rise, then depart, a door opens, more chatter, a door closes.

Silence for a minute, then another door closes. In my mind, that's Ma gone into our cottage and Caroline back to hers. Right, time to get out of this claustrophobic bog and to get on with the business in hand, the delight and luxury of clambering through a field with Mikey and Stevie.

I'm up and out and halfway over really rather quickly, stomping as I leave to submerge the duvet, but my descent is slowed by memories of barbed wire and worry of where I may land, should I take the leap. The darkness at the foot of the wall could contain anything – Stevie, Mikey, sheep shite – I do not want to land on any of them. I do not want to crush a skull on impact or skid on shite and shatter my own or slip and be gutted by these damn scissors…

Johnny, GET DOWN, we're o'er here.

I'm well off. Ten feet away. Slide down, between wall and wire, push the wire low and carefully hoik myself over. I scurry over to Stevie and spy the darkened shape of Mikey, hanging on the barbed wire as though he'd attempted to climb but been shot, looking for all here like a memory of the First World War.

Christ. I close my eyes, attempt to re-set. Every now and then, within this enterprise, the bewildering realness of the situation gets to me. We are disposing of a body. And now, we are disposing of a body that is reminding me of millions of bodies of a time long gone, when a great load of Mikey and his ilk died far younger than Mikey is now. He is hanging, he is hung, arms outstretched like a scarecrow. His time is over, we need to move things along now, get this over with. The longer we are out here, the more normalised the situation will become. I don't want it to become normalised. I want to be freaked out and disturbed. Stevie's not moving – he looks, in the gloom, as though his head is in his hands.

Stevie, we have to move. This won't do.

There's no reply.

We can still make this work, but we have to get going. We can still…

And he's up. Has he been crying, waiting for me? I don't know. It's impossible to see.

You okay?

Aye – his – he's snagged likes, in the wire. Cut deep, I think, in his arms. We'll have to be careful no' to rip his claes and his arms, then reach his body o'er the wall.

Okay. Right – well, let's get started –

I move over, the cold of my clothing causing as much of an impetus as anything else. I need to get inside and I need to get warm. Every time I'm still, my bones complain, my skin creeps, my neck tightens. I need to get this done.

Arm Number One is mostly just clothing; there's one snag in the middle, but he's soon freed. Stevie is in control of Arm Number Two and maybe he's being more cautious than I, but he's taking longer.

Christ, how the fuck did this happen? It's a' caught up, like it's been a' birled roond...

I make to move over but Stevie waves his arm, making contact with me, pushing me away.

Ach, it's nae use, I cannae free it – the wire must have turned as he fell.

Do you want the scissors?

Eh?

The scissors. Get him cut, and then away. We can't be here forever.

The rain has stepped up again. I'm wiping the water from my forehead, my eyes... I should have grabbed a waterproof whilst I had the chance. This East Neuk temperature is not intended for dancing about sodden-clothed, even in summer showers.

Aye – hand them over.

And I do just that, handle first, as I was taught by my mother. She'd be pleased now, if she could see. Jings, she's still inside oor wee hoose. I hope she's lighting a fire...

Snip snip, a curse, a rip of clothing, a pronounced tug and finally Mikey's loose. His neck is bent, his head looking down towards the grass, but there's no wire in him there, thankfully. He's an easy lift now, almost, if we're careful, which we are. Before long he's up and over, joining us in the freedom of the field. There's a car door and we cease movement, but then an engine starting and surely, surely it's my mother driving off. A relief, her car slowly getting further, her headlamps visible at the top of the field, lighting her way, far away from us. Oh, for the warmth of that car; I'd gladly take the natter and the nagging for a minute to unchill my aching bones.

Couldnae Flee At A'

I've got him now, Mikey, his left arm pulled over my shoulders and his right the same over Stevie. He is our injured-to-death fallen comrade and we are rescuing him from the insult and indignity of the clasping barbed wire, we shall be bathing him, sheltering from this pelting, driving rain. Any thoughts of crouching carefully have been dismissed; the weather now too hard, too present for any such luxury as *not being seen* to matter. The two of us, the three of us, sludging through the field, top-runny now after the day's watering, slipping, losing hold of Mikey, his head lazily shaking from my side to Stevie's, Stevie's to mine. There's no discussion, no working out of the route, we both know where we're going and how we'll get there, we just avoid any sheep that aren't wise enough to get out of our way and stand staring at us three, or perhaps to them, the one being: three-headed, two arms, six dangling, struggling feet. We have made a wall. This is primary school football and we have made a wall. Nothing can get by us, escape us, except the heat draining from our bodies and our tongues, pushing the rain water out of our mouths, licking our noses. I've wiped my eyes on Mikey's arm now a dozen times on one side and a dozen times on the other, clearing my vision, catching a smell of his clothing, just present still through the sooked, sponged evening it's encountered.

And down the hill now, our feet slipping on the glaur and wet grass almost every step – but I've no desire to stop, the heat of the movement warming me and still very aware how cold we'll be, still and exposed in this miserable field. Another rabbit hole to avoid, a rhythm to keep, just keep on going, moving forwards, towards our destination.

There's no-one, no cars, nothing in sight. No sounds other than the rain and the movements and efforts of our excursion, an occasional sheep, the approaching purr of the sea. With this weather, only a fool would be out. My breathing is heavy, Stevie's too. Mikey is silent. What a fucking bother this guy's been. If only I'd missed the bus – decided to stay down there – gone a week later – had that extra pint – sat beside someone else – telt Mikey tae fuck off sooner – been better at art – drawn better cocks – pulled better pints… Mikey's shoes are dragging behind us. See if one of those cunters comes off and we have to search the entire field? I'll be well pissed off.

Through another field – another good ten minutes of struggles, slips and wet – and we are almost here. The last hurrah, reaching the dunes, the thin tree line, the slight shelter from the fierce sea wind. My back is cursing me, a hot knife slowly being inserted to the base of my spine, turning, punishing, ridiculing my life decisions. Still, at least it's hot though, eh? My body could do with some warmth.

It's lighter here, with the reflection of what little moon there is poking through the clouds, but it's still almost impossible to see in this weather, at this time of night – for it is almost night now, absolutely. All the sensible people are tucked up in their beds, enjoying the luxury of the sound of rain and the cold air padding their ears and faces, thinking *I'm lucky I'm not out now, who'd be out on a night like this?* And the answer is us – us three dafties, fate entwined lang since, our feet collapsing in the sand, the beginning of the dunes. Finally, Stevie speaks.

Whaur the fuck is it? There should be a path through…

I'm exhausted, my body seems frozen with the soaking and the gusting chill and on the point of collapse, my head spinning. I cannot talk or stand tall, my spine curved and set at the point of carry, forever to haunt me of the evening's activity.

Johnny – Can you see it?

But I can't, just reams of sea grass, the sand lighting the floor slightly, but – fuck it, we can just climb through, surely? It's only reeds…

Stevie explores, quietly, gingerly – *here we go.*

He's found a path, a slim break, down through the dunes themselves and onto the beach.

* * *

Christ, how did I get here Johnny?

He doesn't mean the beach. I can't answer though, struggling as I am with Mikey, watching not to drop him. The one respite is that here, slightly lower, closer to the dunes, the wind is lower. The rain's still coming, of course, but within this relative shelter of the dunes, it almost feels warm.

I mean – I didnae like this guy, but, ken, he wisnae – he wisnae TOO bad. What the fuck was I playing at?

Stevie has stopped, so I rest too, the pair of us holding Mikey up, as though he's going to join in, chat away.

I don't know, Stevie. It was pretty daft. I mean – I know the guy was a – dare I speak ill of the dead? – *I mean, sometimes he could come across as a bit of a* – his hair is now tickling my ear – *a bam, but, I mean…*

He drops him. Stevie drops Mikey, leaving Mikey hanging from me like a ventriloquist's dummy, waiting to be pulled into life. Stevie crouches down, head in his hands, clearly crying. I crouch down myself, letting Mikey rest gently, no throwing, no disrespecting. But what do I say here? How can I console my Stevie, my good ol' friend Stevie? I stand and move over towards him, placing my hand on his shoulder *Hey…* but there's no more words. I crouch down, the sheets of rain still pouring upon us but my body happy just to be still and not to be carrying the half-weight of Mikey any further. We're almost done now, almost done. *It was just, fucking… too much. Too much. I cannae be…* Stevie's shaking his head, muttering. *I mean, coming back here – wrang fucking move. I fucking hate that wee cottage, this shitey wee hole of a place. I mean…* My hand is grasping his shoulder, just feeling the wet leather beneath through the numbness of my cold and drookit fingers. I have no words of comfort, I have no *It'll be alright* as it won't, I'm sure of that. Stevie's killed a man. Mikey was no sheep or rat or bird; a real, live, living, breathing fellow. Stevie's mumbling, barely coherent – *I fucking knew it, it's just…* and he's greeting fully, sobbing into his hands, his body shaking and rocking. *Stevie…*

WHAT?

And now he's shouting –

What fucking good are you going to say? What fucking good did it do me you turning up, eh? I kent fine it'd be fucking trouble and it is. Ya fucking… prick.

Stevie – Stevie, it wasnae me who brained that guy there, lying right there on the floor. Sure, it was me who met the cunt, but it wisnae me who killed him, was it? Here I am, putting my fucking life at risk, helping you – my auld buddy – but let's get one thing clear, this is your cunt of a mess that I'm clearing up. And now – we have to get on with it. You understand? We cannae just dump Mikey on the beach. He needs to go… I motion to the water, the waves, just fifteen feet or so away from us – *in there. And deep. We need the tide to pull him out. The undercurrent.*

I'm up away from them both, standing, shivering, facing along the coast towards St Andrews. The downpour has got me everywhere; my neck, my front, the sodden crotch of my breeks – I am soaked through, my clothing now mere guttering for the constant flood. The peace of these few seconds removed is somehow welcoming and I stare off into the distance, watching the orange lights of Dundee and Broughty Ferry, far across the Tay estuary. My body doesn't even feel cold now; it's just shaking and exhausted, a resigned nag that *I should be home now,* that I *need warmth, need food.*

The sea is a dark and wide crashing field, a spitting, frothing beast awaiting with interest our gift. I swam in this water so many times in my youth, it was never warm, never welcoming. If you were lucky you could find a patch, a pool without jellyfish, skate or seaweed, a warm clear bath, but mostly it was a constant reminder of what it is – the edgings of a deep and wild northern sea.

Stevie's up beside me, silently weeping. I place my arm around him before remembering that was exactly where Mikey was all too recently. It's time to go, time to move. *C'mon Stevie, let's get this done.* He turns to me and I can just make out his face. There's little movement but I know he's watching me as me him, perhaps attempting to make out my expression, my mood as I am his.

Will ye gie me a hand, Johnny?

I nod. *I will.*

He judders forward and hugs me, a long, tight embrace. I hold on, clutching him close, the warmth off him and the shelter he provides reason enough, but far more than that – I'm holding the Stevie of my childhood, my adolescence – I'm holding big daft Stevie, the smell of musk, earth and sweat in his drenched wet hair, the entwined memories, the years of shared fears, loves, laughter and disappointments.

Then he pushes me away and we're quickly over it, struggling but picking Mikey up now, an arm each, hoik him up, back on our shoulders, shuffle him somehow comfortable and then move off, the familiar tearing muscular aches returning with each step, the sand no easier than the mud of the fields, our legs weighing thrice their usual weight. The water's edge quickly approaches. There's no need for us to remove any of our clothing or footwear – they couldn't get wetter if we tried.

The first step is no different to the ditch; but as we go deeper, we can feel the rise and fall and the pull of the tide. Mikey's feet are dragging behind us, both shoes still on, thank Christ, but dragging all the same, like a scared swimmer, an unenthusiastic dance partner, a hapless drunk who has peaked too soon and let his buddies down. As we three wade deeper, the temperature change between the wet of our clothing and the clasp of the sea seems minimal; but within moments it is clear the sea is far, far colder. This cannot be a good thing. It's briefly interesting, feeling the currents whip through my footwear and weighten my breeks, but I cannot feel the urge to carry Mikey beyond waist level. I am only here because of Stevie, his strength pulling both Mikey and me forwards, deeper, colder, less visible, less in control. And over my waist the water goes, crawling within every crack and gap of skin, any last scrap of a memory of warmth quickly snuffed out by the all-encompassing grip of this great body of icy water. When this creeping, devilish freeze reaches my armpits, my heart skips and my feet slip – on a rock, maybe, or some seaweed – and I dook completely under the water, briefly, into the black, the extreme cold tightening around my neck instantly, flooding my ears and causing inner waves of astonishment. I let go of Mikey. Of course I do. I panic and attempt to re-emerge, to upright. And I do surface – after only two seconds, or maybe three, later – choking, coughing out water, periscoping my neck to clear the rising, swelling water. I attempt to find my bearings; I see Stevie's face turned towards me, but still moving away, a hand pulling Mikey, who is floating somehow – his inflated leather jacket perhaps – deeper, deeper into the water. They are too far, Stevie and Mikey both. I cannot follow, I can barely move. All I have is the strength to turn and wade from this near chin-high bewildering crush of cold, pull myself home, forwards, away from Stevie, towards the shore, concentrating on each foot hold but slipping, the tide pushing, toying with me, slipping down below once more and swimming, briefly, a fully submerged doggy paddle, fearing the worst, screwing my mouth closed, tasting the salt-water through my nostrils and then somehow up, lungs screaming, breathing deeply, shaking, panicking wrists rubbing water from my eyes, my mouth, my ears. And continue, wrench forward, one leg at a time, damn these heavy jeans, the tide just at my waist now, then my knees, then my ankles, my shoes of watery lead. And out.

I cease every movement except for erratic fitting shakes; I'm bent double, unaware of the reminder of the torture of the cold, barely feeling it now. I need to slow my heart down and am struggling for slow, long, deep breaths, attempting to focus on where I am, where I need to be. But it's not easy, my head is light, my thoughts just a random, uncontrollable dwam – but from somewhere – *I need home, I need home…*

As I stand, the shock of my sodden clothing ambushes me once more, sticking, soaking to my chest, my back, my legs. I turn, maybe expecting to see Stevie nearby, but nothing, no-one. Maybe it's the dark? Maybe he's out already and missed me when I was dooked below the surface? I have no idea and I can no longer care… I wait, I resolve to wait, but I cannot. I give him ten, maybe twenty seconds, but I need to go. I cannot be here, frozen and exposed, numb and exhausted on this beach. A calm has descended, the purr of the waves more distant, my body fooling itself that it's adjusted to the elements – for I fear I cannot feel a thing, other than an unkind, drilling pain in my head. I need to walk and begin just that, wearily talking out, carefully, quietly – *Stevie! Stevie!* – but not looking, listening or expecting response. If he needs my help, then he is fucked already, for I have no more to give.

Epilogue: A Wonderful And Welcome Strong Easter Sun

Here in this small hollow of the field, we are sheltered from any wind and deep in thought, Stevie holding the lamb by its head and me, well-sharpened knife in hand, beginning a precise incision, just under the neck, then round, all around the beast, creating a small, bloodied collar *that's it, that's it*. Returning now to the chest and cutting a thin, straight line, all the way down to the rear legs that are firmly in Stevie's grip, the soft, wet body tight, my other hand pushing it toward me, onto the knife *okay, okay* and then marking it little socks; toward the barely formed hooves, but aware the pelt, the skin, will need to *peel* off, so keeping it on the shanks. *Good knife!* Then joining the cuts, creating a cardigan, almost, but with flappy, witchy 1970s arm-wear and off – begin the peel, the grey and purple innards exposed soon enough but very little blood, the creature long since dead, never really alive in this world. Stevie moving both hands to the head, grabbing on under the jaw, me using force now, but also the knife to tease the quarry, release any clinging, stuck skin. It's mostly easy enough, though glad of my gloves, tight leather like what was on the sheep itself, enough *purchase* to allow me to floor the knife and use my fingertips to adjust, undress and finally free the pelt, holding it solo and unattached. I'm careful with it now, don't drop it, don't fanny about. Stevie puts the carcass straight into a thick green seed bag already containing two more still-births or *narry-langs*, stands and collects from a make-shift pen another new-born lamb, but this one very much alive. Quickly, so as not to transfer his own scent too much, he brings the lamb down and I begin the process of tying the old pelt around the neck – a leathery batman cape, hanging loose – and then using the rear leg flaps I tie again, this time around the body, all the time the weak, young lamb, just hours old, doing its best to escape, to get to its mother, a mother who died during the birth. Once tied, we walk the short distance to another ewe, but this one alive and calling for its young, who'd been born dead and just been skinned by me. *Here, here, here's yer wee lamb* – leaving it ten, fifteen feet away and quickly retreating, hoping the old ewe will take this young one as her own, recognising the smell from the hanging pelt and cherish her, feed her, mother her. We watch in quiet now, the peerie lamb wobbling towards the ewe, the ewe apprehensive at first but then smelling, licking, accepting. All good. *Is that the last one Stevie?* It is, today it is. I know my duty next and am happy to do it; I return to the sack o' died, skinned lambs and hoik it into the wooden neep crate attached to the back of the ancient, basic tractor. Fire it up and ride off, down towards the edge of the old woodland, away from prying eyes, footpaths – *Bury them deep mind, we don't want any dugs digging them up* – dragging the sack along now, well off the path and deep within the trees, hidden – finding a spot and choosing it, but no hurry here, just myself, my own boss, digging deep through the thick clay soil, cutting through roots, moving muckle big stanes. An hour to myself, hard work, but glad it's the holidays and beating schooling. *Just a few more feet, a few more inches* finishing, measuring and realising, *I'll need deeper still,* stopping for a cigarette, sitting on a log and sooking through filthy grey clay fingers, looking up at the trees, an eye out for treecreepers below and buzzards higher, enjoying the breeze, the day, the sunshine reaching through the branches, lighting up the dust and stour. There, in the seed bag, wait three of the unlucky ones, barely lived at all and now bound for the earth and dirt of the forest.

James Yorkston is a celebrated songwriter and musician who has released over a dozen albums, mostly on Domino Records. His most recent musical project, *Yorkston Thorne Khan* (2016) received 5★ reviews in *Roots* and *Record Collector*, with *UNCUT* saying "It could just be one of the albums of the year". In 2011 Faber published his tour diaries *It's Lovely to be Here* to great acclaim. *Three Craws* is his first novel